D1058847

Praise for Edward Schwarzschild

Responsible Men

"From a complicated business deal to a teenager's first kiss, Schwarzschild works with the quiet authority of a master. This is one terrific debut."

— *Kirkus Reviews* (Starred Review)

"Early in Schwarzschild's marvelous debut novel, Max Wolinsky issues a warning: 'Let the buyer beware.' But it's impossible to avoid falling for Max, even if he is a small-time con . . . That's how appealingly the author has designed our hero, not to mention his cohorts."

— *Entertainment Weekly*

"*Responsible Men* . . . takes the generations that separate Arthur Miller's *Death of a Salesman* from David Mamet's *Glengarry Glen Ross* and condenses them into one panorama, so that you can see all the way from Willy Loman, 'riding on a smile and a shoeshine,' to Willy's cutthroat contemporary heirs . . . Schwarzschild writes with compelling insight and emotional power. It is a rare authorial gift."

— *Chicago Tribune*

The Family Diamond

"The trials and tribulations of relationships are at the heart of this collection of nine tales of modern life; sparkling with wit, compassion, and sometimes whimsy, the vivid characters will not be quickly forgotten . . . Schwarzschild has a hit with his second work; the writing is polished, well paced, and exceptional. Heartily recommended."

— *Library Journal*

"In *The Family Diamond* . . . Schwarzschild squarely faces obdurate aspects of life—illness, aging and death—with curiosity, respect and humor. He is the sort of fiction writer whose prose is so lucid, psychology so convincing, characters and action so surprising and intriguing, you forget you're reading."

— *Chicago Tribune*

"Linked by the author's generous attention to his characters and by the mixture of generations and cultures that enrich them, these nine stories sparkle with humor, insight, and heart."

— *Boston Globe*

In Security

Also by Edward Schwarzschild

Responsible Men
The Family Diamond

In Security

A Novel

EDWARD SCHWARZSCHILD

ee

excelsior editions

AN IMPRINT OF STATE UNIVERSITY OF NEW YORK PRESS

Published by State University of New York Press, Albany

© 2020 Edward Schwarzschild

All rights reserved

Printed in the United States of America

No part of this book may be used or reproduced in any manner whatsoever without written permission. No part of this book may be stored in a retrieval system or transmitted in any form or by any means including electronic, electrostatic, magnetic tape, mechanical, photocopying, recording, or otherwise without the prior permission in writing of the publisher.

Excelsior Editions is an imprint of State University of New York Press

For information, contact State University of New York Press, Albany, NY
www.sunypress.edu

Library of Congress Cataloging-in-Publication Data

Names: Schwarzschild, Edward, author.
Title: In security : a novel / Edward Schwarzschild.
Description: Albany, NY : State University of New York Press, [2020] |
    Series: Excelsior editions
Identifiers: LCCN 2019055337 | ISBN 9781438480916 (hardcover : alk. paper) |
    ISBN 9781438480930 (ebook)
Classification: LCC PS3619.C489 I5 2020 | DDC 813/.6—dc23
LC record available at https://lccn.loc.gov/2019055337

10 9 8 7 6 5 4 3 2 1

For my wife

It's easy to see the ball, but not so easy to notice the exact pattern made by its seams as it spins.

—W. Timothy Gallwey, *The Inner Game of Tennis*

1

IT WAS MID-APRIL, EARLY MORNING, and I signed in at the checkpoint: *Gary Waldman, Transportation Security Officer.* I was almost ready to focus through another shift at Albany International Airport. Before I could get down to it, though, I needed to stop daydreaming about the run I'd take later, after work, when I'd hustle over to the campus of Haven College and huff it up the winding gravel path on Monument Hill. I called it the Hill of Sorrow now and it offered the best, most economical therapy around. Up at the summit I'd stand wheezing before the sandaled toes of the thirty-foot-tall marble sculpture of young Mary Haven. She remained frozen there, leaning against a cross while holding her broadsword forever aloft, brandishing it at the distant sky, as if vowing revenge against someone up there for her terrible fate. Poor girl, mauled to death by a black bear in the woods of Albany when she was twelve. Her father rushed with his Remington toward the sound of her screams. He managed to shoot down the bear, but failed to save the child. The bear's pelt still hung in the college museum, right next to a few framed, carefully preserved locks of Mary's curly red hair. There was no statue to mark the grave of that father, just a plain, well-worn headstone for yet another powerless man with a gun—another man who lived unaware of doom until it was far too late.

I snapped out of my reverie when my straight-up, no bullshit supervisor, Carelli, pointed me to the divestiture spot on lane three. Carelli was five seven or so, trim except for his beer belly. He kept a photo of his two hay-blond toddlers pressed behind his ID in the laminate pouch clipped to his chest pocket. The guy was a lifer, a grunt, a fellow grinder, and because of that I felt at ease with him.

I grabbed a radio and a few extra pairs of large blue gloves, stepped into position, and launched right into the script about liquids, gels, aerosols, laptops, jackets, sweaters, shoes, belts, and empty pockets. It was the part of the shift that reminded me most of coaching, how, back on the courts, I could spend hours repeating the same phrases I'd lifted early on from Gallwey's *The Inner Game of Tennis*: *Show interest in the ball. Be aware of your racket. Find your quiet mind. Let it happen.*

I had become accustomed to a different set of phrases during my almost seven years at the airport. From day one on the job, it was 9/11, 9/11, 9/11, and War on Terror mantras. *Not on my watch. Not in my airport. Never again.* The higher-ups liked to invoke the fact that some of those terrorists started their fateful September morning in airports even smaller than Albany. "Albany *International*," they insisted, because of the daily commuter flights to Montreal and Toronto. They felt the need to fight against complacency and they talked about it like this: *We're 150 miles from New York City. The terrorists have as many chances as they want; we only get one chance to stop them. It could happen here. If you see something, say something.*

But what if you don't see something?

Apply the guiding principle of my thirties and forties—of my whole life, really: *What you don't see is what you get.*

Still, no matter what they said, no matter how much fear they mongered, I believed Albany would always resemble the old fluffy sitcom *Wings* far more than the flashy, high-body-count dramas of *24* or *Homeland*.

Or, to borrow another popular TSA mantra: If you've been in one airport, you've been in one airport.

There's a useful concept with many possible applications. A bleak version of how much experience will help you prepare for the future. Or maybe it was a celebration of the particular. Or, most likely, it was both, and more.

If you've been an only child, you've been an only child.
If you've had one kid, you've had one kid.
If your wife died in your arms, your wife died in your arms.

Better to move from position to position—divestiture to bag search to X-ray to walk-through metal detector to document checker to exit to the scanner then back to divestiture and round and round—more or less like that for eight hours with breaks for briefings, occasional online training, coffee, and breakfast, lunch, or dinner, depending on the shift. *Never the same day twice*, some said, because the passengers were always different. Even when the passengers were the same, taking one business trip after another, their moods varied widely. Still, the tasks could get repetitive and tedious; rotation from position to position helped keep everyone alert and engaged. Walk up to a fellow officer, say "I'm tapping you," and you could feel the gratitude flowing back your way. When we were short-staffed or slammed or a supervisor slipped up, the rotation rhythm could get thrown off and we'd all start looking over our shoulders for relief, eager to move on. If we couldn't move on, people would get irritated, and woe unto the passenger who pushed back at such moments.

But most of the time, especially in the mornings, the rotation stayed smooth and close to peaceful, which was just what I needed, now more than ever. When I was surveilling the lines I wasn't agonizing about the fast-approaching birthday of my dead wife.

"Everything out of your pockets," I repeated. "Laptops get their own bin. Coats off. Shoes off. We recommend belts off as well. All liquids, gels, and aerosols need to come out of your bags."

My crowd-surfing gaze caught a young woman in purple yoga tights. She was sipping a bottle of water, enjoying it, as if it were the best beverage she'd ever had. Early thirties, right around the same age Laurie had been when she died. If the situation were different, if I were in a different place, at a different time, with a completely different personality, I might have told her I had a break coming up and I'd be honored to buy her more water and I'd buy one myself and we could drink together and maybe talk about life and death and love on the other side of the checkpoint.

Unfortunately, August Harnett was nearby, working the walk-through metal detector, otherwise known as the mag. August was not a grinder; he was a cowboy, a wannabe cop who had so far failed the Albany Police entrance exam twice, in part because he'd lost most of his left foot in a snowmobile accident. "You need to drink up, Miss," he barked.

The woman smiled, a bright flicker of grace added to my shift. "I spent the whole morning on the phone with my mother," she said. "Forgot to hydrate. I'll be done in a second."

"When you're done isn't up to you," August said, and I watched him limp forward, apparently ready to shunt her directly to a full-body standard pat-down, which he'd no doubt perform himself, if only the rules didn't interfere. But I didn't want an incident. I saw an old man approaching with a small yippy dog in a carry-on bag. The man and his pet would need to pass through the mag, so I directed them that way. "Here comes one for you, Officer," I said, and August had no choice but to stay at his post.

Then I turned to face the woman again. Her thin-lipped mouth was half-open, her emerald-green eyes showing sadness and hurt. Maybe she'd been up all night. Maybe she'd never done yoga in her life. Maybe she was a runner with a terrible headache. How could I possibly know the precise ways she might be lost? All I knew was she was enjoying that water and I was enjoying her enjoyment. She had slender, toned legs, but her heart could still be broken. I imagined her standing in this checkpoint line after an awful night, an awful week, an awful year. I didn't have to stretch my imagination very far. "Take your time," I said, hoping to make the simple words soothe, hoping she'd see beneath my starched shirt, the shoulder patches, the ridiculous epaulets, all the way through to my own flaws, my own errors, which, I'd be the first to admit, were legion.

She smiled again and I stood taller, which still wasn't very tall, five eleven, on a good day. She offered the water bottle to the older man standing behind her. Was she a trophy wife? The guy looked wealthy, ready for business in a soft, gray sport coat, thick silver hair gelled back. "I'm fine," the guy said, brushing the bottle away.

Yoga woman shrugged and drank some more. It would have been a pleasure to continue watching her, but August was glaring over, eager to reassert himself. I wanted to keep the peace. Isn't it funny, I could have peacefully pointed out, that the abbreviation on the job for passengers is PAX? Instead, I said, as calmly as I could, "Please move along when you're ready."

I yearned to speak more with her, but I switched my attention to a little boy, six years old or so. Same age as my son, Ben. He was speed-drinking from a fist-sized purple juice box. Then I caught yoga woman flashing her sweet smile my way before she entered the scanner. Did she mouth "Thanks" at me? Sure looked like it, and I felt grateful even as the boy's stern mother scolded the potbellied father about how all the sugar was going to make the kid hyper for the flight. "I'll let you deal with it," the mother said, and they shuffled toward August, who was once again on the correct side of the mag, finishing up his rigorous inspection of the pet owner's palms.

～

I spent the next hour trying to sink deeper into the rhythm of the job. August chattered away with his cowgirl buddy Gloria Sanchez about the latest push at TSA HQ to arm at least a few TSOs on every shift.

"We'd get a lot less flirty talkback that way," he said.

Sanchez had a boxy head, and the way she wore her curly black hair accentuated the squarish shape. The straight lines and sharp angles added to her authority. "That's right," she said. "And we'd be ready to help if any demonstrations went south."

I didn't bother to point out that Albany International had no history of demonstrations. Instead, I drifted toward Laurie's old dream of moving to one of those countries where people shunned guns and cars while pedaling around on sensible bicycles. Amsterdam, that was her ideal city, and had been ever since she'd spent her junior year abroad studying history in Leiden. In Amsterdam, we'd find a real social safety net in place. Significant maternity leave. Dependable public education. She could live life to the fullest, raise a bunch of multilingual kids, get stoned with impunity, and fantasize occasionally about a tall, slender Dutchman while staying true to our marriage. I wondered, for the millionth time, what would have happened if I hadn't raced her, if I hadn't tried to pull in front, if I'd let her lead the whole way down the hill.

If this, if that, if the other thing.

Meanwhile, August and Sanchez were complaining about how ridiculous it was that TSOs always had to defer to the Law Enforcement Officers. If someone ran, TSOs weren't supposed to intervene directly. We were supposed to follow, keep the person in sight, await those LEOs. We'd be easy targets for any TSA-hating moron with a fancy rifle and bag full of ammo, like the guy who terrorized the checkpoint at Los Angeles International. It was exactly the sort of protocol that Laurie's older brother, Hank, loved to mock. Hank, who'd been working in and around the military and the FBI for more than twenty years. Hank, who'd called in late last night to say he'd be in town for the birthday. "Still with the TSA?" he'd asked, as usual.

"Affirmative," I'd answered.

"Thousands Standing Around," he'd said. "Tough Shit for America."

I took a breath, focused back on the job, and a few minutes later I was at the scanner being tapped for break. I wandered out of the checkpoint. Any chance yoga woman was still around? Should have stolen a glance at the gate number on her boarding pass. It might have been nice to look her in the eyes and wish her a relaxing trip. Or I could keep my distance. No conversation required. Buy her that water and get someone else to give it to her. Let her live the rest of her life never knowing it was a gift from me. Maybe an anonymous act like that would boost my beleaguered karma.

Instead, I headed for the men's room and locked myself in a stall to take a piss. When I opened the stall door and saw a guy rushing toward me, I panicked. Then I realized I was face-to-face with a flustered, terrified traveler who was desperate for help. "An old man collapsed over here," the guy said, pointing. "I was standing by the sink. I don't think he's breathing."

I considered running to get Carelli. That would be standard operating procedure. More TSA protocol for Hank to mock. Defer to the LEOs and defer to the EMTs. But maybe this was something minor, and why create unnecessary commotion? Create calm, right? One look at the man on the floor, though, and I sensed a real emergency. Two college-aged guys were trying mouth-to-mouth on the lifeless, splayed-out body. A once-white V-neck T-shirt partially covered his silver-haired chest. There was a bright-blue button-down shirt balled up next to him. Pungent aftershave, sulfuric like a polluted stream. Something about the man was vaguely familiar—maybe it was the smell—and then I noticed the soft, gray sport coat. My heart raced. I watched as one of the college guys did the compressions, counting them off, while the other guy clamped the old man's nose and breathed into his mouth. The guy doing the compressions needed to lock his elbows and move his hands lower.

I radioed Carelli and told him to send the EMTs over. As I spoke, I realized I was the one person in the room who knew exactly where the closest AED was. I quickly adjusted the college guy's arms. Command presence. "Get that T-shirt off while I'm gone," I said. "You're doing great here. Don't panic. I'll be right back."

I hustled out of the bathroom, thinking the old man was about to die. He was so pale and pasty. Those college kids would be the last ones to see the guy alive. Where was the yoga woman now? I didn't see her anywhere. I grabbed the AED off the wall. The traveler who'd surprised me by the stall trailed behind, repeating what he'd seen, maybe to get the images out of his head, or maybe to explain how it wasn't his fault. "He was standing by the sink. He reached down for the water, then his hands clawed at his chest. He didn't say a thing. Looked like he decided to sit down and then he just plopped over backwards."

"Don't worry," I said, shocked at how relaxed my voice sounded, as if I spent everyday rushing through the concourse with a defibrillator. "You did the right thing. Less talk, more hustle now, and we might do some good."

I stepped through the crowd of people, knelt down, opened up the AED, and it started squawking out instructions as soon as I switched it on, just like in the first aid course I'd taken before Ben's birth. All I had to do was follow the directions, get everyone to stand back, place the pads correctly. Then the man vomited and that changed the situation. The college guys, so brave at first, couldn't handle it and they backed away. I was disgusted too, but I didn't flinch. Credit fatherhood, I guess. I looked at the chunky, peach-colored mess and wondered what the man had been eating. The image of a smorgasbord, like the ones I used to love in college, flashed by. The steam rising from the buffet. The Sterno fumes.

Ponderosa, baby, I'd say to my willing friends, and off we'd go, ready to graze those tables.

Without more thought than that, I took over completely. I wasn't going to wait for the EMTs. I cleaned the area as best I could and kept the mouth-to-mouth going. I felt so calm. Was something wrong with me? What diseases can you catch from someone's puke? Maybe this was Ebola and not a heart attack. Then it got spooky for a moment when I felt the weight of the man's head. Nothing more or less than a heavy round object, awkward to lift, and the extremely oily hair didn't help. There was the pull of Laurie, what it was like near the very end. I'd never felt so powerless and there was no one in sight and I couldn't move her and I had to move her. I was breathing for this stranger and I felt as if I were inhaling death and I'd had enough death, thank you very much.

But I shook that off, backed away again, and listened as the machine did its work. *Do not touch the patient. Analyzing heart rhythm. Preparing shock. Move away from the patient. Shock delivered.* I focused on the body in front of me, observing it as carefully as I could for signs of life. Lately, Ben and I had been scouring Washington Park for signs of spring. Crocuses. Robins. Hyperactive squirrels. A hint of green in the tree branches above our heads. I worried again about the dictates of SOP. Should I really have waited? The first order of business must be to help everyone survive. Shouldn't you save someone if you can?

Then, in an astonishingly short amount of time—it felt like seconds—the old man stirred. The room smelled of barf and barbeque now. The man sat up, nearly bashing his head into the long row of sinks. His skin flushed, his lips reddened, and he seemed to start talking before he was breathing. I tried to take it all in, but my wandering mind seesawed back to Ben's birth, back to when he wasn't even Ben yet, just a waxy, motionless, tiny body the midwife was lifting out of the bathtub's reddening water and settling onto Laurie's chest. I kept trying to be the best labor partner ever, leaning forward, waiting, in my boxers and T-shirt, right behind Laurie in the tub, hands on her shoulders. The baby didn't breathe and didn't open his eyes and the candles I'd balanced on the shelf above the sink guttered off black smoke, as if they were about to be snuffed out too. I kept staring at the bruise-blue baby's blank, unmoving, shut-eyed face and I heard only the sound of murky water sloshing in the tub, and I felt overwhelmed by the fear that I was the father of a stillborn baby, soon, no doubt, to be divorced, because how could we recover from this? Fatherless myself for most of my life, I would now never become a father. I'd die alone, remembered by no one, which must have been my destiny all along. But then the midwife interrupted my pity party. "We're good here," she said, and the boy we'd name Benjamin opened his tiny mouth and gasped and wailed away, his cries an answer to the cries Laurie had pushed out for hours. His skin pinked up and minutes started speeding by again and in a daze I was cutting the umbilical cord. It felt like slicing into a thick piece of sashimi. Octopus. And before I could get my mind around what I'd just done—what Laurie had just done!—I was standing in front of those bathroom sink candles—still burning!—holding the towel-wrapped baby to my chest while the woman I loved more than anything in the world showered herself off and then stood beside me, leaning in close, warm, so completely alive. At that moment I felt a sparkling in my lungs I'd never felt before, like a torch igniting inside me, burning brighter, until the heat could barely be contained within my body. I closed my eyes and the torch flared higher and it was almost blinding. Was this what people meant when they talked about a third eye opening? Transcendence? I had no clue, but I could not stop grinning.

And that's when the airport EMTs rushed in, two rail-thin guys, both tall and twitchy with caffeine or something stronger to help them through the long hours. They probably had plenty of options in the enormous bags slung over their shoulders. But they looked devoted to their work, and they immediately took charge. They kept the man seated and checked his signs. "He's stable," said the one with the mullet. "Nice work. Way to save a life."

The EMTs who eventually found me carrying Laurie down Monument Hill Road never said anything remotely like that. In the ambulance, in the ER, in the waiting room, they left me alone, in silence, except when they interrupted my dread with useless questions: *How fast was she going? What did she hit? Where did she land?*

The question I saw on every face was: *Why her and not you?*

Now this mullet EMT was asking something different. "What's your name, Officer?"

I rubbed my eyes, wondering if I should keep my last name out of it. "I'm Gary," I said. "I didn't do a thing."

The EMT leaned in closer and then, too late, I remembered my name tag, pinned to my shirt pocket. "Gary Waldman," he said, writing it down.

The old man tried to stand. "I'm feeling much better," he said. "Where are my shirts? It's chilly in here."

"You'll be coming with us for a bit," the other EMT said. "We need to run some tests. We'll talk on the way."

"My stepdaughter and I have a flight to catch," the man said. "I don't think I have time."

The mullet EMT laughed. "Actually, you do have time, and for that you can thank Officer Waldman and his two samaritan assistants. I'll have someone make an announcement for your stepdaughter. What's her name?"

"Diane Percy Strand," the man said.

The people who'd been milling about, including the once-frantic traveler, chose that moment to break into a round of applause. The echo of it made my chest swell and helped me refocus. I waited for the yoga woman—Diane—to appear.

"Nice to have the TSA stepping up," Nonmullet chimed in. "Last time I flew, one of my boots disappeared in that damn X-ray machine. They shut the whole line down. Took them twenty minutes to find it in there. Must have irradiated the shit out of it. Foot cancer's coming my way."

"I think I remember a Waldman," the suddenly very alive old man said. "You're Lloyd's son. Gary, right? Tennis player?"

"Smallbany," I said, nodding. But I didn't know what to do next, especially since there were twenty-some people still lingering in the tight space. Were the hangers-on expecting more? Would they have a happy or sad story to tell when they arrived wherever they were going? Would the old man offer something to the TSA employee who'd just shocked his heart back on track?

"I'm Alex Strand," the guy said. "Knew your father slightly. Still hitting the courts?" I laughed and searched for the right response—*I gave it up after my wife died. Dropped all forms of competition for a year and now, well, sometimes I think I should shut it down for the rest of my life.* But the EMTs wanted Strand on a stretcher stat. And then Diane rushed in. "Dad!" she shouted.

"Where were you?" Strand asked.

"Another lousy call with my mother," she said. "Here's your phone back. What happened?"

"My heart started racing," Strand said. "I couldn't get enough air and I was sweating. Then I felt myself going down and I reached for the sink—"

"Let's continue this happy reunion in the ambulance," Nonmullet said, and they started wheeling the older Strand away.

"We'll have you over for drinks," Strand called out. "That's Gary Waldman, Diane," he said. "Saved my life. Get his contact info."

"I'm staying with you, Dad," Diane said, her hand resting on the stretcher, but she followed his gaze and looked my way. "You!" she said, shaking her head. "I'll come find you again."

And then they were gone and it was like when the house lights come on after a show. No encore, not tonight, the band left it all on the stage, and, quickly, that seemed okay. Sure, I might have treasured a few more grateful words, a heartfelt handshake, a hug or two, but I was pretty sure I hadn't seen the last of the Strands.

That thought helped me find a path through the short conversations that arose as I tried to leave. "Anyone could have done it," I said, chewing three pieces of wintergreen gum at once. "I was only doing my job. The real heroes are those guys who started right in with the mouth-to-mouth."

And in that way I left the bathroom behind.

Some break.

I had plenty of adrenaline still flowing, but I'd need more than that to get through the rest of the shift, so I bought another coffee and drank it by one of the large windows, trying to remember when I'd ever felt so alive at work. It didn't take long to drift toward the obvious thought: I hadn't felt anywhere near this alive since before Laurie's death.

Back at the checkpoint, Carelli was nowhere to be seen—he might have rotated to break or some sort of training class—and news of my bathroom "heroics" had not yet traveled very far. *Never the same day twice.* I knew how to *keep it simple, stupid.* Rodgers, another solid, grinding supervisor, an older woman with thick black glasses and steel-gray hair styled into the shape of a knight's helmet, steered me toward bag check, lane two. I grabbed more blue gloves, slipped on a pair, stuffed a few extra pairs into my back pocket, and took up my position, trying to be friendly to each and every weary traveler, concentrating, again, on standing taller, presenting my best self to the world parading by. This was the way the job should be done. Touch people. Save lives. Make a shitty world a little less shitty, one person at a time. Why not, for a change, try feeling proud?

2

AT THE END OF MY SHIFT, I left the checkpoint, walked to the break room, and watched the clock. Punch out too early, discipline. Punch out too late, discipline. And just as I was thinking I might actually escape into the rest of my day without anyone mentioning the CPR incident, Anderson Neffer poked his big head out from his office and said, "Come sit with me a sec, Officer Waldman."

I did as I was told and found Neffer reclining in his chair, feet on his desk, a plate full of buffalo wings resting on his lap. There were two dozen wings at least, half of them already eaten, their bones sucked clean. Neffer had a wing in each of his large, pudgy hands. "You look hungry," he said. "Have one of these. They're fantastic."

"Thanks, but I'm hoping for a short nap when I get home," I said. "Those wouldn't be good for my dreams."

"Come on," Neffer said. "Don't make this big man eat alone."

The guy remained something of a cipher to me, probably a grinder, maybe with cowboy tendencies. There were plenty of rumors or, as some called it, intelligence. Neffer was the TSA employee with the most seniority at the airport. He could have been fifty or sixty, his bulk made it tough to tell. He tended to speak cryptically and at length. His official title was Program Analyst, though he doubled as a Behavior Detection Officer. He could read your intentions on your face, if you believed in that stuff. The boards buttoned to his epaulets had three stripes. He worked whatever shifts he wanted and he held ultimate control over the schedule for everyone else. He also had an encyclopedic knowledge of SOP, and word was that before

Albany he spent time outside DC at TSA headquarters. Some said if he lost a little attitude, shed a few pounds, and learned to shave, the suits would eventually give him his own big-city airport.

I'd dropped papers by his office from time to time, but I'd never before been invited to sit down. I hoped to move up to a higher pay grade, sooner rather than later, to combat my imposing stack of bills. So, I reached for a wing. I took a bite and my head spun. "Hot," I said.

"Intended to be a merit," Neffer said, grabbing a bottle of Saratoga water from a tower of cartons near his chair. He handed the bottle over along with some napkins.

"Thanks," I said, shaking my head, as if that would cool down my torched tongue. "Is there something—"

Neffer cut me off. "Let's eat. Then we'll get to the talk. That's Interrogation 101. Or is it Psychology 101?" He pushed the plate of wings across the desk.

I picked up a few napkins and plucked out three more wings. While I ate, my attention drifted from the sauce in Neffer's silvering goatee to the walls of the cluttered office. No signs of the family Neffer, though the man did wear a wide, smooth gold wedding band. There was a New York Giants pennant, a photograph of Neffer himself in a black suit and tie at Ground Zero, and a standard TSA poster that featured two photos of a shark swimming in the ocean. One photo showed rough seas; in the other photo the seas were placid. It was, of course, much easier to spot the shark's fin—also known as *the threat*—in the calm water. A clear and basic reminder: don't make waves while working at the checkpoint.

Neffer dumped the bones into the trash and set the suddenly empty plate on the desk. "Okay," he said. "Anything you want to tell me?"

I glanced at my watch and looked back up. Was I about to get in trouble? I stared at the paper stacked everywhere, on the desk, by the walls, on the shelves, like some kind of insulation, but the room was still chilly. There was one small window above Neffer's head. It didn't look like the kind of window you could open. At the moment, it offered a view of two fuel trucks, exhaust pluming toward the gray sky. Nothing good could come from spending time in a space like this. It had to be killing him, but Neffer appeared content, ruler of all he surveyed.

"Let's skip the leading questions," Neffer continued, leaning forward, his voice sharper. "Shut the door." When I'd done that, he went on. "Now, personally, and off the record, I think you did something truly fabulous. Performing CPR in an emergency situation is a courageous act. What you did was brave and humane and it sets an extraordinary example for everyone fortunate enough to have witnessed it."

"Thank you," I said.

"Almost everyone is on your side," Neffer said. "Including me. I believe I would have done the same thing. As long as the guy was good-looking." Neffer paused, opened a fresh bottle of fizzy water, and guzzled most of it in one gulp. Then he belched—a deep rippler—before going on. "However, what happened is that someone heard about it and it got back to a few sticklers and they checked the surveillance tapes and asked me, first, and most importantly, to thank you for your extraordinary service and, second, to remind you that we need to remain very careful about that kind of behavior. The TSA's reputation has been in the toilet long enough without some sort of CPR-gone-wrong video hitting the YouTube."

"Am I getting written up?"

"You are not. I addressed the matter with the sticklers and told them they were being ridiculous."

Neffer paused to polish off the backwash from his bottle. He stared at me, as if awaiting further reaction. I kept quiet. He went on.

"But you've noticed that Albany's been receiving a little extra attention lately, haven't you?"

I nodded. There'd been more tests than usual during the last few weeks. An up-tick in Air Marshalls passing through.

"Glad you're aware," Neffer said. "There will be an important briefing soon. In the meantime, I wanted to make sure you know who your friends are. And I wanted to speak to you first, *as a friend*, so you can tell me how absurd it is to search people in wheelchairs while warning our officers away from saving lives. That is some deep-ass dysfunction, ladies and gentlemen. It's exactly the sort of bureaucratic bullshit that makes people laugh at us, isn't it?"

"I sure think so."

"Is there more you'd like to say about the matter? Now would be the time. It is a genuinely fucked-up response to basic ordinary human heroism, correct?"

"I agree."

"Go on. I don't want this sort of feeling to fester within you. Get it out of your system. The door's closed. I watched the man not breathe and not breathe and not breathe because I was following orders. I wanted to watch his mortal soul depart the terminal unimpeded. I mean, give me a break, right?"

I hesitated, but Neffer clearly wanted me to say something. "We're supposed to save lives when we can, aren't we?" Once I began, it was easy to keep going. "We're supposed to make people feel more secure. Wouldn't they feel secure knowing that officers will rush to assist them if they happen to collapse?"

"That's what I'm talking about, Waldman. We are all brothers and sisters, are we not?"

"If I were to collapse on the job—"

"That's it, Gary. Yes. That's it exactly. Go on."

"I wouldn't want anyone pussyfooting around. I'd want someone to give me CPR ASA-fucking-P."

Neffer nodded. "Excellent," he said, grinning. "*Pussyfooting.* Nice touch." He lightly applauded with his stove mitt-sized hands. Then he grabbed a pack of gum from his desk drawer. He took two sticks for himself and offered one to me. Doublemint. Gum to dull the taste of death before; now gum to mute the hot-wing haze.

"Thanks," I said.

Neffer folded the Doublemint into his mouth. "No problem, but here's something I'm curious about. Who would you pick?"

"What?"

"One of those hot part-time ladies, right? Myself, I'd go for Sharona. You've met her, haven't you? That mouth? Forget about it. And her bazongas would be right there. I'd be all, yes, thank you, please, I could use a few more breaths, just like that, and, perhaps, if you wouldn't mind, I mean, if it wouldn't be too inconvenient, could you slide your hands a little lower, a little lower—"

I could feel my face reddening. "Anyhow," I said.

"I'm not trying to embarrass you," Neffer said. "What's the matter? You're single, aren't you? You don't like Sharona?" Then he leaned forward again, his face more serious, intent, like in his Ground Zero photo. I half expected him to reach out and put a hand on my shoulder, but that didn't happen. "I get it," Neffer said. "Too soon. How long has it been now?"

I didn't want to talk about it with him, or with almost anyone. At the same time, the fact that he'd remembered was surprisingly moving. "Almost a year," I said. "Saturday would have been her birthday."

"Still is her birthday. Always will be. Never forget."

"I know."

"Well," Neffer said, shaking his head slowly, "I remain impressed by how you've been holding up. It does not go unnoticed. You have any family coming in to mark the moment?"

He was still leaning forward and, despite the gum, I could smell his wing-singed breath. "My son's here," I said. "And my brother-in-law is on his way."

Neffer exhaled. "Mrs. Neffer would say it's good not to be alone."

Now wasn't the time to talk about how cold and distant and condescending Hank could be. "I need to punch out soon," I said.

Neffer glanced at his watch, a dainty gold antique. Probably had to wind it himself every morning. "Thank you for your focused attention," he said, repeating another familiar TSA phrase that connected with my coaching years. How many times had I told my players to pay attention to the ball, to their racket head, to the moment of contact? "You did good today," Neffer added. "That's the takeaway here. Now hustle up. I'd hate to see you get in real trouble, especially with Albany under the spotlight."

"I appreciate that," I said, and then I hurried down the hallway and punched out just in time, reliable as ever, doing my best to follow all the rules. I headed toward the employee parking lot, wondering what that spotlight was searching for.

3

AFTER THE FUNERAL, THERE'D BEEN counseling, and there were people who did their best to offer sympathy and support, dropping off food, volunteering to babysit Ben. I was grateful for the kindness, even though I couldn't really talk about it and I wasn't eating much and I wasn't seeking any time away from my son. "Grief can alter your brain," said the therapist I saw for ten weeks, and I didn't doubt it, but it felt more like a reset than an alteration. Sleeplessness, racing heart, twitching eyes, the inability to corral my thoughts—it was all familiar. I'd been shut down before and now I was shut down again.

I would have shut down more than ever, over and out, if not for Ben.

In a very different way, there were the occasional hours I spent with Paul Fasch, my old friend and high school tennis-team doubles partner. Paul's wife, Tara, had died three years earlier following a long struggle with breast cancer that became a short struggle with pancreatic cancer. After that, Paul left town for a while to live near his daughter in Philadelphia. When he'd returned to Albany, I got him back on the tennis court and Laurie used to talk about fix-ups. "No rush," she'd tell Paul. "Whenever you're ready." Then she was gone and it was my turn to take a break from tennis. "So we'll run," Paul had said.

One or two afternoons a week, we'd meet at Haven College, one of Paul's marketing firm's many clients. My connection to the place was more intense. It was where I used to coach and where Laurie used to work in HR. It was also, of course, where she'd had her fatal accident. I liked to believe it was doubly healthy to keep exercising at the site of the disaster, but I had my doubts.

As usual, I met Paul at the gym and then we headed out on what we'd come to call the afternoon mourning route. Not quite five miles and we did our best to bang it out in less than forty-five minutes. On this particular day, Paul pushed the pace hard from the get-go. Spring had begun a few weeks ago, but it was chilly. There'd even been talk of snow in the forecast. I could almost smell it in the air, as if someone had reopened a vast freezer.

"Let's pick it up," Paul said.

There was a gentle downhill zigzag past the president's mustard-colored Georgian mansion. We startled a family of deer and the buck snorted before prancing into the forest, his doe and two scrawny fawns right behind. Far ahead, I glimpsed a line of horseback riders, some of Haven's equestrian studies majors, a holdover from the college's single-sex days, when it was Mary Haven College for Women, striving to be one of the Seven Sisters. Before the riders disappeared into a tall stand of pines and boxwoods, they kicked their horses into a gallop for the homestretch back to the college's high-class stables.

I followed Paul to the base of Monument Hill. The gravel path ascended like a long circular staircase. I used to lead the tennis team on runs like this, pushing them and myself past the point where conversation was possible. Breathe and keep going, I'd urge them. Use your arms to pull yourself along, lean forward, push and push and push. As I neared the small grove of pine trees atop the hill, I remembered how Laurie and I would circle Mary's statue, slap the side of her marble foot, gaze up at her broadsword, and then walk or bike back to the bookstore café. Later, in those weeks after the birth, I'd swaddle Ben tight against my chest and urge Laurie out for as long a walk as she wanted. Then there were the years of pushing the stroller up through the shifting gravel. Pause for a while at the summit, inhale the piney air, and pray the kid would nap all the way home.

The hilltop was a natural destination because of the tough work it took to get there, but it also offered a great view of Albany.

There was Empire Plaza, a Rockefeller-era "gift" to the city filled with concrete towers and underground tunnels, home to thousands of state workers who commuted back and forth on the highways that ran along the banks of the Hudson River. Then there were the still expanding medical complexes out on New Scotland Avenue. You could see Pine Hills and Buckingham Pond, the four tall towers of SUNY's dorms off in the distance. Washington Avenue ran out that way, one of the patchwork city's many dividing lines, separating areas of urban renewal from areas of urban decay. Center Square, with its increasingly well-tended 1880s brownstones, was somewhat successfully gentrifying on one side. Arbor Hill, with its once-grand brownstones increasingly abandoned and boarded up, stood—or failed to stand—on the other side. Over the last few generations, my family had managed to migrate across that dividing line, moving from North Albany to the fringes of Center Square.

This was the city where I'd grown up. I hadn't chosen it. I suppose I had chosen to stay, though I couldn't say why. What did it mean that I still remained a renter? Was I keeping my options open, ready to relocate to some other city when the right time came? Or would I, like Laurie, forever yearn for a small brownstone of my own to fix up just around a corner or two?

"Awfully quiet today," Paul said.

"I can barely breathe at this pace," I said. "You want to talk, talk."

Paul had two fingers pressed lightly into his neck, checking his pulse. "I figure if I make these last few runs miserable enough, you won't have any second thoughts about switching back to tennis."

"Back to tennis," I said, testing it out. "Won't be pretty."

"This won't be pretty either. Time to sprint."

Then I was flying down the hill toward the gym. Paul was pushing harder, gaining strides. I didn't mind. It was fun to accelerate after my old partner. He'd always been the popular guy and the better athlete. During high school, all I had to do was play steady while Paul put away shot after shot. When we were really clicking, it felt like we were unbeatable. A grinder and a gifted wonder. The human backboard, chasing down everything, and the amazing acrobat, leaping skyward to snatch lobs out of the air and smash them for easy winners. I kept pushing and then the runner's high kicked in at last, the whole point of the exercise, and my mind whirred forward. Maybe the return to tennis will be a relief, and healthy too. Maybe the time off will have made me a smarter player. My cardio must be better, my heart stronger. Laurie would want me to play. And maybe Ben would begin to show some interest in the game. No pressure, but whenever he asked, if he ever asked, I'd be there with a racket ready.

We bumped fists at the gym's door, laughing, and by the time we'd showered and changed, my mood had shifted so much that without thinking it over at all I shared my life-saving story. "Shit," Paul said, when he heard about the puke. "That's above and beyond."

"It felt nice to save the guy's life."

"Who was he?" Paul asked. "I mean, thanks to you, who is he?"

"Alex Strand."

Paul reached over and clapped me on the shoulder, like he used to do after we'd won a tough point. "Nice choice," he said. "Strand's one of the richest guys in town. Any mention of a reward yet?"

"I was trying to think of it as a quasi-redemptive pay it forward and backward karmic wheel kind of thing."

"I see."

"New life. More life. I mean, I wasn't looking for money when I grabbed the AED."

"I get it," Paul said. "But maybe this will jumpstart a search for better work."

I rolled my eyes. Nearly everyone I knew encouraged me to quit the TSA. Paul believed a career change would be a healthy way to deal with grief. Almost as healthy as getting back on the tennis court. He wasn't wrong, but I wasn't ready. I more or less still hated myself, and it felt accurate to have a job where many people hated me every day. I didn't need a therapist to understand that. "The work felt good today," I said. "Which isn't bad timing, since Hank could show up any minute now."

"I'll leave the badgering to him then," Paul said. "Might be nice to go out a winner, though. Save a life. Drop the mic. Move on."

As we walked back outside, Paul adjusted the knot of his bright-blue tie, sliding it tight to his neck. He'd probably log a few more hours at his office over on Swan Street. Meanwhile, I had to pick up Ben. I paused by my aging Subaru and studied the outrageous campus, the stately red brick college buildings lining all four sides of the grassy, well-manicured quad, so pastoral, so out of place smack in the middle of Albany. The buds on the trees were fighting the chill in the air. Barely visible up close, they made the sides of Monument Hill shimmer in the breeze and the Helderbergs out on the horizon looked greener than they had in months. I was well aware that the students strolling among the buildings were often weighed down by real worries and troubles, but even when I tried to observe them with my sharpest surveillance gaze, what I saw was one carefree kid after another, all of them lucky to frolic in this bubble world for as many years as their parents could afford.

Paul beeped his slightly newer Subaru unlocked. "So let me change the subject for a second. Can I ask you a favor?"

"Of course."

"There's a woman coming to visit me from Philly—"

"The one you've been talking about?"

"You got it. Her name's Vanessa."

"Visiting? This is a major step."

"Just trying to be a good role model for you."

I was tempted to remind him about the significant differences: three years versus one year; a teenager versus a kindergartner; a long sickness versus a sudden accident; getting to say goodbye versus getting to say nothing. "A major step," I repeated.

"I'd like to meet her at the gate somehow. An old-school welcome. Can you make that happen?"

"Not if I quit my job," I said. "But, seriously, shouldn't be hard. You can usually get a pass from the airline. When is she flying in?"

"Friday morning. She'll stay for the weekend. You'll come out for a dinner or two?"

I wasn't going to speak of Tara, but I couldn't help thinking about how hard she'd fought, how frail and off-balanced she'd looked the last time I'd seen her, tightly clinging to Paul's arm as they walked up the steps into their house. "You sure you're ready to do this?" I asked.

Paul laughed. "Ready? What a joke. I'll never be ready and neither will you. You know that much, don't you?"

"I'm not an idiot," I said, though I wasn't so sure. "So, you're not ready?"

"I'm not ready and I'm doing it anyhow. I have a plan."

"Let's hear it."

"I'm going to surrender everything and expect nothing in return."

"That way you won't get hurt?"

"I might get hurt. But I won't be disappointed."

I admired his bravery, but that wasn't the kind of thing we said to each other. "Inspirational," I said.

Paul laughed again, harder this time, a cartoonish sound loaded with more good memories. "I can't remember," I said. "Does this Vanessa have a sister?"

Paul smiled as he climbed into his car. "That's the spirit. I want to hear what happens next with Mr. Strand, so keep me posted. Then after this weekend it will be tennis again, right? At long last."

4

As soon as I saw my son, I lowered my window and started waving. Ben was sitting by the flagpole along with a few boys from aftercare. Ben's main teacher, Irene, was a sweet woman my age who looked a least a decade older, in part because she had five kids and a weakness for tanning salons. She steered Ben's attention toward the line of cars and he jumped up, waving back. He looped his bag over his shoulder and followed Irene down to the sidewalk.

She opened the back door and leaned in. "I hear you have a tough birthday celebration coming up," she said, shaking her head. "That generated some interesting conversation today."

Irene struck me as a woman who'd seen it all. Maybe she'd have some advice about what we should do. "It wasn't my idea," I said. I didn't bother to explain that Shannon, one of my ex-players and, since Ben's birth, our go-to babysitter, had been the first to mention the possibility of a party.

"What exactly will you do?" Irene asked.

I didn't have an answer ready. "I guess I haven't figured it out yet. Any suggestions?"

"Can't go wrong with cake."

I laughed. I hadn't even thought that far ahead. "Cake," I said. "Sure."

She stepped back from the door, clearing a path for Ben, who rumbled into the booster seat and buckled himself in. "Dad Dad Dad," he was saying.

"You tell me if I can help out in any way," Irene said, stepping back more and waving goodbye. "You know I'll do what I can. Laurie remains in my thoughts, as do you two boys."

I drove off, making room for the eager parents in the cars and minivans behind me. Ben was eager too. "Dad Dad Dad, can we go to CVS?"

Ben's current obsession was first aid kits—it had been dinosaurs before, and before that clocks, stuffed animals, ambulances, and firefighters.

"Can we, Dad?"

I glanced in the rearview mirror and tried to gauge my son's interest in this request. Soon after Ben was born, Laurie had started calling him a "mini-Gary." It could sometimes bring her down. She was exhausted. Her old life was gone. She didn't know what to do. She was trapped and people kept echoing what she said, telling her the baby was indeed a mini-Gary.

I had joked about it as best I could. "His face might be my face," I'd say. "But his head is the shape of your vagina."

She was silent for a few seconds the first time I used that line. Then she laughed. "Funny man," she'd said. "Let's hope he gets your sense of humor too."

I smiled at my son and thought: If she could see Ben as I see him now, she'd see herself everywhere. Then I said, "CVS, here we come!"

"Yes!" Ben shouted, and as we drove toward the nearby strip mall, Ben kicked the long, spindly legs that came from Laurie. Her curly brown hair blew in the breeze from the window he insisted on opening (she always wanted the windows open). He smiled her irresistible smile. In the parking lot, he hopped out, held my hand until the sidewalk, and then he was off, all pointy elbows and knobby knees, running her gawky run to the automatic doors.

Inside, in this blandest of stores—*if you've been to one CVS, you've been to every single CVS*, though CVS workers would probably disagree—there was so much Ben wanted. He brimmed with excitement by the shelves of bandages and ointments. He grabbed an aerosol can of something called Wound Wash and declared it his choice. I looked it over. Ten bucks for a saline spray that would eradicate a little more of the ozone he'd need when he got older. Well, part of a parent's job is to teach children how to tolerate frustration. That was some of Laurie's wise language, language she loved to apply to many of our politicians. Like everyone else, she'd encouraged me to bid farewell to the TSA. "No one should work for such a dysfunctional government," she liked to say.

So I knelt down, looked Ben in the eye, and said, "Sorry, partner, you'll have to pick something else." I referred to climate change, price, and the waste of buying unnecessary products. I counteroffered with a host of other possibilities—ACE Bandages, boxes of gauze, spools of waterproof tape, scissors, tweezers. But the boy, like his mother, could occasionally be stubborn and inconsolable.

Would he actually go to tears on this one? I sat down on the cold linoleum floor beside him. I wasn't going to be impatient, but that was an available path, old and well-worn. It used to hurt my tennis game. Far better to create calm.

"What was your favorite part of the day?" I asked.

"I don't remember."

"Let me tell you my favorite part of the day then."

"Okay."

"Too bad I don't remember."

Ben turned away and stared at the Wound Wash cans on the shelf. "Come on, Dad. I'll tell you if you tell me."

I wondered if I should have asked what it was about Wound Wash, but that felt like backward movement now. "I saved a man's life at the airport this morning," I said.

"What was wrong with the man?"

"His heart had stopped."

"How did you restart it?"

"I knew where the defibrillator was and we used that."

"What's a defibrillator?"

"It's a machine that shocks the heart and gets it going again."

"Can we buy one of those?"

It was progress of a sort and I mussed his hair. "Afraid not," I said. "They're superexpensive."

"But don't we need one? Our hearts are broken. That's what Shannon says."

Shannon had been essential throughout the year. These days, she worked in the Student Services office at UAlbany, but sometimes it seemed as if her main job was caring for Ben. The extent of her influence occasionally surprised me—the whole birthday party idea, for instance—but I trusted her. Had the Wound Wash idea come from her too? "Shannon's talking about a different kind of broken heart," I said. "It might be nice if defibrillators could shock sadness away, though."

"But it's okay to be sad, right?"

"You bet," I said. Would I wind up being the one with the tears? To stave them off, I grabbed an extra-large ACE Bandage, a box of Toy Story Band-Aids and a thick roll of tape. Was it too much of a mixed message? *It's okay to be sad, but let's cheer up!* "All this," I said, "plus a Ring Pop. Then pizza and frozen yogurt. What do you say?"

Mixed message or no, it was good to see that smile again, and in it I could see the old mini-Gary I'd heard so much about. Stubborn, but maybe not inconsolable after all. "Plan!" Ben shouted, reaching out for all the stuff.

I held onto it. "First let's hear about your favorite part of the day."

"My favorite part of the day," he said, moving in for a hug, "is right now."

I could call that "right now" a victory, some sort of pitch-perfect Zen wisdom, and from there I could try to follow a fun, enjoyable route through the next few hours. We coasted to pizza and frozen yogurt and then, later, bellies full, bath rituals completed, we wound up pajamaed and stretched out in Ben's bed. He begged for an extra book before lights-out and I said okay and read the one where a kid describes in detail the incredible house he plans to build someday. If I stayed in the bed too long, I'd fall asleep too. It wouldn't be the first time. I'd made the midnight, sleep-stupored stumble back to my bedroom more nights than not during the last year. Ben turned to face the wall, like he always did just before drifting off, and I started to tiptoe out. Then Ben stirred. "Daddy," he said, "when is Uncle Hank coming?"

I'd often been tempted to tell him not to trust Hank. When I coached, I taught my players to be on the lookout for deception. Learn how your opponents disguise their serves. Learn how they vary spin and speed to keep you off-balance. Hank seemed to keep everyone he knew off-balance, but he was the only family we had left. And it was late. So I simply answered the question I'd been asked. "Sometime tomorrow," I whispered.

"What about the man?"

"What man?"

"The one you saved. What did he look like?"

I perched on the bed again. I kept whispering. The kid would be asleep in less than a minute. "Well," I began, "I wasn't really studying his face. I was just trying to help him breathe again. It didn't matter what he looked like. But here's something you won't believe."

His breathing slowed, grew steady. That should do it.

"What won't I believe?" he asked.

"The man knew who I was," I said. "He said he knew my father." This time I listened to the steady breathing a little longer, just to be sure.

"How did he know you were you?" Ben asked.

I almost laughed. I stretched again and put my head down. Ben was at least half-asleep, but he was also a fighter. A tough little grinder. "He remembered my last name," I said.

"He remembered my last name," Ben mumbled, as if he were already dreaming, or maybe as if affirming that he too was, for better or worse, a Waldman.

I was thinking it over, staring at my son's smooth, peaceful face in the faint greenish glow of the T-Rex night-light. I stared in part to make sure Ben was really asleep, in part to keep myself awake. Plus I was always on the lookout for changes, as if I'd see something on my son's brow, cheeks, or chin that would reveal, with undeniable clarity, that Ben wouldn't be scarred for the rest of his life. Such a sweet impossibility. People often tried to connect my TSA work with the desire to keep Ben safe in the wake of Laurie's accident, but I was a TSO long before Ben was born, back when Laurie seemed indestructible. I'd known for years that I couldn't keep anyone safe. My father died of natural causes—an aneurysm—when I was twelve and my mother died of different natural causes—lung cancer—when I was thirty-eight. In between, there'd been too many years with my lousy stepfather. I'd been scarred, or euchred, as an old coach used to say after each defeat. *We've been euchred by this loss, everyone of us,* he'd declare. But that's not where he'd stop. He'd take a short breath and then he'd raise the volume of his voice a few notches. *Now let's do better when we hit the courts tomorrow!*

So, or course, Ben would be scarred. Was scarred already. But what about tomorrow? Tomorrow, I noticed, I needed to remind my son to do a better job washing the little folds in his flabby, baby-fat neck. I also noticed his moist, warm breath. It seemed enough to heat the whole room. And it would be no big deal if I fell asleep for a few minutes in his bed. I'd be right there in case of a bad dream, though if Ben had nightmares, he'd yet to share them. I certainly didn't share mine. I didn't talk about the ways Ben, years older, in various locations—kitchen, car, campus, park, checkpoint—would yell at me. He'd grown so tall, broad-shouldered and strong. Sometimes he was standing next to Hank, sometimes he stood alone. But he always had his child face and the lungs of a baby. He yelled louder and louder. *Get out of here! Leave me alone! I don't ever want to see you again! You ruin everything!*

"*Shh,*" I said. And I kept whispering to myself as my head sank deeper into my son's pillow. "I'm sorry. It'll be all right."

5

THE NEXT MORNING, I WAS WALKING up to the checkpoint for my shift and I couldn't remember if I'd packed a fork in Ben's lunch, and then I was thinking of how many other things I couldn't remember that had happened just minutes ago. Which echoed one of my long-held fears: My brain only fully kicked in when I was at work, whether on the court or at the airport.

Right now it was easy to see the suits, Behavior Detection Officers, and new recruits milling about on the observation deck, one floor above the checkpoint. The walls were glass up there, making it the perfect spot to see the remarkable amount of dust that gathered atop the scanners. More importantly, it was also the perfect spot to surveil the lines, measure the throughput, note the choke points, and teach the newbies while also identifying those who were underperforming. Obviously, yet another test loomed. I switched on my A game as did everyone else around me.

I rotated in on X-ray, lane three, and it wasn't long before I saw Carelli off to my left shutting down lane two. Looked like they'd snagged a woman with some contraband pinned up in her hair. The rules for dealing with hair, turbans, hats, and wigs seemed to change constantly. What should you touch? What should you ask the PAX to touch? Hats off (so to speak) to the TSO who'd made the catch.

The powers that be tended to use new airport workers in these tests—unfamiliar faces to keep us TSOs on our toes—and the girl they'd pulled aside was blushing, more embarrassed than scared. I looked up and saw that almost all of the people in the observation deck had stepped away from the glass. No sign of real urgency or panic in any eyes that I could see. So I carried on, allowing myself to feel at least a little relieved. A passed test was good for everyone on the shift, even if solidarity wasn't always Albany's strong suit. The patches on the uniform emphasized three attributes that supposedly united everyone working for the Department of Homeland Security: Innovation, Integrity, and Team Spirit. But at Albany, as far as I could tell, it was a pretty narrow version of *to thine own self be true.* In other words, look out for number one. Take the rule around security doors: You step through those doors one at a time. If there's someone behind you, even if it's a friend, even if it's someone you work beside every day, someone who has passed all the same background checks you've passed, someone you've known for years, you follow SOP. You walk through the door and you close the door in your coworker's face. Let them unlock it themselves with their own secure code.

Eight others were hired at the same time I was. We trained together and we started losing people almost immediately. There was a former sociology major who was compelled to cover her blue-dyed hair with a wig. She left after failing the first test about SOP. There was a burly Harley-Davidson biker guy who was compelled to cover his neck tattoo (a pirate flag) with a bandage. He left because the uniform gave him a rash. When we moved out of the damp, windowless basement classroom and shifted to early-bird on-the-job training, four more people quit. By the end of the first month, my training group was down to three. We met up for happy hour at the TGIF in Stuyvesant Plaza when our badges came in. A former middle school teacher, an out-of-work car salesman, and me. We talked about doing happy hour again, but we never got around to planning it, and after six months, I, the former tennis coach, was the sole survivor. Over the years, attrition only got worse. They started bringing on more and more part-timers and even though the salary and the benefits remained decent, people struggled to build a life around a twenty-hour workweek.

But if you did your job, the raises came through, the benefits accrued, and no one bothered you too much. Know your SOP, show up on time, pass the tests, deal with the repetition and the tedium, and you could survive. You might even succeed.

So I watched the screen, my attention focused, and then I noticed an odd three-ring binder and two large bottles of water in a rolling duffel bag. A very deliberate distraction, or so it seemed to me. They usually ran one test per shift. Usually, however, wasn't always. August was on bag check, so I called him over.

He peered at the image and said, "I'll grab the water and run it through again."

"Check the whole thing," I said. "Binder looks fishy too. Do people even use binders anymore?"

"Not on your watch, right? CPR samaritan wants more glory."

I kept the bags moving along. I'd have to trust August to do his job, even though I knew he'd be happy to see me fail. Still, I'd get another look at the bag when it came back through the machine. In the meantime, I glanced over at the passenger who stepped up to claim the bag. Male, thirties, nervous eyes. I looked up at the observation deck again. Empty. Lane two had reopened and the young lady they'd been patting down was nowhere in sight.

"Pulled the water," August said when he returned. "Coming back through now. Seems okay to me."

I stopped the belt and took my time. The binder probably hadn't been touched at all. "That color around the edges looks like a threat to me," I said. "I still don't like it."

Sanchez stepped up to study the image too.

"He still doesn't like it," August said.

"Lord knows we want our hero to like it," Sanchez said.

I moved the belt forward. "Whatever," I said. "Search it."

About a minute later, when August used the ETD machine to test for traces of explosives in the bag, the reading was off the charts. The alarm sounded and Carelli shut the line down. The suits and LEOs were suddenly everywhere. The bomb squad guys cleared the area. Two of them were helping their short, squat chief climb into his big green armored outfit. Neffer himself magically materialized from his office. He sauntered over and shook my hand. "Well done, son," he said. "You just did your whole crew a solid."

∾

Soon after the two-part test, a bunch of us rotated down to the break room for a briefing. There would be a few more or less identical briefings throughout the day. That way everyone could be on-message. Maybe these briefings had been serious gatherings in the past. Maybe they remained serious in other airports. At Albany, though, they'd come to feel like short detentions. Sit quietly while one of the supervisors shared announcements, updates, and some heavily redacted sensitive security information, otherwise known as SSI. The supervisors followed their scripts and the TSOs were supposed to listen carefully. Most people surfed their devices, wolfed down food, joked around, tried not to laugh. Still, given what Neffer had said, I had a feeling this briefing might be different.

Carelli stood in front of the microwave. He requested everyone's focused attention and then began reading from the pages on his clipboard. He started with a recent event in Yemen that led some mullahs to issue statements citing American weakness and disarray, urging militants everywhere to feel uplifted and emboldened by yet another successful operation as well as by the lowering of American flags on the rooftops of various US embassies. "The takeaway here," Carelli said, "is that we need to remain vigilant at our posts."

I was sitting next to Kevin, a big African American guy who had to walk through the scanners sideways. Definitely the most intimidating officer on the floor, until he chuckled. It was almost a giggle, surprisingly high-pitched. Rumor was he'd played football at Syracuse until he feuded with the head coach and quit the game. He inspired fear and didn't seem to have much of it himself. I had helped train him and had come to trust him. We shared a sports background. And I liked that he'd once talked about how, as a kid, he'd dreamed of being a Boy Scout. "I dug those sashes," he'd explained. "My father said there was only time for football." Still too early in his TSA career to tell if he was a grinder or not, though he didn't seem likely to be a cowboy. Probably a short-timer, waiting for something better to come along. He was twiddling away on his phone. He slid his device over to me, showing off how he'd cut and pasted a photo of Carelli into a disaster montage that featured a wave of gunfire followed by a series of atomic explosions.

Carelli kept following the script. A man had created a level-one disturbance by praying in the aisle of a 747 during its approach to Phoenix. The man was asked to move. He refused to move. He protested. He said it was time. Fighters scrambled from a nearby base. A deadheading pilot, assisted by two flight attendants, saved the day, restraining the kneeling man until the plane was safely on the ground. The takeaway from this event supposedly had something to do with command presence and team spirit.

"You believe this shit?" whispered Kevin. "Man was praying and they scrambled the goddamn fighters?"

I shook my head and stayed quiet. Carelli soldiered on. Overtime opportunities would soon be available. Canned food was being stockpiled for future emergencies in the region. All donations would be appreciated. And Officer Sanchez had made a good catch of an inert replica grenade artfully concealed in the hidden compartment of a backpack. "Which brings me to today's drill," Carelli said, finally looking up from his clipboard. "Well done, with special shout-outs to Officer Singh, for catching that batarang hair piece, and Officer Waldman, for his sharp eyes on the bags."

Carelli paused to slap at the clipboard with his hand a few times. A brief titter of applause spread across the room and then Carelli got back to business. "I need to add one more thing about Officer Waldman, however," he said.

"Uh-oh," Kevin whispered. "Better sit up straighter, Holmes."

I put my shoulders back, lifted my head higher.

"We all know the SOP about calling for EMTs and letting the professionals do their jobs," Carelli said. "And yet, you may have heard that Officer Waldman's instinctive medical assistance saved a life yesterday. While we absolutely applaud and celebrate his efforts, I'd also like to remind you all that what looks like an emergency might be a staged distraction, creating an opening for real terror. Luck was on our side on this occasion and Officer Waldman's timely intervention has been recognized as heroic by our airport's director of operations. But it could just as easily have been a tragedy. For that reason, and for many other all too familiar reasons, we need to remain vigilant and error-free. We can afford no mistakes. Heightened scrutiny will continue here at Albany International. So, no slip-ups, understood?"

People began to push their chairs back. They knew the closing notes when they heard them, but Carelli raised his voice. "Before we disperse," he said, "we need to hear vital information from a special guest who is here with us today."

I heard the footsteps and recognized the exaggerated throat-clearing behind me before I turned. Carelli went on. "Our colleague from the FBI, Hank Bell, would like to say a few words. He'll be working with Albany's Joint Terrorism Task Force for a little while and he's been visiting all of the Upstate airports to spread the word about a high-level threat. Everything you'll hear is, of course, SSI."

Hank was in a standard dark-blue suit, with a matching tie, and a starched white shirt. The creases in his pants were military grade, as was the buzzed head. His black steel-toe boots were buffed to shine like two dark mirrors. With the possible exception of Kevin, he was the biggest guy in the room. He held a thin manila folder in his hand.

"No way," I whispered.

"You know this dude?" Kevin whispered back.

"My brother-in-law," I said, shaking my head.

"You're shitting me."

"Afraid not."

Then Hank began to talk, his familiar sharp, drill-sergeant squawk echoing around the room. "I'll keep it brief," he said. "I don't want to interfere with your crucial work." He opened the folder and held up three photographs, one at a time. It was difficult to see them clearly from where I sat. "These three men are part of a terrorist cell last known to be working outside of Buffalo, near the Canadian border. Homegrown ISIS fans. They have expertise with explosives and we have reason to believe they're targeting one of the smaller Upstate New York airports. Albany International has been mentioned as a possibility. Officer Carelli will post these images here, along with the vitals we know. Please study them carefully. If you see anyone even slightly resembling any of these individuals, alert your supervisor immediately." Hank handed the folder of photographs to Carelli. "Any questions?" he asked.

The room had grown very quiet, quiet enough that I felt I could hear all of our hearts beating faster. The air seemed a few degrees hotter. Hank scanned the room. When his eyes caught mine, he nodded, and then kept talking. "Thank you for your focused attention."

Hank shook Carelli's hand before marching back out of the room. "Now take a look at these photographs and then get the hell back to work," Carelli said.

I joined the line to the bulletin board, where Carelli was posting the photos. While I shuffled forward, I tried to catch sight of Hank, but he was gone.

"That's your brother-in-law?" Kevin said. "What's the story?"

What could I tell him? All I really knew was that the guy had served in the Air Force for more than a decade before shifting over to the FBI. He didn't talk about his work, which, of course, was part of the nature of the work.

"Let's keep it to ourselves," I said to Kevin. "I know almost nothing about him. He's got kind of a gruff exterior."

"No kidding."

"I haven't managed to get much beyond that. Laurie's death didn't bring us any closer, that's for sure."

"Interesting times," Kevin said, as we approached the images.

I nodded. I was tempted to say more about how shocked I was, but August and Sanchez moved up beside us and we all studied the images together. They didn't fit my ideas of a stereotypical terrorist. They were clean-shaven. They were all in their thirties. Two of them had pale white skin. One with thinning black hair, the other with bowl-cut reddish hair. The third struck me as European, tan, bald, with a tattoo of the word *DEVOTED* on his neck.

"It's the Three Stooges," August said. "Larry, Moe, and Curly."

"Curly looks hot," Sanchez said. "You think I can fuck him before he gets shot?"

"Curly's the bald one, right?" said August. "You go for tattoos?"

"It's those blue eyes I like," she said.

August looked my way. "Meanwhile, our persistent little savior went lip to lip with that old geezer. Bet that was fun."

"That's not who he wants to be lip to lip with," August said. "He was practically drooling over some yoga tights yesterday."

We'd been shown photographs of suspected terrorists before, but never by a visiting FBI agent and never with the news that Albany had been identified as a possible target. August and Sanchez were clearly more excited than shocked about the special briefing, so they joked with more cockiness than usual. Maybe it came from nervousness too. Also, as always, they wanted to get under my skin, find a way to push my buttons so they could use it against me when the time came around for promotions or transfers. Sanchez often talked about her dream of a posting out west or in the Caribbean. When August wasn't talking about the next police exam, he talked about applying to the FBI. Maybe he thought Hank could give him a hand. In any case, snide comments from the two of them hadn't fazed me for a while, but I didn't appreciate having Kevin witness this round, especially when Kevin chimed in. "Yoga tights?" he asked. "She have a sweet ass?"

I left the break room and walked silently toward the checkpoint, passing by one of my favorite pieces of airport art: a pair of matching stainless steel triangular objects that hung suspended beneath a row of ventilation ducts. The circulating air kept them always moving, light shimmering on their burnished metal, and they looked like fighter jets in tight formation. I watched them bob and weave while Sanchez, August, and Kevin walked on ahead. Then I turned my attention to another favorite piece: a giant ball built from plywood and laminated with a layer of red cedar. The thing was seven or eight feet high, centered on a black stone platform right in the middle of the concourse. The artist had attached more than a hundred hand-made wrought-iron rings to the sculpture; they were all circular, some thick, some thin, some the size of a pinky, others almost as large as small bicycle wheels. The piece was called *Lubber*, but I liked to call it "Clobber." Apparently, the rings were meant to be used. Out of habit, I stepped over and clobbered one against the wood. I felt the clatter in my teeth and temples.

Then it was just a few short steps back to the checkpoint. I grabbed more gloves from the table in front of the supervisor's podium and waited for my assignment, but suddenly Neffer was standing next to me again, this time with a young woman by his side. "Officer Waldman," he said, "I've brought over someone who wants a few words with you."

August and Sanchez were on their way over to bag check on lane three. Before they moved off, I could hear August mumble, "Speak of the devil. Here comes the reward for the life-saving widower."

"Woman doesn't have a prayer," Sanchez said. "Goody-goody Gary's a walking bag of lady catnip right now."

I tried to ignore the ribbing. I also tried not to stare at Diane. Just about my height, sweet smile and stunning legs, a flash of Laurie through my body. Was this the way I'd be for the rest of my life, glimpsing my dead wife in every woman I met?

She wanted to shake hands and I discovered I could do that. I could also remember I was in uniform, with a familiar role to play. Hard to overemphasize the comfort of that. Surveil. Focus. She kept her dark brown hair short, almost as buzzed as Hank's. She was fine-boned, birdlike, with those emerald-green eyes. She was wearing a tight T-shirt that said Question Authority and even tighter black jeans. She had a strong grip and I guessed she was a runner, too.

"Thank you again for helping my stepfather yesterday," she said. "The whole family is extremely grateful to you."

One of Laurie's occasional criticisms, way back when, was that I wasn't very spontaneous. Once, in a huff, tired of the same old charge, I'd responded without thinking: "I can be spontaneous," I'd said. "I just like to know when." Laurie had cracked up and I'd wound up laughing along with her.

Now this woman, Alex Strand's stepdaughter, was waiting for me to say something spontaneous. Or at least appropriate. Polite. Neffer seemed to be waiting as well. So I spoke. "I'm Gary," I said.

"Man of few words," Neffer said. "The tough, silent type treasured by TSA HQ."

"Didn't you coach over at Haven?" Diane asked. "Odd career change."

How did she already know about me? And why was it so difficult to keep talking? I'm her family's hero, right? "I get that a lot," I said. Then, like a true dolt, I asked, "Are you traveling somewhere today?"

Neffer clapped and rubbed his two hands together. "Let me help move this along," he said. "Apparently Mr. Strand would like to offer his thanks, but he didn't know how to contact you, so he sent his lovely stepdaughter over to extend an invitation."

"We're hoping you can stop by for a drink or two tonight," Diane said. "My stepfather wants to know more about you. Let me text you the address."

She stepped closer as we traded information and I caught a foresty scent. Maybe it was lingering around me after my recent contact with "Clobber." "I was just doing my job," I said.

"Well," Neffer said, "technically—"

Diane somehow tucked her phone into the back pocket of her tight jeans. "As you can tell from my T-shirt," she said, "I'm not a big fan of the TSA."

"Neither was my wife," I said, surprised that I'd brought her up so soon.

"I'd love to stay and chat," Neffer said. "There is so much we could expound on and explore together. The discoveries would surely be scintillating. But this is not social hour and it's time for me to escort Ms. Strand back to her car. In addition, I believe Officer Waldman has a shift to finish."

"Look," I said, glancing at Neffer. "I'm not sure the regulations allow—"

Neffer interrupted. "I've asked around upstairs," he said. "I've been assured there are no special considerations being offered here. Stop by their house. Accept the thanks of the man whose life you saved. Understood?"

"So," Diane said. "We'll see you at six?"

"I'll have to bring my son along. It really might be better—"

"I love kids. Please bring him. We'll be waiting for you."

Then Neffer and Diane were walking away and I watched them go. An unlikely pair—a lumbering ox leading an exquisite ballerina. I wouldn't be a good match for that ballerina, either. Too shut down. Too graceless. But I kept looking anyhow, admiring the sweet curves of her ass, remembering the warmth of her hand in mine, the tightness of that T-shirt.

"Waldman," Carelli barked. "Divestiture. Lane two."

6

WHEN I PULLED UP AT BEN'S SCHOOL, I was still rattled by Hank and his arrival. Then there was Diane and her invitation. I was tempted to ask wise teacher Irene for advice, but she was escorting other students and then Ben was strapping himself into his seat. " 'Puff,' " he said. "Can you please put it on?"

What parent would object to Peter, Paul, and Mary? I glanced into the rearview mirror, hoping a quick read of my son's face would answer yet another familiar swirl of questions: How would I know when Ben was really mourning? How would I know when to help? How exactly should I help when it was time to help? I couldn't force Ben to talk about it. The therapist had advised me to remain "receptive."

For now that seemed to mean loading the CD. It felt good to sing along until the dragons were living forever and the little boys weren't. Our last family road trip before the accident was a drive up to Saratoga Springs to hear Peter and Paul play a concert (add Mary to the list of things that don't live forever). Peter shuffled onto the stage, a withered old man with the spine of a fading rice farmer. Paul, right next to him, was tall and hale with the posture of a world leader. Whatever Paul's lifestyle and/or gene pool was, he was the clear winner.

I sat up straighter and the CD moved on to "If I Had a Hammer." Ben had a sweet, high voice, like Laurie, and he sang with real feeling. We'd had a fantastic time at the concert. We might have been the youngest people in the whole crowd. Even back then, Ben knew all the words and everyone who saw him couldn't help but smile.

Next up was "Leaving on a Jet Plane." A heart-crusher. *Now the time has come to leave you.* Probably not so safe to drive and listen. I checked the rearview mirror to see if I was the only one tearing up in the car. I was. I was also, it turned out, the only one awake. Hadn't even managed to mention Hank or the Strands to Ben. How would an introduction to Diane, a young woman who'd set my insides humming, help Ben with his mourning? How would it help either one of us? And how would it possibly help to have Laurie's unforgiving brother lurking around?

I turned the volume down slowly—no sudden changes, preserve the nap at all costs—and then switched it off. I checked the address and found a spot nearby, right across the street from Washington Park—an Olmsted-inspired green space complete with a small lake and a defunct art-deco boathouse, right in the heart of the city's never completely resurgent Center Square neighborhood. Ben and I lived nearby, but not on such an upper-crust street. For years, I'd heard talk about how Albany was on the verge of a serious boom. *Time to buy,* the boosters said. *This is the most vital urban center between Manhattan and Montreal.* Their broad stroke historical argument brought together such elements as the Hudson River, the Erie Canal, the fur trade, some relatively open-minded Dutch settlers, a few devious bootleggers, a few even more devious politicians, and a once-dazzling music scene.

If the boom ever hit, the Strands would be sitting pretty. In the meantime, they lived in what looked like a lovely mansion that would go for millions if they could just haul it a few hours south to Brooklyn. When Laurie wasn't dreaming of Amsterdam, she'd fantasize about moving closer to the park. Sometimes she'd pause in front of one of the tall, big-windowed row houses and talk about how the sunset light would flood the rooms. And the kid (or kids) and dog (or dogs) would love having a giant playground always waiting right outside the front door. Her favorite houses were on the other side of the park, closer to Haven College, because she liked the idea of shortening her walk to work, though she liked riding her damn bike in too.

I glanced away from those thoughts and saw two people walking briskly toward the car with their dog, an imposing German

Shepherd. A pair of older parents, I guessed, dignified empty nesters clinging tightly to each other and to the dog their long-gone kids used to love. It was the kind of dog I'd see at work, running drills at baggage claim. I didn't want any barking dogs to disrupt Ben's nap. If the kid stayed zonked for a full hour, the evening would almost certainly be easier, so I tracked the couple in my mirrors and considered closing the windows.

When Laurie had glimpsed old couples like this one, she'd often drifted to talk of dying. "If I die before you," she'd tell me, "I want you to find a good woman. I don't want you to wind up all alone in some antiseptic assisted living community."

I'd remind her that I was ten years older than she was and the actuarial tables strongly predicted a different outcome.

Then she'd talk about exceptions. Outliers.

I focused on the couple again just as the dog caught sight of a squirrel and, barking wildly, dashed after it. The man managed to hold his ground and then began yanking on the leash in retaliation. The dog's head jerked back hard and the barks switched to whimpers. Poor creature. How was it supposed to resist the squirrel? I checked the mirror again and found my son still sleeping, eyes closed, breath steady, legs crossed, neck bent at an angle that couldn't possibly feel good.

I rubbed at my own neck. The old couple walked forward hand-in-hand, the chastened dog heeling beside the man's legs. I checked the time. Down the block, the Strand's mansion waited. This wasn't a date or anything remotely like that, and yet how would I explain it to Ben? The only woman other than Laurie that Ben ever asked about was Shannon and I knew it wasn't simply because she was the babysitter. She was a sweetheart, a good tennis player, and cute, like a small-town librarian from an old film, down to the black-frame cat eye glasses. She'd make a fine mother and at times she didn't seem uninterested in me. She was also thirteen years younger than I was. Plug that into your actuarial tables.

I'd had sex exactly once since Laurie had died and it had been a disaster, some sort of consolation hook-up with Nora Flint, a bitter, single mother with a kid at Ben's school. "A guilt-free sorrow fuck," Paul had called it, after I shared a few of the glum details. "Forget about it and move on." But it wasn't a pleasant memory and it hadn't done much for my confidence. Apparently, Nora was dating a guy in the sheriff's office these days. If that kept going, some sharp-edged jokes would no doubt find their way back to me. August and Sanchez would love to put that kind of intel to use.

I was steeling myself against these as yet unformed jokes—about my inability to demonstrate authority, my failure to perform my duties, my lack of convincing command presence—when my phone buzzed in my pocket. Ben stirred even though the ringer was off. I hoped it was the Strands, calling to postpone, but it was Hank. "Cruised by your house," he barked. "Where the hell are you?"

I reminded myself that Hank had talked exactly the same way when Laurie was alive and well. "I've got a meeting in a few minutes," I whispered, still aiming to preserve the nap.

"The Strands, right? The big money grants an audience to the everyday hero."

It wasn't worth asking how he knew so much. He wouldn't say. Best to push on. "Didn't know you'd be hitting town so soon," I said.

"Couldn't believe I scored an Albany-based assignment. Perfect timing. What are the odds?"

"It'll be good to catch up."

"Next time say it like you mean it," Hank scoffed. "But, seriously, about your CPR heroics: Are you trying to give the TSA a good name or something?"

"Just doing my job."

"Well, keep it up. I've got more calls to make. Tell the kid I say hey." Then he hung up. No one seemed to know why, but the guy didn't believe in saying goodbye. Laurie tried to laugh about it. "Goodbye, you asshole," she'd say, long after he was off the line.

She also used to try to laugh at her brother's self-absorption, the way he never offered to hold the baby, the way he never understood why their plans revolved more and more around Ben and not him. "Hank's older," she'd say. "Always wants to be in charge of everything and everybody."

I shoved the phone back in my pocket. I still had about fifteen minutes before I was supposed to knock on the Strands' door. Ben had uncrossed his legs and moved his head to the other side of his seat, still asleep. It was starting to feel contagious and, exhausted by the thought of Hank and his questions, I decided to chase my own power nap. I reclined my seat, cracked the window open a little more. Checked on Ben again. I'd been so curious about Hank when I was first falling for Laurie. I fell for her parents, too, and I believed it would be an incredible gift for the whole family—and to myself—if I could make peace between the brother and the sister. I could grab a few beers with Hank. Play some tennis. Heal whatever had gone wrong.

My eyelids grew heavier and I could almost hear Laurie whispering into my ear: *It wasn't possible back then. Neither one of us had a chance. But now, maybe now, it might not be impossible now. . . .*

I bolted awake and for an ecstatic heartbeat I was ready to embrace her, welcome her back, and tell her that I'd do anything for her, absolutely anything.

7

BUT, OF COURSE, I DIDN'T SEE Laurie. I heard the sound of Diane's footsteps and she was standing by the door, her open hand pressed against the window, as if her fingers had frozen there midwave.

I rubbed at my eyes, waved back, and opened the door as quietly as I could.

"I was on my way home," she said. "I saw you guys, but I didn't know whether I should wake you or take a nap myself. You both looked so peaceful."

"Peaceful," I repeated, tempted to tell her we'd both probably been dreaming of Laurie, how she'd been just a breath away. "Well," I said, checking my watch and doing my best to focus on the alive woman in front of me, "I believe nap time is over."

Diane was more dressed up than she'd been at the airport. Tight jeans again, but instead of a T-shirt, she was wearing a heavy cardigan sweater over a loose turtleneck, shiny black elfish boots that scraped against the sidewalk as she stepped back. Her beauty made it difficult for me to think straight. She seemed more out of my league than ever.

Ben stretched in his seat. "Where are we?" he asked.

Diane hadn't moved much, so I had very little space to climb out beside her. I remembered the therapist advising me, surprisingly soon after Laurie's death, to notice which female friends stood extra close. "Notice who touches your arm," he'd said. "Your wrist. Your thigh. You don't have to respond. No one will expect you to respond, but it's worth filing away."

That kind of thinking had led to the ill-fated night with Nora. And yet, as Diane stood beside me, waiting for Ben to climb out, I was wondering if we'd touch.

She hooked an arm around mine and leaned her head close to whisper in my ear. There was that foresty scent again. Cedar, I decided. New green leaves were bound to unfurl from the budding trees in a week or two. "Still don't see you as TSA," she said. "Especially without the uniform."

"I don't look the part?"

"How can I put this," she said. "I don't think the TSA workers I see ever coached tennis. They always seem pretty pathetic to me."

"I don't seem pathetic?"

"Nope," she said. "Though that question is kind of pathetic."

I was going to have to remember how to flirt. My method, if it could be called a method, had always involved getting the woman-in-question on the tennis court. Maybe that was another reason I'd stopped playing.

Ben was staring at us from inside the car. I opened his door and studied his groggy face. "This is Diane," I said, "the daughter of the man whose life I saved."

"Stepdaughter," she said.

"I want to go home," Ben said.

"The man I saved is inside," I said. "He wants to say thank you."

"I want to go home," Ben repeated.

In such moments, my parenting philosophy was to keep moving forward. If I remained in motion, Ben would usually follow. I reached in to help with the car seat. Diane peeked in, too. "Come on out here, you sweet shy little boy," she said. "I'd like to thank you for having such a fine father."

The compliment warmed me. At the same time, I felt a pulse of irritation. *I've got this*, I almost said. But Ben's eyes opened wider and he seemed close to a smile. Then there was music blaring—Elton John—and a sleek, silver Lexus sedan pulled in front of the house. The music vanished as suddenly as it had appeared and a younger version of Alex Strand stepped out of the car. He had a meticulously trimmed dark-brown beard and a blue pinstripe suit with flecks of gold that sparkled a bit in the light. He was still singing along about living alone or choosing to live in the city or a family home. He had a decent voice, but he was no Captain Fantastic. He stopped at the word *whippoorwill*. "It's my least favorite line," he said, putting his arm around Diane. "What the hell is a 'whippoorwill of freedom' and how does it zap anyone between the eyes?"

"Shine the light," Diane said, stepping away from him. "Won't you shine the light?"

"That's what our man Gary did the other day, I heard. Shined the biggest light around. I'm Thomas, Alex's son." He walked closer and put out his hand. "It's a pleasure to meet you."

I shook his hand and nodded.

Thomas released my hand very quickly and peered into the Subaru. "And who is this little dude?" he asked.

"I was just trying to lure young Waldman out of the car," Diane said.

"We all know how alluring you can be," Thomas said. "What's your name, son?" he asked. "Climb on out."

Ben kept quiet, pressing himself deeper into his seat.

"Kid's mother died less than a year ago, knucklehead," Diane whispered. "Don't rush him.

Had Neffer told her? Or had she been doing some internet research? Thomas stepped back.

"Her birthday would have been this weekend," Ben said, suddenly wide awake, jumping down onto the sidewalk. "We're going to have a party."

"Is that so?" Thomas asked.

"Dad," Ben said. "When can we go home?"

I heard the change from *I want to* to *When can we?* The nap had worked its magic and Ben would follow along, well-rested, in fine spirits. "Come on," I said, holding out my hand. "I'll tell you all about it inside."

Ben took my hand and together we climbed the steps to the Strands' front door. Leading the way, Thomas chattered at Diane. "Good calls from Saratoga today. That horsey set has money to burn. Unbelievable stuff."

Diane barely paid attention to her stepbrother. Instead, she looked over her shoulder at me. "Listen," she said, "Alex is not taking his doctor's advice, and he's preoccupied, which isn't the best combination, and—"

"He's doing much better," Thomas said.

The front door opened and there stood a surprisingly vibrant Alex. Clean-shaven, dashing again, he was dressed in something like expensive golf gear, creased khaki slacks, an elegant light-green V-neck sweater, a small bright gold chain around his neck. The picture of what it meant to look "happy to be alive."

"Hey Dad," Thomas said. "We've got your lifesaver here."

"So glad you made it," Alex said, offering his hand. Then a phone rang. "Excuse me for a second," he said. He and Diane exchanged glares and then he walked away, phone pressed to his ear. His gait looked shaky and Thomas stayed close to him.

"Pour the man a drink," Alex shouted. "And get something for the kid too. I'll be right back."

I watched him shuffle and talk, amazed by the vigor of his voice as he spoke into the phone. "No. That does not sound like a good idea to me. Foolish. Unnecessary. We need them around, but I suppose I can't change your mind. Fine. So be it." Then he stepped into another room and closed the door behind him. Soon after that, the landline started to ring.

I noticed Diane's bare fingers. The uncluttered rooms were large and airy. Laurie would have loved the open space, but the wood floors and high ceilings made the sound of the ringing phones hard to take.

"Are you going to get that, Thomas?" Alex called from behind the door.

"On it," Thomas said.

Diane shook her head. "I guess that leaves me to drink with our lifesaver."

"Of course we'll fight it," Thomas was saying, and then he shut himself in a different room.

I followed Diane toward the immense designer kitchen. "So," she said, "you're observing the two Strands already, I'm sure. Alex, always charming his way forward, thinking about future connections. And then there's uptight Thomas."

I was paying more attention to the kitchen's marble counter-tops. Light fixtures made from large whisks. You could almost take a bath in the sink. The stainless steel refrigerator was the size of a barn door. Diane reached in and grabbed two bottles of Stella. Before she could open them, Alex walked in. "I'll take one too," he said. When Diane shot him another glare, he quickly added: "I promise not to drink it."

I smiled and mussed Ben's hair. The two of us hadn't socialized much for months. When was the last time we'd gone to dinner at someone's house? At a restaurant? There'd been plenty of hours with Shannon, but those hours tended to be in and around the apartment. I'd taken Ben to movies and diners. There'd been school-related activities, a few birthday parties. Pizza. A bunch of nights over at Paul's small, cluttered bungalow. But dinner with fashion-plate people in a mansion? I wasn't prepared, so how could I have prepared Ben?

"Follow me," Alex said.

"Take these with you," Diane said, handing frosty mugs around. Mine was filled to the brim with beer. Ben's was filled halfway with orange juice. "Do you like tire swings?" Diane asked him.

"Yes," Ben said.

"Then there's something I want to show you."

The sliding glass doors off the kitchen led onto their split-level deck. Benches had been built into the railing and Alex sat on one that looked out toward the backyard. Diane took the stairs down to the yard and Ben followed her without even glancing back. Ah, the power of a good nap. I sat beside Alex. The surrounding houses weren't shabby, but they appeared less grand and, for a moment, I felt as if I were sitting with the ruler of the neighborhood—a distant, benevolent patriarch. Diane pushed Ben on the tire swing. Alex raised his mug. "To you," he said, "with my sincere gratitude. I will never forget what you've done for me."

"I was just—"

"Shh," he said, moving his mug and tapping it against mine. Then he took a tiny sip and set his mug back down. "Too bad I can't drink yet. It was a pleasure to hold it, though. You go ahead, please."

I did as I was told, aware that I'd have to watch it with the beer. I had a habit of falling for whole families, always on the lookout for substitute fathers, substitute siblings. I'd loved my own father, fought against and fled my stepfather. I'd gravitated toward Paul's family and

I'd spent days and nights in their busy house. There were coaches I'd tried to make into fathers. I'd tried to make Haven College's dean into a father. When I'd first met Laurie, her parents were alive, and her father was a loving, caring surrogate dad.

As the alcohol from another long drink of the cold Stella rushed into my brain, I watched the gorgeous stepdaughter playing with Ben, pushing him high, then higher, one, two, three, and Ben screamed like a thrilled kid on his favorite roller coaster.

More often than I'd admit to anyone, I fantasized about Laurie returning. Sometimes I could almost see her walking through the front door, asking me about my day, telling me about an overheard conversation on Haven's quad, calling out for Ben to come over and give her a hug. Now one of her old dreams was beginning to materialize right in front of me. If I could just keep doing what I was doing, could I possibly have a chance at something like this? The big backyard for Ben. Washington Park for a front yard, just across the street.

And then, a heartbeat later, I felt guilty for the grandiose way my mind could run on and on.

It was the same sort of grandiose thinking that had deluded me for years into believing I could make a career out of playing tennis. I was good, but not that good.

Alex took a deep breath and stretched his arms. "I love it out here," he said. "It's a beautiful afternoon. And it doesn't hurt that Diane looks happier than she's been in ages. Hear her laughing? A rare sound around here lately."

I was curious about the family situation. The phone calls had a high-stakes energy. And why didn't Diane have her own place? Did that connect to the obvious tension between her and Thomas? "She must be relieved to see you recovering so well," I said.

"I don't want to talk about myself," Alex said. "I want to talk about you. I told you I used to know your father, way back when?"

For almost three decades now, I'd heard other people tell me what they remembered about Lloyd. He'd made good money in real estate by maintaining solid relationships with his clients. People who'd played tennis with him had the best stories, though, so I was hoping for a tennis memory. Whatever it happened to be, I'd listen and nod.

"We met a few times about an office park," Alex said. "It wasn't long before he died. I was sorry for your loss back then. Sorry to this day. We didn't get to talk much, but he mentioned you." He picked up his beer again and poured most of it into my near-empty mug. Then he drank the few ounces that remained. "You didn't see that," he said.

"See what?"

Alex smiled. "I remember looking forward to working with your father."

Why? I wanted to ask, but I'd learned long ago to avoid such questions. I'd just wind up sad and quiet. Might as well drink a little more.

"Let me ask you something," Alex said.

I sat up straighter and imagined Alex pacing in front of a boardroom table. People would listen to this guy. "Ask me anything," I said.

"What do you think your father would make of you in the TSA?"

I looked back out over the yard. I could say that after Laurie died I'd felt a sudden, overwhelming desire for security and the job felt like a perfect fit. No one, including my father, would question that. But the truth was I'd applied right after Laurie learned she was pregnant.

The sun was dropping lower in the sky. Diane would have to bring Ben back in soon, but for now they'd moved from the tire swing to a game of hide and seek. Ben was counting out loud, not really covering his eyes, watching as Diane dashed behind a red toolshed. She had a nice stride, a good midfoot strike, and it was easy to imagine her banging out seven-minute miles. It would be a struggle to keep up.

I tried to zero back in on Alex's version of the perennial question. I could use the sad story of Lance Ostrow, an unlucky guy from my high school tennis team. Wound up a bigwig at Cantor Fitzgerald and never made it out of the Towers on 9/11. I could say I'd heard the news and applied as soon as I could. But the truth wouldn't back me up there either because Ostrow had been a bully. A smart, vicious doubles player, though I'd never had difficulty beating him in singles. Never saw him after graduation and rarely thought of him at all.

"We can talk about something else," Alex said.

"It's okay," I said. "You know, my father had his heart set on tennis for me."

"Long odds," Alex said. "You think he'd be disappointed?"

"No more disappointed than I am."

"What do you mean?"

"A lot of people ask me about it. My wife really wanted me to resign. I don't know, maybe I believed in the whole saving lives things a bit too much. Make a difference and all that. Still, sometimes—almost all the time, I guess—I can't help wondering if I should do something else."

"Don't we all think that?" Alex asked. "Something else? Something better? Just proves we're alive. And I know from extremely personal experience that you definitely make a difference." Alex had his right hand in a fist and he tapped it against the top of my knee, as if he were midpresentation, making an important point.

I studied that fist, the puffy, blue-tinged veins on the back of the hand, and then I could see that splayed-out body again, my own hands on that unmoving chest as I tried to breathe life back into it. The taste of the dead air returned. I needed more beer. Or less beer. I remembered Paul talking after our run: *Drop the mic. Move on.* "I don't know," I said again.

"You *do* know," Alex said. "And your father would know too. I hope you don't mind if I talk to you straight. It's what I do."

He waited for me. "I don't mind," I said.

"I'm glad," he said. "Now, I believe we all labor on and what matters most is that we do a good job. I don't care if Diane ever becomes a veterinarian as long as she brings an excellent work ethic with her wherever she goes. I have my doubts about that these days, but we don't need to get into that. You're here. I am in your debt. I never got to work with your father. Maybe I wouldn't have chosen my path to this moment. Maybe you wouldn't have chosen yours. But that doesn't mean it isn't an opportunity."

I set the beer down and told myself to lay off the rest. Ben was running behind the red shed now, giggling like a maniac, shouting, "Found you!"

"Such a beautiful sound," Alex said. "I like to sit out here by myself. I like to travel by myself. As does Diane's mother. Her name is Faye. She happens to be in Japan for a little while. I may have to go visit her. And not for the finest of reasons. But, again, I want to talk about you. Your boss shared a few things with me. I hope you don't mind. You're an only child. You're a widower. Too many losses."

I tried to interrupt, but Alex held up his hand. "You understand what it is to be powerless. I don't mean that to sound harsh. It's just that I realize these are challenging times and I understand the desire to protect others, but I'm familiar with the TSA pay scale. I have some ideas about rewards, but I need to figure out a few things first. For now, here's my proposal: I'll explore the possibilities and you keep the whole heroic CPR story as quiet as you can. I prefer not to share signs of weakness. Does that sound all right to you?"

I nodded, but I wondered why he wanted the story quiet. Then Thomas walked out onto the porch holding another phone. "I don't think this can wait," he said.

Diane and Ben climbed the stairs back up to the deck, both of them rosy-cheeked, breathing heavily. Diane looked back and forth between her stepfather and stepbrother. "Done with the drinks already?" she asked.

"It's looking more and more like a busy night," Thomas said. "Maybe you can take Officer Waldman and his son out someplace they'd enjoy?" Then he spoke back into the phone. "One moment for Mr. Strand."

Alex stood up slowly and offered his hand. I rose to take it, too quickly, and the world shimmied. "We'll chat again soon," Alex said, reaching for the phone.

"Thank you," I said.

"I have a life of my own, you know," Diane said, but she seemed to be play-acting, and once Alex and Thomas walked back inside, phones pressed to their ears, she looked down at Ben and smiled. "You like pizza, don't you?"

"I do," Ben said, a big grin spreading across his flushed face. He turned to me. "I invited her to the party, Dad," he said.

I watched Diane walk into the kitchen and grab a bottle of beer from the giant fridge. Ben was drinking the last of his orange juice. I leaned down to him, but I didn't lower my voice. "What did she say?"

Diane stepped back out, drinking from her bottle. "I told him we could talk about it over dinner," she said.

8

I DIDN'T DRINK ANY MORE BEER at dinner. I needed to pay attention. Plus I wanted to savor my son's happiness. As we ate, Ben and Diane gabfested, the two of them gleefully trading stories about school and Albany and dinosaurs and art projects and book show-and-tell. Then Diane talked about her mother, Faye, who was taking a class on flower arranging—ikebana, it was called—in faraway Kyoto, where they had a temple made of gold named *Kinkaku-ji*. Ben repeated the word—*Kinkaku-ji*—enthralled. Then he started talking about a cartoon ninja and a special wooden temple and he talked about his mother, who had also gone far away, but not because she wanted to—it was just something that happened and then she was gone. I fought my urge to intercede, wondering how and if the gabfest would go on. Ben took two more bites from his second slice of pepperoni pizza, and as he wiped sauce from his mouth and the tip of his nose he again asked Diane if she would come to the party at the cemetery.

Later that night, stretched out in bed, I kept reliving that dinner, and even though I was utterly exhausted, I still couldn't fall asleep. My head spun and the apartment was quiet so I couldn't listen to anything except my own racing thoughts about how strange it had been to sit down with Neffer and Strand, to hear from Hank, to dine with Diane. I decided as usual to keep my eyes open, watch my step, work hard because, yes, I was a grinder, and I didn't overreach, but when it came to women, on those extremely rare occasions, a special dispensation seemed to apply and I was permitted, even encouraged, to aim higher, far above my station, because, obviously, Karen, in high school, was way beyond my pay grade, as was Melissa, for a while, in college. And there was Laurie—most of all, utterly improbably, there was Laurie. These women appeared in my life and seemed to choose me for reasons I'd never understand. I was uplifted each time, which is not to say it was always easy—it was not always easy—but I almost never lost sight of how fortunate I was to have been found. Even bitter Nora Flint fit in somehow, though in that case I had not been chosen for long, just long enough to climb feebly back up. And now here was this gorgeous, alluring Diane, and while I felt guilty and uneasy because maybe it was still too soon, my body and mind were telling me that I was being chosen again—why or for precisely what I wouldn't know right away, if ever. But when the dinner was done she walked beside me all the way back to the old Subaru and she helped Ben into the booster seat and then walked around to my door and asked me, in a surprisingly sexy way, what it felt like to do pat-downs all day long. Before I could think of how to respond she told me I didn't have to answer, she could ask another time. What she really wanted to say was she'd had a nice night. She thought I was doing a great job with Ben. When I said I had no idea what I was doing, she said she didn't either and that didn't really matter since the results couldn't be clearer, shining bright for anyone with eyes to see. Then she hugged me tightly and kissed my cheek and said she'd love to spend more time with me. Okay, I said, I'd like that too. Then I drove home, carried my sound-asleep son inside and tucked him in. After I left his room, I climbed into my own bed where I couldn't sleep, my brain buzzing, my body yearning, feeling something I might as well call Kinkaku-ji. And in my dreams she was golden too, like a woman out of James Bond, one of the good ones, unharmed, unarmed, happy, and I was all over her.

9

FRIDAY MORNING, BACK AT THE checkpoint, I tried to finesse my way through the start of my shift. But Carelli wasn't missing much and he was right there when I let a passenger step into the scanner with shoes on. "Does this look like the Pre line to you, Waldman? Or maybe you think this guy is seventy-five? Or under twelve?" The man couldn't have been any older than fifty. "Get his shoes off and get them through X-ray," Carelli said. The passenger acted as if he were the one in trouble. His hands shook as he fussed with his laces. "Take your time, sir," I said. "It was my mistake."

"Look who's making mistakes now," August said, studying the shoes at the X-ray position.

Two rotations later, I was at the walk-through metal detector, wondering about rewards and what I should have done differently at the end of the night. Lindsay, another TSO, rushed up and flashed her ID. I waved her through. I didn't notice she was carrying her purse, but Carelli did. "Wake up, Waldman," he said. "I don't care how well we know her. Purse comes off. Jacket, too."

After that, it was back to divestiture and my familiar script. As I spoke, I remembered Diane asking her pat-down question, and then I walked right into a flight attendant who'd bent over to unzip her knee-high boots. She wobbled but managed to keep her balance.

"Smooth," Sanchez said, cracking up over by bag check. "Maybe the heightened threat level is too much for you."

I apologized profusely, hoping Carelli hadn't noticed, but no such luck. He was beside me again, shaking his head. "You not sleeping at all? You look like crap. Take a break and then I know you have your friend stopping by. Drink some coffee before you come back."

I headed for the men's room and splashed some water on my face before locking myself in the stall to piss. I listened for footsteps rushing my way, another PAX with news of an emergency, more rush, chaos, another life for me to save. My heart began to race and that helped clear my head.

Back on the main concourse, I checked my watch. I was supposed to meet Paul downstairs in a few minutes. When I hustled back to the checkpoint, though, Paul was already standing by the supervisor's podium, a bouquet of red roses in his hand.

"Wow," I said. "You're going all out."

"Doing the best I can," Paul said, looking around anxiously.

"Guess you got the gate pass already."

"I think the flowers helped. Either that or they saw how nervous I was and took pity on me."

"Time for a quick coffee?"

"A shot of whiskey might be better."

I hadn't seen Paul so on-edge in a long time. "Let's just sit for a few minutes then," I said, and we wound up in the pleather cushioned chairs in front of Starbucks. The PAX passed by, pulling their rolling bags, poking at their devices, chatting with other PAX and non-PAX in distant locations, and I wondered if Paul could perceive the odd, pulsating beauty of it all. I could occasionally wax philosophical, find some comfort and stability in my own set of somewhat cheesy airport mantras. It was the kind of thinking my mother would have loved. PAX of the world, we are but a swirl of souls. We lift off and we land, like so many drops of water, bound for our time in the clouds. We're carried aloft for miles and then we descend back to the surface of this forever spinning planet. Why bother being annoyed? Why bother being sad? Why bother being happy? Whoever we are, we won't be for long. The world spins and we spin upon it; it is beyond our control. The tickets can say whatever they say. Everyone knows the person who arrives is not the same person who departed.

Or as Gallwey would suggest, and as I used to echo back out on the Haven College courts not that long ago: *Let it happen. See your strokes as they are. Let go of judgment, for you become what you think. Be aware of what actually is.*

But Paul was the one who'd told me, more than once, "You're at the airport hiding out, just because you think you failed."

Maybe I could use some whiskey too. Down some shots with my friend. Instead, I zoomed back in time to a familiar prematch moment, late teens, trying to get psyched up, out by the aluminum bleachers in front of the Albany High courts. Together, bouncing on our toes, we'd volley the ball back and forth, and then, silly as it might seem now, right before we walked onto the court, Paul would shout, *Band time!* We'd both reach into our pockets, pull out our matching set of bright-blue headbands and wristbands, and put them on. Then we'd rush toward the net to meet the opposition.

Now, though, I noticed a twitching near the corner of Paul's left eye, and that made me recall more recent history, just three years ago when I'd stood next to my friend by Tara's grave and then moved forward to take my turn with the shovel and dirt. I didn't need to follow that memory any further, so I started talking.

"Go ahead," I said. "Tell me what you're afraid of."

"What I'm afraid of," Paul said. "I don't want to talk about that and we don't have enough time anyhow. Let's hear what's new with you."

I told him about the Hank surprise appearance, the Strands, the reward "possibilities," the pizza out on Lark Street with Diane. Paul set the flowers on the table in front of us, put his feet up, leaned back, and relaxed into the story. "Sounds like fun," he said. "But tell me more about this Diane woman."

"What about her?"

"Did Ben like her too?"

"Too?"

"It's okay if you like her, man. You don't have to pretend. Did you make a plan to see her again?"

"Not exactly a plan. I don't know, though, shouldn't I wait?"

"Until?"

"Until the right time?"

Paul leaned his head back and looked up at the ceiling. "I tried to clean the house last night and this morning, but it's still

Tara's house and I had no idea what to put away and what to keep out. And what if she can't stand Albany? What if tonight doesn't go well? Maybe I should call the whole thing off. I could wait until the right time, even though I'm a forty-three-year-old widower living alone in Albany. You asked what I'm afraid of, didn't you? But you already know the answer."

I remembered how we'd rush the net together. In doubles, that's where you win your points. *Close, close!* Paul would shout as we charged forward. *Here we go!* "Maybe I thought you weren't afraid at all," I said.

"Sure," he said. "I'm only afraid of being alone for the rest of my life. And I'm afraid of waiting around forever. You're afraid of the same things, partner. I hear it in your questions. I mean, I used to think I had to wait."

"And now?"

"That's the answer. As you know, Mr. Inner Game guru. The time is always now." Then he stood up and walked over to check the big screen. "Time really is now," he said. "It'd be silly to get the gate pass and then be late."

"Can I say I'm proud of you?"

"No."

"Can I say you're an inspiration?"

"Not again."

"How about good luck?"

"You can say that," Paul said, and then he started down the concourse.

I lifted the roses off the table. "How about don't forget these?"

"Thanks," he said, taking the flowers and giving me a fist bump. "You want to walk up there with me?"

"It's not doubles today, man. But I've got a few minutes before I have to get back to work. I'll wait here and hope to meet the lucky lady."

I watched him speedwalk down the concourse, past "Clobber," past the wine bar, and I remembered a time, years ago, when Laurie came to meet me at this same airport. We hadn't been dating long. She'd volunteered to pick me up. She'd brought flowers, too, but she must have felt unsure about bringing them inside. They were waiting for me on the passenger seat of her car. Orange lilies. I saw them there, watched her nervously hand them to me, and I didn't know what to say or do, but I knew everything had changed. I was stupefied. Nothing like that had ever happened to me before.

I bought more coffee and perched at a table, watching the PAX move through the checkpoint. August scolded an old man who couldn't figure out how to stand in the scanner. The poor guy—stroke-slowed, I guessed—faced the wrong way. He curled down into a ball. Fetal. August's voice grew louder until the guy got it right at last. A tough, mean scene to wax philosophical about.

Drop the mic. Move on.

And then Paul was walking back up the concourse with a short, smiley woman. He had his arm around her, holding her close, and she looked radiant, burying her nose in the roses again and again. I'd expected someone younger, more classically striking. Tara had been tall and thin, blonde. Norwegian. Vanessa looked like a bubbly cherub. "You must be Gary," she said. "I've heard a lot about you and I'm sorry about your loss. Forgive me, but I wanted to say something out front. And I don't know what Paul would have done without you. So I guess I want to say thank you, too."

Paul was smiling, watching her, happy to let her go on.

"I'm glad we're going to get out on the courts this weekend," she said.

"I've heard about your game," I said. "You'll need to go easy on me. I haven't played in a while."

"Don't fall for that bullshit," Paul said. "I bet he's been visualizing his stroke twenty-four seven. Does this Diane woman play tennis, by the way?"

"Seems like a runner to me," I said, "but I didn't ask her about tennis."

"Maybe you should."

I glanced over to the checkpoint and there was Carelli, pointing at me. "Duty calls," I said.

"We'll see you tomorrow night," Paul said.

"You bet," I said, and then I was watching the happy couple walk away, arm in arm. I expected to feel jealous and I wanted to guard against that, but as I approached the supervisor's podium, I felt myself standing up straighter, almost as if something I'd been carrying had suddenly grown lighter.

"You look a little less peaked," Carelli said. "Now go tap in at exit."

10

PEOPLE WHO DON'T WORK THE JOB think exit is the easiest part of the rotation. Newbies think this too, and why wouldn't they? You're alone, you're resting, and most of the time absolutely nothing happens. You're allowed to get off your feet a bit, sit on a stool, and all you have to do is make sure no one crosses the bright, clearly marked red line on the carpet. Watch out for kids darting forward to hug their mothers or fathers, lovers running to swoon into each other, maybe a few small crowds carrying hand-made banners rushing up to welcome home a soldier or a high school team. There are well-placed, boldfaced posters to help with your job. When someone approaches the red line, hold up your hand, say "Halt" if you have to, and point to the poster.

But, of course, it's not that simple. Each and every kid dashing your way could be a devious distraction. Be careful not to draw attention to the concealed-weapon-carrying Air Marshalls flashing their badges at you as they wait to check in with the supervisors. Remember there's a camera right on you the entire time and if you doze off, even for a second, you'll be hit with serious discipline. If one of the suits from upstairs walks your way with a guest, you'd better ID that guest and call the supervisor, even if that guest bears a startling resemblance to the president of the United States. If you allow someone—anyone—going the wrong way to get past you unchecked, you've created a breach, which will shut down the airport and you could be fired on the spot.

In other words, like many tasks, this one is more complicated than it appears. But if the love of your life died young for no reason bicycling down a slippery hill and you never got to say goodbye in any real way even though she was right there warm in your arms as she breathed her last breath, well, then here's the most challenging part of working exit: As you watch people reunite in absurdly peremptory fashion, again and again and again—peck on the cheek, no eye contact, handshake, slap on the backside, hug, fist bump—you'll have to restrain yourself. You'll find it difficult not to shout at them, tell them this moment won't return, shake them until they understand once and for all that they shouldn't take each other for granted.

∿

I never risked sitting on that stool. I stood, inhaled, exhaled, spine straight, chest out, shoulders back, until I could feel my head resting lightly atop my neck, as if I were a mere marionette—god's invisible string attached to my fontanel, tugging me skyward—and there was Laurie again, out in the parking lot, offering me those lilies. Once they were in my hand, I had no idea what to do with them. It was a crisp, fall afternoon. I'd been in Lynchburg, Virginia on a job interview, even though I didn't want to move to Lynchburg, Virginia. I was hoping to pressure the dean at Haven to shift me from contingent to permanent employment, but I knew it wasn't going to work. The college was losing money. Lacrosse had been "retrenched," as they say, and tennis and soccer might not be far behind. Plus I'd only gotten the Haven job because the UAlbany coach called in a favor. I didn't have the credentials or record to win a job like mine on the open market. Meanwhile, Laurie was wearing a long black overcoat that could have come from her father, or her brother, or an ex-boyfriend. I set the flowers on the roof of her tiny blue Ford Fiesta and wrapped my arms around her and then I was undoing the coat's wide belt to get my arms and hands closer to her skin.

"I never use that damn stool either," Neffer said, startling me back into the present. "Always looked like a trap to me."

How did the guy keep sneaking up on me? I glanced down at his shoes. Some kind of brand-new shiny black Nikes.

"Pricey," Neffer said, "but they're worth it. Make me feel positively buoyant." The black shoes glittered like a sun-dappled lake as Neffer rocked back and forth, heel to toe. "You're a size ten and a half?"

"Eleven."

"You keep on saving lives and I'll see what I can do. In the meantime, I told Carelli I needed to talk with you."

"I can't leave in the middle of—"

Sanchez was there before I could finish the sentence. She looked like an older, sourpuss version of Vanessa. "Tapping you," she said.

"Follow me," Neffer said.

I figured we'd head to his office, but he led me down to baggage claim, out past the loading docks, and we started walking toward the employee parking lot. Once we were alone on the sidewalk, Neffer pulled a cigarette out of his shirt pocket. "I'm allowing myself one a day," he said. "Helps curb my appetite. A little bit, at least. Want one?"

"No, thanks."

"Good for you."

I'd never taken a midshift stroll with a supervisor before, let alone with Neffer. I wanted to see it as an honor. Why not try to be open? "Those Strand drinks turned into pizza on Lark Street with the stepdaughter," I said.

"I hope you did more than stare at her bony ass."

A little too open, I decided, shaking my head.

"I'm sorry," Neffer said, lighting the cigarette and taking a long pull. "That was inappropriate. I'm on edge lately, that's all."

"It's okay," I said, "but I should probably get back."

Neffer paused and turned in a circle, as if to make sure we weren't being followed. "We've got time," he said. "There's something I need in my car. You might like it. It'll give us a chance to chat." He flicked the half-smoked cigarette into the street. "Filthy habit. Don't tell anyone about it."

I nodded. Then Neffer began walking forward again, faster now. One of the parking shuttles rumbled by, heading for the long-term lot. Leroy, an obese, diabetic driver, honked and waved. I looked out toward the runways. Below the layers of asphalt and concrete, there was marshland. Along the chain-link fences, cattails still grew tall, rustling in the wind. They were stiff from the stubborn cold and I listened to them brush like bamboo against the fence, an oddly soothing wind chime. I paused to pluck and pocket a dandelion that was sprouting at the edge of the sidewalk. I'd show it to Ben later, if I remembered. Another sign of spring. Out on the tarmac, red lights glowed, and a Southwest jet stuck a smooth landing.

Neffer turned onto an access road that led into the employee lot. He paused by a shiny white Jeep Cherokee and brushed a hand over his chest, as if trying to get rid of a few stubborn ashes. Then he beeped the car unlocked, grabbed a small cooler out of the backseat, and said, "I have no intentions of sharing this jalapeño venison jerky with everyone who walks past my office." He set the cooler on the hood, opened it, and pulled out a sealed plastic bag and two bottles of Saratoga water. As soon as he opened the bag, I felt the hot peppers in my eyes. Neffer handed me a piece. "I get it from a friend in Maryland," he said. "No one will smell smoke on my breath, that's for sure."

I wasn't going to brave the stuff until I had a bottle of water in my hand. Then I took a small bite. The dried-out deer tasted better than I'd expected, not nearly as blazing as Neffer's hot wings. I took a real bite. "Not bad," I said.

"Food like this will help you live longer."

"Depends how much of it you eat, I guess."

"True that," Neffer said, reaching back into his bag. "You want a little more?"

I nodded and Neffer handed over a bigger piece. This one evoked the deer more directly. I saw sinew, the muscle of a foreleg, something furlike in the grain of it. I drank more water.

Neffer glanced at his watch, the opposite of an antique today. Stainless-steel band the width of a belt, face the size of a silver dollar. Could have been scuba equipment. Navy SEAL gear? "I'll say no more about that Strand girl's bony ass," he said, "but would you like the general Neffer advice about women?"

"Here we go," I said, bracing myself for more Neffer-speak. It could be frustrating, but I'd also begun to develop a fondness for it.

"In this world," Neffer began, "we all experience reversals. Our compasses spin, our polestars become more difficult to locate, the firm ground beneath our feet shifts like sand and we feel it being washed away. Nevertheless, we continue making decisions. Not because we have sought out decisive moments. We might, in fact, be seeking to disappear. We might be well aware that we need time to recalibrate our lives, recover our balance. We might want to wait for the polestar to reveal itself once again. But decisions are demanded of us."

Neffer reached into the bag for the last piece of jerky and took a few bites. He leaned back against his car. "Now, Mrs. Neffer and I haven't yet been blessed with little Neffers. We haven't given up hope, however, and they are often in my thoughts. There was a time, long before I got the assignment to come up here to Albany, when I lived in DC and I fielded my share of what you might call merger and acquisition opportunities. My career was on the rise. My weight was down. I was as charismatic as ever and I was not smoking at all. Do you think Mrs. Neffer was the only woman I met?"

"Of course not."

"What kind of women do you think I met?"

"Do you want me to answer that question?"

"You don't have to. Use your imagination and you won't be mistaken. There were more exciting women. Edgier ladies. Women of mystery. Plenty of intrigue available. Then there were my reversals. I wouldn't say they were equivalent to what you've experienced. I would never say that. But they were real. Substantial. Deeply felt. And Mrs. Neffer—"

Neffer paused to wipe at his eyes. I couldn't tell how much of this was theater. Too much hot pepper, or real tears? And where exactly was it leading? It would eventually circle around to Hank and those photographs, wouldn't it?

"Of course," Neffer went on, "she wasn't Mrs. Neffer yet. She was my Chloe-clo-clo. And she needed to know if I was in or out, on a permanent basis. I'm proud to say I didn't hesitate. *I am yours*, I told her. *Eternally*. I had no doubt. I still have no doubt."

Neffer paused again and stared at me for a moment. I didn't know what to say. Did I have doubts? About him? About Diane? About myself?

Meanwhile, Neffer licked his index finger and used it to pluck the last jerky crumbs from the plastic bag. He caught sight of the piece I was still holding. "Are you going to eat that or not? I don't know when I'll get another shipment."

"I'm good," I said, handing it over.

Neffer snapped it down in two bites and closed up the cooler. "All I'm saying is that terrible events lead to many things, including possibilities for growth—"

"What doesn't kill me makes me—"

"You've seen it. You've bought in already. The uniform becomes you, does it not? Everything changes, a security industry emerges, expands, and then what? Checkpoint Charlie to the nth degree. Do we pretend it hasn't happened? Just go along? Hunker in the bunker, draw the blinds down low? I'm not saying we'll improve. I'm not saying we'll get better. It's highly unlikely anything will get better, if you ask me. But that doesn't mean we can't *do* better. If every single one of us does a little bit better—"

"Sure," I said. "Never again and all that."

"Don't get cynical on me now, Officer. You're a good listener. You observe well. I know you do because I observe many things, including you. I'm convinced you see the airport clearly. You under-stand the security we provide is mostly an illusion. There are threats everywhere and our defenses, even at their best, are minimal. But we pay attention and we learn and we utilize the time we have. This is the way it is. Sometimes there are events that are larger than ourselves and we have to let those events unfold in order to learn more. We do what we can to stay safe and we don't jump in too early. We wait and we learn and we study and we pay attention and we decide when to act. *We* decide. Whenever possible. We prefer not to let others dictate. Here's where you and I are the same: We know we can't keep people safe, but we also can't not try. The useless job I had before this made me pull over and throw up on the side of the road too many mornings in a row. I feel happy and proud to come in here every day. You need to love what you do. That's the only path to real individual security."

I tried to keep up. I wiped my hands on my slacks. "Are you talking about women or the TSA?"

Neffer stowed the cooler and locked the car. "Maybe you've heard rumors about where I worked before I moved here. I hear people whisper about my time in Vienna, Virginia, or wherever it is they think I've been. People believe I need to trim down. Like

I haven't heard that my whole life. I can do it. I will do it. But my theory is that the rest of the world needs to beef up, and fast. Someday, we'll see who's correct."

Neffer checked his watch again, pulled a bar of dark chocolate out of his coat pocket, broke off three squares and offered them up. "Do you hear what I'm saying?"

Hearing was the easy part. I took the chocolate and ate it. It tasted bitter, like burnt sugar. Salted almonds were in there somewhere. But I couldn't really begin to parse Neffer's entire midshift mumbo-jumbo performance. Can't keep people safe, can't not try—that resonated with me. We started walking away from the Cherokee, out of the employee lot, and then, finally, Neffer eased toward his ask. "I've been studying your brother-in-law," he said. "Seems like a real professional."

"I agree with that."

"I'm trying to learn more about him and I'm trying to do it quickly. People I trust trust Mr. Bell. So there's that. Still, I'm a talented reader of people, but I'm struggling to get my own clear read on him. Do you trust him?"

It was a simple yes-or-no question, and yet it was more complicated for me. I wasn't even sure how much Laurie had trusted him, but that would steer us into an even longer conversation. "I want to trust him," I said. "He's the last one left from my wife's family. But sometimes I think he blames me for his sister's death."

"A natural part of the grieving process," Neffer said.

"He's also been trying to get closer to my son these last few months, and I bristle at that sometimes, but it's probably natural too."

We were closing in on the terminal again. A plane drifted lower on its approach. "Even before Mr. Bell appeared on the scene," Neffer said, "I was interested in helping you advance. I'm not saying you need to do anything extra to get promoted. You understand that, right?"

"Yes," I said, though I couldn't help feeling a little suspicious.

Neffer clapped me on the back. "It's good to have that out in the open," he said. "Still, I would appreciate hearing more if you ever have more to share. Are we clear?"

The plane seemed to hover toward us, wheels down, tires enormous. I tried to make out the lines of the tread. "We're clear," I said.

"Excellent," said Neffer.

The breeze picked up, blowing distant clouds in front of the sinking sun. The roar of the jet engines overpowered every other sound. I covered my ears. The plane seemed to float, ever so slowly, right over our heads. When it was gone and I could hear again, we were a few steps from the terminal. "What should I do now?" I asked.

Neffer accelerated toward the sliding doors. "You know what to do," he said. "Punch out, pick up your kid, and consider yourself blessed as you keep your attention focused, twenty-four seven. Have a nice night and get some rest if you can. You're going to need it. I'll be lucky if I sleep at all."

11

I DROVE AWAY FROM THE AIRPORT, sped across town, took my place
at the end of the car line at Ben's school, and started inching forward
behind an enormous white, freshly washed Land Rover. The older
kids horsed around in the schoolyard while I puzzled over Hank and
Neffer, wondering what they were and weren't telling me, and then
I daydreamed toward my father and tennis and there's Lloyd, back
in town after weeks away. It's the summer I turned twelve, twice as
old as Ben, as yet unmarred by loss. My father steps over to hug
me and then gives me the heavy blue racket bag, draping it over
my shoulder. I smell the Aqua Velva and feel the heat of the coffee
thermos warming one of the bag's side compartments. My mother,
Joyce, has been hinting that Lloyd might not be traveling as much
anymore. And there's a brand new silver Saab 9000 in the driveway.
My family is changing and the changes seem awfully good to me.

Deep breath in, deep breath out. Might as well let it come. As
Paul once said, *You'll miss the memories after they stop haunting you.*

"Wait until your mother sees this new one," my father is saying.

"She'll hate it," I say.

My father shakes his head. "That might be what she'll tell you,
but it's not what she'll really feel. She'll be surprised and it will make
her happy." He tosses over a single key. "You unlock it," he says.

The key weighs almost as much as a tennis sneaker. I'd swear the
car, bathed in sunlight, is brightening as we approach, the reflection
of the blue sky pulsing on the hood. I beep it open, push the button
to unlatch the trunk, and set the racket bag next to the hopper of
balls. Then I toss the key back to my father. Inside, the black leather

is hot to the touch, slippery, and it smells like lemon shampoo. As soon as my father starts the engine, the air conditioning blasts away and the alarming sound of trumpet voluntaries kicks in. He loves brass. He cranks it louder. Maybe he thinks blaring Bach will make me decide to play trumpet. I don't mind the music and the sound is impressively clear. I can hear the soloist breathe during the pauses. But the only thing I want to play is tennis.

I study my father behind the wheel to see if he changed at all while he was away. The bushy mustache is still there, the thick black hair halfway down his neck like a lion's mane. His right forearm remains thicker than his left from tennis. He works the wheel and those forearm muscles move like a tide beneath his skin. I can't wait to be that strong. I want to have the exact same mustache as soon as I can. A few nights ago, I used my father's razor for the first time, on my chin and upper lip; I'd heard the whiskers would grow faster once I started shaving. The sting of the Aqua Velva surprised me, but I still slapped on a second helping of the stuff, like I'd seen my father do. I'm a half-inch taller than I was when he left. What will he notice?

His attention stays on the road. He drives to the Washington Park courts and on this sunny, new car morning, all the courts are open. My father pops the trunk and pulls out the hopper full of balls. I grab the bag and sprint ahead to get the best court before anyone else shows up.

I stretch by the fence and keep my eyes on my father. He walks over, sits on the wooden bench by the net, removes the thermos from his bag, and pours some of the steaming coffee into its red plastic cup. He takes a few sips before sealing the thing back up. He stands and starts windmilling his old Jack Kramer racket, holding it in his right hand and then his left. He turns his head from side to side and does a quick, high-kneed sprint in place. That's it for stretching. "Time, gentlemen," he says, and he serpentines to the T of the service line where he bounces up and down on his toes, ready to send over balls from the hopper.

He's been hitting the courts for a few years already and I go with him whenever I'm invited, trailing along, chasing down wayward balls like a high-strung ball boy, watching the points intently, as if

I'm working the latest US Open Final. When he's on his game, he calmly coils and uncoils himself, crouching low as the ball approaches and then exploding through it, finishing the stroke standing tall on his toes, racket arm upraised, like a statue of himself, frozen, until he bounces again and shuffles toward the next ball, racket back, crouching low once more. In those moments, he looks like a few different people all working well together.

Now he's on the other side of the net in his tennis whites, his socks pulled halfway up his calves, waiting, and I do not want to disappoint him. Maybe if I play well, my father will ask me to play more often. In fact, I've been doing my best to prepare myself for a chance like this. For almost two months, I've been getting informal lessons three times a week after school.

"We'll start off easy," my father says. "Remember to get a feel for the ball on the strings."

To this day, there's nothing I ever tried harder to do. I focus completely on hitting the ball straight back, a game of catch, my racket to his racket, and this one is a perfect strike that smacks dead-center into the sweet spot of his Jack Kramer.

When I started the after-school lessons, I strove to imitate my father, but I was shorter and weaker and I tended to stay low even during my follow-through. I imagined myself prowling the baseline like a panther. My father has a pretty one-handed backhand—is there a prettier stroke in any game in the world?—but I've been learning to hit the stroke two-handed, Jimmy Connors-style, though the coach said at the end of the day Harold Solomon, the original Human Backboard, might be the better model.

I don't want to reveal all I've learned right away. I don't zing the first few balls, but I put a little more on the fourth one and watch my father react. He looks up, opens his eyes wider. "That was unexpected," he says.

I keep quiet, just shrug my shoulders, as if it's a surprise to me, too, but I can't help grinning.

My father picks the hopper up and carries it to the baseline. "Let's see more," he calls out.

I retreat to my baseline and bounce up and down there. The two-handed backhand is the stroke I've been practicing the most, but he keeps sending balls to my forehand, my strongest shot. I've learned to rip it back full of topspin, using tough angles whenever I get an opening. After some softballs down the middle, I put as much pop on one as I can. My father watches it go by. "Duly noted," he says, and then he feeds me another, to see if I can do it again. He smiles as I zing it back, loaded with even more topspin, and we manage to keep the crosscourt rally going from there.

When the hopper is empty, we gather up the balls, stacking them on our rackets before dumping them back in. My father is laughing and I treasure the sound. "You really like this game, don't you?" he says. "Could be a nice way to make a living."

I don't answer. I haven't been thinking much about winning and losing or making a living. And I can't really see past the thrill of watching my father suddenly look at me differently. It's more than enough just to feel this glimmer of the grace available. My body a tuning fork struck just so, thrumming its perfect note. Within the straight-line confines of that hard court, I can make everything right, and I can do it again if I simply pay attention, watch the ball, let it happen.

My father takes a short coffee break, then pulls a clementine from the bag and peels it, glancing back toward the car. I use the time to savor what's happening. I wait close to the bench while my father polishes off the clementine and pours more coffee. I'm not asking anything about anything when he starts talking again.

"So, you've been playing on your own?" he says, smiling, and I still believe he's happier than usual. Maybe it's the new car. Maybe he's excited about a summer of tennis, too. Maybe a nice surprise is a rare thing for him.

"The coach gives free lessons," I say. "He's been helping me—"

"I'm glad," my father says. "Keep after it. And here's some advice for later, just in case I'm not around to give it to you when you need it."

For years, he's been crisscrossing Upstate New York, selling buildings and land. So I assume my father is telling me there will be more travel after all. No need to be downhearted. Take the news like a man. Why else would he have bought a new car?

He makes room for me to sit beside him on the bench. So close, now, and we're both sweating, and I can see the way our shirts grow damp in the same places—underarms, midchest, and a circle above our belly buttons. We have the same odor, muskier than the Aqua Velva, like a towel that came out of the dryer a little damp.

"You need to keep your head down a bit more," my father says. "But that's a minor point. In my line of work, I discover some unfortunate facts."

I haven't finished reveling in that "duly noted" and our shared scent. Now there's more. Tennis can do so much! Why hadn't I started younger? I always want to hear more details about my father's work.

"You'll be a teenager soon," my father says, "so you can probably understand what I'm going to tell you. You'll learn that with certain people, it's important to be careful how you win."

"I'll be careful," I say.

"You've got real skills and you'll get even better quickly. It's obvious. I'm not telling you anything you don't know. But you'll find there are people who don't like losing. Reprisals appear when you don't expect them. People can be resourceful when it comes to hurting others."

"Who's going to try to hurt me?"

My father finishes his coffee, shakes out the cup, and puts it back on the thermos. The muscles in his forearm twitch as he tightens the lid. "I'm not just talking about tennis," he says. "In business. In love. Other places, too, I'm sure. There are hostile people who can't help retaliating when you win or when you get something they want. They'll use their own loss to justify anything."

He sounds proud, but also upset. I don't want to look in his eyes. I just want my time with him to be perfect. When it doesn't go well, I grow nervous and worry the time won't last. "Are you a hostile person?" I ask.

My father slaps my back and laughs and I feel safe again, breathing in a deep whiff of our smell. "Me?" he says. "You know that's not me. I'm just your old man gabbing away after a rough week." Then he puts his hand on my cheek and rubs a finger gently above my upper lip. "Wait a second," he says. "Did you shave while I was gone?"

I smile, embarrassed and pleased at the same time. "Did I do it right?"

"Looks dynamite to me," he says, and then he stands and speeds through another round of stretching. "Good for you. You really are growing up, just like I was saying. And, unfortunately, you will get hurt. Like everyone else. The key is to keep hitting the ball through it all. So, how about we smack a few more?"

Which is exactly what I want to hear. "You bet," I say, putting the rest of the conversation out of my mind and rushing back onto the court.

A few weeks later, I'll start remembering that conversation differently. After the aneurysm bursts, my mother will gradually though not completely explain. I'll hear more and more, but never enough, as we prepare for the funeral, which is sparsely attended.

The doctors knew all about it for more than two years but they couldn't get to it.

We thought about telling you.

We thought about it all the time but we didn't want to make you carry that kind of knowledge.

At least not until you were much older.

Also, we didn't know it would burst.

Your father could have lived his whole life with it dormant, stable, safe.

It just didn't work out that way.

And then, all too soon, my mother will introduce me to the strict, controlling bank teller bound to become, for a time, my step-father. Morris, a defeated man very interested in hurting. Had my father glimpsed his hostile successor in the wings? Or was he looking further ahead, somehow aware of Hank on the distant horizon?

For now, I stay out on the court, bouncing on my toes by the baseline, the late afternoon breeze in my hair, my hand loose on the warm grip, my whole body jangly, set to pounce, and I can see my father, bouncing the same way on the other side of the net, the same breeze moving through his hair. It's as if I've been given a brief glimpse into the future and I can peer over at the promise of myself, and I'm surprised by how comforting that is. I don't have to rush toward it, I can simply observe, prepare myself, look forward. It's all there waiting for me while I get to remain the kid I am—the blessed kid with a mysterious, inspiring dad who is eager to offer me lessons about winning, eager to help me face whatever lies ahead. Now, look out! What's immediately ahead is the next ball, and here it comes, and I can see the seams on it, how the topspin makes it accelerate downward once it clears the net. I bounce once more, up on my toes, then I start to turn my body, racket back, and I'm sure I couldn't possibly be more ready.

12

"HELLO IN THERE," IRENE SAID, startling me as she opened the passenger side door. Then she moved on to hand over the next kid and Ben tumbled into the car. "Wagon Wheel," was the song he wanted—*Rock me mama any way you feel.* And his questions turned immediately toward Diane. "Will we see her tonight?" he asked.

I tried to sink right into the conversation. "What did you think of her?"

"She made me laugh," he said.

"How did she do that?"

"It's a secret."

I was just dreaming about what my father kept secret from me, I could have said. *Lots of secrets swirling around these days.* "No fair," I said instead. "Why can't you tell me?"

"I can tell you, but you have to promise not to tell her."

"I promise," I said, and even though laughter could quickly become a complicated subject, I pressed on. "Now, how did she make you laugh?"

"She runs like an archaeopteryx," he said. "Like a fast, funny-looking bird."

"I guess I didn't notice that."

"Mom ran like an antelope," he said. "Almost like she could float."

"It's true."

"I could imagine Diane with feathers."

"She did seem fast," I said, hoping Ben would keep talking about all he noticed and thought, but the car was having its predictable effect. In a few more minutes he'd drop off into a nap.

"What did she say about the party?" he asked, after a long pause, fighting to stay awake.

"I haven't heard from her yet," I said. "But I have heard from Uncle Hank. He's in town. I'm guessing we'll see him soon."

"That's great," he said. "I hope Diane comes too."

"I can't remember," I said. "Was the archaeopteryx a carnivore, herbivore, or omnivore?"

I waited for the answer and when I didn't hear one, I looked back and saw my son sacked out again.

I parked in front of our building, reclined my seat, and checked my phone. When I looked up, there was Hank walking my way. Over the years, I must have logged hundreds of hours in the Subaru with my son napping and I was rarely recognized or disturbed. Now it was twice in a row, and this promised to be far less pleasant than seeing Diane's open hand pressed against the window. Hank stood at attention by the door, wearing his familiar suit. I quietly turned the key so I could lower the window and the first thing I said was, "*Shh*."

Hank didn't listen or didn't care. "Officer Waldman, I presume," he said. Then he registered Ben asleep in the backseat. "Isn't he a little old for after-school naps?"

"He'll probably sleep for a half hour or so."

"I can't stay for that long," Hank said. "Let's sit on your stoop for a bit. We can see the car from there."

I glanced back at Ben before carefully opening the door and was struck anew by the fact that, despite all of Laurie's fears, Ben's face more and more resembled a Bell face, not a Waldman face. I zeroed in on how perfectly smooth his eyelids looked when they were closed. Just how Laurie looked when she was sound asleep. And that was more than fine, but it was eerie to see how Ben could also easily pass for Hank's son.

Maybe that was part of why, during the last year, Hank had begun to take greater interest in Ben. We'd only seen him at the funeral, then at Ben's birthday, but on both occasions Hank had made a point to spend time with his one and only nephew. He brought gifts. He'd begun contributing to a 529 account. He sent postcards every now and then from various locations, sometimes signed together with Elizabeth, a woman he'd been seeing. So, it wasn't at all untruthful for me to say, "Ben will be sorry to have missed you."

"I could wake him up."

"Not a good idea, but you'll be around for a few days, won't you?"

We sat on the barn-red wooden stairs. Soon it would be warm enough to see people sitting out after work, but it was still chilly, so the stoops up and down the street were empty. Hank kept quiet, as he sometimes did when he wasn't going to answer a question, so I tried a different one. "Can you tell me more about this threat?"

"Of course not."

"And where did you say you came in from?"

"I didn't say."

"How's that woman you were seeing? Didn't you mention last time she might be moving in with you?"

Hank smiled, but it was hard to see much happiness in it. "What about you?" he asked. "Almost a year now. You put yourself back on the market yet?"

How to answer that question without adding to his anger about Laurie's death? "I don't know when I'll be ready to meet new people," I said.

"Don't worry about that," Hank said. "At your age, it'll mostly be old people from now on."

Not the friendliest joke, but the attempt at humor was enough for me to try to open up at least a little with him. "It's just hard to imagine," I said. "You remember my friend—"

"You don't have to bullshit me," Hank said. "You must imagine it all the time. Performing those ridiculous pat-downs day after day."

I'd been about to mention Paul and the arrival of Vanessa and how strange that felt. I shook my head and slipped into TSA lingo. "It's clinical," I said. "The job is the job, you know that."

"That woman you asked about?" Hank said. "Elizabeth. She told me we have to be careful who we pretend to be. You know why?"

"I'm betting you'll tell me."

"We have to be careful because we are who we pretend to be."

"Who did she think you were pretending to be?"

Again, Hank didn't answer. He leaned forward and rested his elbows on his knees, his hands clasped between his legs. He seemed to be staring at my Subaru, checking to see if Ben was still asleep. The guy was hard to read, as Neffer had said, and I was no Behavior Detection Officer. Still, I thought he looked sad. Big surprise. He missed his sister. He'd been hoping to spend time with his nephew. He probably had no desire to be stuck in Albany, sitting next to someone he didn't really respect.

While I waited for Hank to say more, I drifted back toward another time when I'd sat outside together with him. To celebrate Ben's first birthday, Laurie booked a cabin up north at White Pine Camp, not far from Saranac Lake. At the last second, Hank drove up from New York City and I was confident some family healing was about to commence.

That night, after Laurie goes inside to put Ben to bed, Hank and I split a six-pack. When it's gone, Hank says, "I need to grab something from my car." He returns with a bottle of Wild Turkey, opens it, and hands it to me. "Take a swig," he says. "I want to tell you something."

Bourbon isn't my favorite. Still, I'm happy to oblige. It's taken a while, but we've drunk some beers, we're moving on to harder stuff, and maybe we'll be playing tennis before long. I pass the bottle back. A loon wails its haunting, mournful call somewhere out on the pond.

Hank takes a swig of his own from the bottle. "Listen," he says, "I'm thinking about getting out. I don't spend time around many young families in my line of work. It's a reminder. There are other things I can do with my life."

I'm drunk and tired. I don't want to push. Let this late-night conversation be a start. That's more than enough. "I think the same thing sometimes," I say. "I'm glad you're here with us."

Hank takes another swig. "Is Laurie glad too?"

"Of course she is," I say. "This whole weekend was her idea. This is exactly what she wants."

Hank raises his glass. "To more nights like this, my brother," he says.

I drink from the bottle again, swallowing so much I cough, and then we decide to head inside.

I can't wait to tell Laurie what's happened. I wake her when I climb into bed and repeat the conversation. She isn't nearly as excited.

"We'll see, sweetheart," she says, spooning herself up against me. "Sounds like he was just pumping you for information. It wouldn't be the first time."

A few hours later, Ben cries us awake and we find a note from Hank on the refrigerator: *Duty calls. Had to rush off. Be in touch.* Almost a year passes before we see him again and nothing about him seems different.

But out on the stoop, as we watched the six-year-old Ben nap, I kept waiting to see what Hank would say next. How would he swerve away from my question this time?

Finally, he sat up and leaned back, stretching out his legs. "The truth is," he began, "these days, I don't much like who I'm pretending to be, and Elizabeth doesn't like that I don't like myself. How's that sound? Familiar, maybe?"

The longer I stayed with the TSA, the more frequently Laurie, and a few others, suggested I was using the job to punish myself for failing to make a living as a tennis player. The therapist had supported this theory. "I don't know," I said to Hank, "but you keep doing the work, don't you?"

"Despite everything," Hank said, "we don't know each other very well, right?"

I nodded.

"I know you're haunted by what happened to Laurie. I know you blame yourself. Sometimes, in my darker moments, I blame you too. I can't help it. I'm sorry for that."

"It's natural," I said. "I wish—"

"It might be natural. I don't know. But what I want to say is I'm haunted by more than you can ever know. More than I can ever tell you. More than I can ever tell anyone. You've had your time in the TSA, but you could quit tomorrow and get your mind around another job. It might take a while, though probably not. It would be different for me. I'm not so sure I could do it, no matter how much I might want to. I've done too many things. On purpose. With forethought. Again and again."

I used to ask Laurie what she believed Hank actually did. *I don't want to know,* she'd say. *I'm glad I don't know.* I tended to fill in the blank space with generic images: Hank jumping from a plane above Afghanistan or Iraq, special night vision goggles over his eyes, his whole parachute and every piece of clothing as black as night. "Still," I said, "you've been thinking about getting out for years. Maybe now's the time."

"There are reasons for what I do, but these days I believe them less."

I wasn't sure how much more I could ask him before he clammed up again. And maybe it was all an act, softening me up again so I'd feed him whatever information he wanted. Still, he seemed sincere and I couldn't resist trying to learn more. "Can't you take a break?" I asked. "A hiatus, or something like that?"

"Someone has to do my job," he said, "and I'm good at it. Better I do it than someone who's not good at it. There's also my version of survivor's guilt. I do the work for the people who died doing the work. It's a debt that must be paid."

"What does Elizabeth say to that?"

"She says she can't stop the clock from ticking."

"Who can?" I asked.

"She's been patient. She wants a family."

"I'd like to meet her sometime."

"I'm not sure that's going to happen," said Hank. "I might have been overcorrecting, reaching out for someone who wants a life too totally different from what I can handle."

"Makes me want to meet her even more," I said.

Hank looked away. "Ben's awake," he said, jumping up and jogging fast toward the car.

I lagged a few steps behind. As soon as Ben climbed out of the car and saw Hank, he ran up for a hug. "Uncle Hank!" he shouted.

"I wasn't sure when I'd see you," Hank said, lifting Ben into the air for a moment. "I've been carrying something around for you."

"What is it?"

Hank rolled up his sleeve and took something off his wrist. "This was your mother's first watch," he said. "You'll need to wind it every day, like she used to."

He launched into a story about Laurie's first trip to Disneyland, about sunburn and misery, and how the watch had been his mother's way of apologizing for not protecting Laurie. I wondered if it was a true story. Without Laurie around, how would I ever know?

"Now, what time does that watch say it is?" Hank asked, and then he leaned in close to point out the difference between Mickey's two black arms.

Ben studied the watch closely. "Five forty-five," he said.

"And unfortunately," Hank said, "that means I have to bolt."

"You just got here," Ben said.

"We'll see Uncle Hank at the cemetery tomorrow," I said.

"Are you bringing anyone to the cemetery?" Ben asked.

"No. Are you?"

"We might bring Diane," Ben said.

Hank gave me a pressed-lip disapproving look and shook his head. "I hadn't heard that," he said.

I hadn't meant to hold the information back. "We don't know if she'll be there or not," I said.

Hank turned his focus back to Ben. "And who is Diane?" he asked.

"Dad saved her dad's life the other day," Ben said.

I waited to see how Hank would downplay this, how he'd try to dim the pride that lit Ben's eyes. Someday, Hank would no doubt tell Ben about the accident from his point of view; he'd say I'd failed and if only he'd been there instead he would have caught up to Laurie, flown off his bike, stopped her in time, or cushioned her fall, and everyone would still be alive. But for now, for whatever reason, Hank seemed to be feeling generous. "I heard about that," he said. "You should be very proud. Your dad was quite the hero. We should all go out to celebrate one night. Which reminds me: I might have some other things for you."

"Really?" Ben asked.

"Really," Hank said, mussing Ben's hair and walking away. "See you soon."

I started to head inside, but Ben wanted to see what kind of car Hank had, so we watched him beep a dark-blue Dodge Charger unlocked. Hank raced the engine and drove toward us. "Bye!" Ben shouted.

Hank came to a complete stop and lowered the window. "Bye-bye!" he called out. Laurie would have been even more shocked by the farewell than I was. Then Hank revved the engine, honked the horn, and sped away.

13

ONCE WE WERE IN THE APARTMENT, I kept an eye on the clock and tried to tai chi everything toward bedtime. Exert pressure without pressure. Move forward. I boiled up some noodles again, wagon-wheel pasta, since it fit the current soundtrack. Ben wanted yogurt, juice, and a waffle while he waited and I brought it all to the kitchen table. The yogurt was gone in seconds, followed by the waffle. Ben jumped to his feet and said he wanted to get dressed up to see what his fancy clothes looked like with the watch. "Maybe I'll wear it to the cemetery," he said, racing toward his room. "Mom might be happy to see I have it."

I wondered exactly what passed through his mind when he said something like that. Was he also waiting for Laurie to reappear? Make her presence known? Then the pasta water began boiling over. I blew into the white foam and turned down the flame. I could hear Ben opening and closing his closet door, hustling into the bedroom, jetting his piss into the toilet. Part kid, part horse. And then I was stirring the noodles and reliving another overwhelming moment, one of millions, long ago in the same apartment, except I'm the one who needs to piss, and Ben is two, screaming from his crib.

"I'll go talk to him," Laurie says, beginning to sit up.

"What time is it?" I ask.

"He was up for a few minutes at four thirty, but he got himself back to sleep pretty quickly. Then he was up again at four fifty-five."

"What time is it now?"

"He's been trying really hard. It's five forty-seven. Much better than yesterday. I think it would be fine to bring him in."

"Don't," I say. "Please, don't."

"Hey Mommy!" Ben screams.

"He'll make it to six tomorrow," Laurie says. "Little by little."

"Please," I say. "We've done this work before. We all need the sleep."

"Maybe we just need a bigger apartment. A house. A master bathroom."

"A king-size bed."

"Mommy!" Ben screams again.

"You know I'll cry if I have to listen to him crying," says Laurie.

"I have no idea what to do."

"Neither do I," Laurie says, "but he's awake and he wants to be with us."

"We are awfully charming. What's the time now?"

"Five fifty-one. And we're better than charming. We're irresistible."

"Speak for yourself," I say. "But right now I've got to piss."

Laurie reaches down and begins to stroke me. "How can you piss out of something so hard?"

Following someone's example, Ben starts counting. "One, two, three—"

"To be continued," Laurie says, releasing me, and then she's out of the bed, almost shouting, "Here comes Mommy!"

"Here comes Mommy!" Ben echoes, immediately happy.

Meanwhile, I linger a moment before hitting the bathroom, still unsure if we've done the right thing. Did we just reward the kid for crying? Shouldn't we all be able to sleep through the night? But I piss for what feels like minutes, a truly visceral relief. Plus it's 6:01 and everyone is happy.

~

I managed to remember the noodles near al dente. I banged the colander into the sink and I was pouring off the boiling water, steam rising before me, when Ben pranced back into the kitchen. "Ta-da!" he said.

He had his arms stretched out, like he was about to bow, and I was tempted to applaud. I was also tempted to call Shannon. She was scheduled to babysit the next night, but I felt the need for a break right now. The dampness near my eyes wasn't just from the steam in the air. I wiped it away quickly and tried to figure out what to say to my son, who stood dazzling in his dark-blue three-piece suit, the vest unbuttoned, the clip-on necktie barely hanging on.

I did my best to channel Laurie. She was so much better at loving than I was. What I wouldn't give to hear her coming our way, calling out, "Here comes Mommy!" I knelt down, looked in Ben's light-brown eyes—Laurie's eyes—and adjusted his tie. "You look fantastic," I said.

"The watch matches perfectly, doesn't it?"

Every time one of Hank's postcards arrived in the mail, I considered throwing it directly into the trash. I considered doing the same with the watch. Even though Hank had just been more open than ever before, I suspected I was being played.

Ben held the watch closer to my face, waiting for me to say something about it. It looked like it still had its original band—wide, bright-red faux leather with an outsized silverish buckle. The thing couldn't possibly be comfortable on Ben's thin arm. "It's got pizzazz," I said.

"What are you going to wear, Dad?"

I was suddenly hyperconscious of my outfit. The goddamn uniform slacks, scuffed black shoes, dumpy white T-shirt, and an old Haven hoodie. I'd left the sky-blue-epaulet button-down in my locker. I hadn't showered in almost two days and I hadn't shaved in four.

We are who we pretend to be.

I turned my attention back to the noodles. I lifted the colander and shook it to drain more water, grabbed the preshredded mozzarella from the fridge, took down two bowls from the cabinet. At moments like this, I longed to be one of those monastic types who could wash the dishes simply to wash the dishes, or set the table simply to set the table. A Gallwey coach not only out on the court, but also deep in my home. My mother went far down that road after she finally ditched the stepfather and it seemed to help her.

I dished out the noodles, sprinkled the cheese, stirred in some butter. I handed a bowl to Ben, my son, beaming in his favorite fancy clothes, pretending as hard as he possibly could to be a man.

We'd talked about death in the past. We'd talked about it before Laurie died and then, in a much more weighted way, we'd talked about it after. He believed we'd all be together in the end. And we'd all be children and we could play with each other. Simple as that. Could it really be that my son was handling all of this better than I was? How much had I been leaning on the poor kid? How was the kid still standing?

And yet, there he was, my six-year-old, *our* six-year-old, wanting to talk, waiting for an answer.

"What *am* I going to wear?" I said. "What do you think I should wear?"

"Something fancy, of course. A suit?"

"We'll go through my closet after dinner, how's that?"

No screens at mealtime, that had been a long-standing family rule. But something about sitting at the table with my suited son made me consider an exception. It was more than the fact of the ridiculously long day. The buzz of Diane, the ghost of Laurie, my father's daydreamy drop-in. Paul with his arm around Vanessa. The looming threat. The jerky with Neffer and the stoop talk with Hank. So much more to figure out. More than anything, I probably just needed a good night's rest. I needed to be strong and get stronger for the impending birthday. The pasta was heaped high in the bowls. I added an extra layer of cheese. Maybe if we filled our stomachs it would be easier to shut it all down for the night, try to do better tomorrow.

But that suit on my son. My father used to wear suits and when he was home for dinner he'd sit at the table and talk about his day. It was like those dinners were part of his job because he'd barely even loosen his tie. Ben had the clothes now, and there was something new in his eyebrows, the sharp angle in the middle when he raised them. I half-expected him to start talking about a difficult client down in Kingston. An annoying phone call. A funny thing he overheard at the gas station. And then I began talking about my own day.

"Guess what I heard at work today?" I said.

"What?"

"Can you keep a secret?"

Ben nodded. "I already told you a secret."

"But you really can't tell anyone about it, okay? Promise?"

"Promise."

"Well, my boss might get promoted and he might help me get promoted too."

"Promoted?"

"I might get a better job. Maybe make more money. Maybe we'll move and then maybe someday we could buy our own house."

I watched Ben's face and wondered exactly why I'd just shared that information. I needed to talk to someone about it, probably. Maybe I thought Ben would be impressed. But the kid quietly ate a few more noodles and then said he was full. The excitement had vanished. Which made me desperate to get it back.

"Ready to help me pick out my suit?"

"Sure," Ben said, but his voice sounded emptier.

I left the dishes for later, the least of my lousy behavior, though the therapist had early on talked about the importance of the little things—get out of bed, brush your teeth, follow your routine and let it lead you forward. Or, to use more familiar lingo: grind it out.

I'd hoped the suit selection would be funny, a chance to laugh, because, as I well knew, I had only one suit, the black one I'd bought at Macy's for the funeral. But when Ben was standing beside me in the closet, looking at the lame collection of clothes, it wasn't funny at all.

"I don't know," I said. "Might be time for a new suit."

Ben was staring at the space where Laurie's clothes used to hang. That stuff was boxed up in the building's basement storage area, probably getting ruined by mold and moths.

"We could go suit shopping," I said, though I had no idea when we'd have time for that. "Could be fun, right? We could find you something new too."

Ben brightened a little. "Maybe a seersucker?"

Sure, it was bribery, but the smile felt more than worth it.

~

Once Ben was in his pajamas, he resembled a child again, and the routine became closer to normal, which meant I fell asleep beside my son, woke up groggy near eleven, and shuffled back to my own room. I rubbed at my eyes as I brought my laptop over to the bed. How hard would it be to get some answers myself? I googled Alexander Strand first. The bio at Strand Consulting's website mentioned Harvard Law School, more than twenty years as a real estate attorney with a focus on Indian gaming and casinos. Then he'd transitioned to real estate investment. Thomas Strand had also spent time at Harvard Law School and then he'd gone right to work with his father. Diane Percy Strand wasn't listed on the website. I found her at Upstate Animal Hospital, where she worked as a certified veterinarian assistant. There was a headshot of her in a white lab coat. She looked pissed at whoever was taking the photo of her. I also found her name associated with a group called the Armed Ladies of the Capital District.

I was about to check out more links when my phone buzzed and, lo and behold, it was Diane calling in. I closed the laptop, suddenly out of breath.

"Is it too late?" she asked. "I was thinking about you and Ben. I just got off the phone with my mother."

Were we both thinking of each other at the same time? Maybe she'd been googling me too. "How much longer will your mother be in Japan?" I asked.

"After the heart episode she was talking about flying back right away, but now that he seems to be doing so much better, she's staying put."

"Will you go meet up with her over there?"

"I don't think mother-daughter time is what her trip is about."

She sounded angry, a harshness in her voice. I didn't want to make her angry. "I'd love to go to Japan someday," I said.

"I think she's enjoying it, but it sounds claustrophobic to me."

"Really?" Laurie and I had looked forward to more travel. Rome. Machu Picchu. Kyoto. We were going to do it when we had more money. When we had more time.

"It's nice to hear your voice," Diane said, "but I didn't call to talk about all the problems of living in an overpopulated xenophobic island nation. It's like this: I didn't know what to say about your son's question, but I thought we should talk about it. So—"

"I'd be happy to talk about it."

"I don't mean right now. I thought we could grab a drink or some food tomorrow night, if you can step out."

I was about to say yes, please, of course, but just in time I remembered the dinner plans with Paul and Vanessa. I explained it to her. "You could join us," I said.

"I could," she said, her voice softening again. "I could do many things. Are you asking if I'd like to join you?"

"Would you like to join us?"

"Yes, as a matter of fact, I would."

After I gave her the details and we said good night, I thought about opening the laptop again. I could read more about the Armed Ladies. And Hank Bell was next on my list, even though I'd googled my brother-in-law several times before. I'd found plenty of other Hank Bells, but never the one I wanted. Hank surely knew how to make himself disappear online, and in other ways. Better to shut my eyes and call it a night. Drop off to sleep with Diane's voice echoing in my ear, the sound almost sweet enough to make me think maybe I hadn't done absolutely everything wrong all day long.

14

THE NEXT MORNING, I ASSEMBLED the usual breakfast—vitamin, oatmeal, orange juice, banana—and set it down in front of Ben. The kid barely moved. He was looking out the window at what promised to be a warmer, clear-skied day. We didn't have access to the back-yard, but the first-floor tenants tended the garden obsessively. Laurie liked to ask them questions, file information away for when we had a garden all our own. Now the first daffodils were popping open and a few tulips showed teases of color, on the verge of blossoming. "More signs of spring," I said. I remembered the dandelion I'd put away for Ben and I fished it out of my pocket. The yellow weed had turned into a gooey brown mess, so I pitched it into the trash.

Ben chewed up his vitamin and dug into the oatmeal. "Is Shannon coming over tonight?" he asked.

"She should be waiting for us when we get home."

"Will she do bedtime?"

"She will."

Ben looked at his new watch. "Let's go," he said.

"What about the banana?"

"I'll bring it for the road."

The relative quiet continued down the stairs, out the door, and into the car. I did my best to wait through the silence. I played more Old Crow Medicine Show, but neither one of us sang along. Once we pulled into the car line, though, the question, or prequestion, came at last. "Can I ask you something, Dad?"

"Ask away. Please."

"Will you tell me the truth?"

I glanced into the rearview mirror, searching for eye contact. *Is that your question?* I could have replied, but Ben was working hard, so I held back, expecting more about the watch and the birthday. "Of course I will," I said.

"Do we have to move?"

The kid was always listening. How stupid I'd been to so cavalierly mention moving, leaving behind the only home he's ever known. How many other stupid mistakes had I made, without a clue? "I'll totally answer that question," I said. "Just let me park first so we can really talk." I didn't want to be late, but I pulled the car out of the line, parked in the lot behind the school, flicked my seat belt off, and turned to face him. "We don't have to move," I said.

"Do you want to?"

"Sometimes," I said. "Sometimes I do."

"Why?"

"Why do you think?"

"So we can have the kind of house Mommy wanted."

"That's part of it, but you said you wanted the truth, right?"

Ben nodded.

"I'm slowly learning to live without Mommy," I said. "We both are, aren't we?"

Ben nodded again.

"Well, sometimes I think it would be easier to live without her if we lived somewhere else, somewhere new." I kept my attention on Ben even as my mind raced: Why had I never left Albany after all my local losses? Why had Paul left and then returned? How could I expect Ben to want to leave?

Now the kid was eager to get going. "There's Alison," he said, reaching for his door. "Can I go in with her?"

"Sure," I said, stepping out of the car. "Give me a second." When I was by Ben's door, I noticed the banana untouched on the seat so I put it inside the schoolbag. I knelt down to hand it over. "One more thing, though. I promise we won't move unless we both want to, okay?"

"Okay."

As we crossed the parking lot toward the sidewalk, I wondered if Ben felt reassured. He was standing tall, bright-eyed. Alison was up ahead, almost at the school's front door. "How about a race?" I said.

"On your mark," Ben said. "Get set." Then he was off, shouting "*Go!*" and sprinting away, the bag bouncing against his body.

I was soothing my son, offering, I hoped, a healthy distraction, but how would others see a man in a bulky TSA jacket dashing toward a school? I wasn't going to worry about it. I ran, staying a step behind my son all the way to the door.

~

At work, Neffer was pacing in the break room, but I almost didn't recognize him because he'd buzzed his hair and shaved his goatee. He was wearing a pair of boxy black glasses. The changes somehow gave him the face of a session musician or an investment banker. They also made him look like he'd dropped a lot of weight overnight. It was more than a cigarette a day could do. The fact that he'd dressed up didn't hurt, either. He was wearing a stylish blue suit, not all that different from the one Ben had been wearing the night before. His shimmering Nikes were the brightest things in the room. Before I could comment on the makeover, Neffer said, "Good morning, Waldman. Punch in and stop by my office."

I hit the clock, dumped my coat and lunch in my locker, put on my work shirt, and hustled to meet Neffer. His office had been spiffed up too. The whole massive desk was visible and, without all the stacks of paper, it didn't look like standard-issue furniture. Old wood. Oak, maybe. The scent of Pine Sol hung in the air. And there was no food to be seen. "More attention focusing my way all of sudden," he said, speaking quickly, leaning back in his chair. "Need to look my best, even if it makes my face itch. Not my favorite. But it's necessary. You give any thought to what we talked about?"

"We talked about a lot," I said.

"Indeed we did," Neffer said. "Might as well shut the door."

I did as I was told. I took a seat, trying not to stare at Neffer's new face. "I talked to Diane on the phone last night," I said. It was the kind of line I might have said to my therapist, back when I had a therapist.

"Booty call, I suspect," Neffer said, sounding nothing at all like my therapist.

"No."

"No?"

"It's complicated."

"I bet it is. She's basically starving, but she won't eat enough food, so she's down to skin and bone, and that affects her ability to reason. Probably loses track of time. Did she make any sense at all?"

"She's not that thin."

"You feel the need to defend her already?"

"Anyhow. My son invited her to the birthday ceremony or whatever it is that we're having this weekend. She suggested we get together and talk about that invitation. Looks like we'll go out for dinner tonight with some of my friends and—"

"Smart money says she orders a salad. Kale chips. Brussels sprouts."

"She wolfed down her pizza the other night."

"I bet she wolfed it all down," Neffer said, laughing. Then he covered his mouth and shook his head. "I don't know why I give you so much guff. Mrs. Neffer keeps telling me to cut back on my banter. Says it will get me in trouble. I'm sure she's right. So enough banter. Anything else to tell me?"

"I talked with Hank for a while too, but he was professional as always."

Neffer nodded. "Of course," he said. He looked up and kept talking, as if addressing the dropped ceiling and the fluorescent lighting. "Somehow," he said, "I know we'll pass this test."

"How worried are you?" I asked.

Neffer stood up. "Nice to chat with you," he said. "As always. Keep on keeping me posted. But for now you'd better stop dawdling. Get up to the checkpoint. Save some more lives."

~

As I rotated from position to position, I noticed heightened security around, though nothing that would register with the average PAX. A few more LEOs than usual, a little heavier on the bulletproof gear. The regional canine patrol was running some playbook drill in Concourse C. And when I was working exit, I had to radio the supervisor twice for Air Marshalls I didn't recognize and five times for DC-based suits I'd never seen before. Not one of them cracked a smile.

The PAX might remain unaware, but everyone on the shift was on edge. Would there be another test to keep us on our toes? Nothing materialized before my first break of the day. I bought my coffee and headed down to the break room, banging "Clobber" on my way. Then Sanchez and August caught up to me, and they had Kevin with them.

August and Sanchez leered at me. "Waldman and Neff-man," Sanchez said. "Wonder what it's all about?"

"Maybe they're planning a double date, now that our hero has snared a grateful lady," August said. "They want to advance together."

Any response from me would be a victory for them and their cowboy bullshit. If it had just been Kevin, I would have slowed down to talk. But maybe the guy was leaning cowboy after all. Had he told August and Sanchez that Hank was my brother-in-law? I stood up straighter and kept walking down the concourse. Demonstrate command presence. Move forward. They followed along for a few steps before stopping. I heard Kevin say, "We agreed I'd lead." Then he jogged up and started talking even as he was catching his breath. "They used to bug me too. Don't let them get to you."

"You're friends now?"

"They were heading upstairs to tell one of the suits they saw you and Neffer walk outside before the end of a shift yesterday. I told them we needed to stick together. They said you wouldn't stick with us, so—"

"So?"

"I said I'd powwow with you."

Something about the sound of *powwow* reinforced my trust in him. Plus it wouldn't hurt to know their current thoughts about the potential threat. "Okay," I said, "now we're powwowing. What's up?"

"I'll tell you what concerns me," Kevin said. "Number one, those Three Stooges, of course. But, number two, will we have to rebid our shifts if Neffer leaves? Is he going to take some of us with him wherever he's going?"

Plenty of gossip, even in secure environments with a threat looming. That was nothing new. I didn't think the shifts would change, no matter what might happen with Neffer. Still, the worry flashed to me for a second. What would I do if I somehow got switched back to Tuesday-Wednesday "weekends"? Laurie used to wake up with me when I was stuck with four-to-noon shifts, even though she really needed the sleep. We'd look in on Ben together before heading to the kitchen. She'd sit with me while I brewed coffee and inhaled a bowl of cereal. Thankfully, the result of all the attrition was that I'd managed to move up quickly and get a conventional schedule before Ben had his first birthday. That clear ability to advance was part of the job's early appeal. The stability of it, how dependable it felt. A comfort offered amid the overwhelming chaos of new fatherhood. And maybe that comfort amid chaos continued, for me, for Ben. At least that's what I told myself, though Paul still called it hiding.

Neffer had said it right: Can't keep people safe, can't not try.

Which reminded me of more gossip: I'd heard that Kevin's wife was pregnant. In any case, I didn't want to lie to the guy. "I don't think the shifts can change like that," I said. "But I'll see what I can find out."

"Sounds good."

"What are those two cowboys saying about the Stooges?"

"Same old, same old," Kevin said. "They're hoping they can start packing a sidearm. Sanchez keeps melting over Curly's baby-blue eyes. August says he's already revising his old FBI application."

"I'd stay wary of those two," I said.

"I'm wary of this whole place, man. Aren't you?"

I smiled and said, "Guess I'm not too wary of you."

"Let's keep powwowing," Kevin said, then he put out his big fist and we bumped. He reunited with August and Sanchez. I sipped my coffee. It was getting cold, usually a sign that break was almost over, so I hustled back to the checkpoint to rotate through the rest of my shift.

15

WHEN I PICKED UP BEN, HE jumped into the car, full of requests and questions. He wanted "Wagon Wheel" again and was Diane coming to the birthday in the morning and could Shannon take him out for pizza and when were we going suit shopping?

I was jonesing for a run. I was wondering if I could drop the boy with Shannon and dart out for a solo dash to Haven and back, but if I did that I'd wind up being late for Diane. I'd have to settle for some calisthenics while changing out of my uniform.

In the meantime, I cranked the music, rolled down the window, and studied the Helderbergs on the horizon. Ben sang along about looking down the road and praying to see headlights. I inhaled. Exhaled. The rolling hills appeared so soft from a distance. *Rock me mama* goes the irresistible chorus and I see my own mother in the kitchen of the old house after her last trip out West and she's rubbing at her eyes—hazel like mine, but redder from travel. Her hands are quivering. "Big Sur was lovely," she says, "but I shouldn't have spent last night in the city. And the train up here was packed with people blabbering away. So much negativity. You wouldn't believe how peaceful it was out there."

I know the proselytizing is next, so I cut her off. "I was thinking of heading out for a run, but maybe we could walk together instead and catch up a bit?"

"Sounds perfect," she says. "Let me stretch out a little first. And I'd like a cup of tea. Would you mind putting the kettle on?"

While I fill the kettle, she loops a set of long, thick, multicolored rubbery bands onto the pantry's doorknob. Then she begins to perform intricate stretching exercises. It looks like she's being attacked by oversized, hostile pasta. For someone who loves to meditate, she has an awfully tough time sitting still.

She'd been born Joyce Duncker, lived married as Joyce Waldman until Lloyd died. During the lousy years with stepfather Morris, she reclaimed her maiden name. Once she dumped Morris, she became increasingly interested in Werner Erhard and started calling herself Joy Duncker. Through it all, I usually stuck with *Mom*, though as I grew older I wondered why she hadn't concocted a new last name to go with Joy. Erhard, after all, had once been Johnny Rosenberg. Joy Duncker seemed like a failure of imagination and I razzed her about it sometimes, but I didn't push too hard. I was well aware that my own imagination left much to be desired.

In this memory, she pulls and pulls on the bands, as if keeping time with her breath, her arms above her head, out into a T, flat against her sides. She's sick, down to her last months, and yet she remains surprisingly flexible and whatever she's doing makes her appear almost fit, far younger than sixty-three. She lets the bands dangle from the doorknob, takes her big toe in one hand, and manages to keep holding it while she stretches her leg straight out, parallel to the floor.

"What's that pose called?" I ask.

"Leg-straight-holding-big-toe," she says.

"Everything should be so simple."

"I could teach you how to use these bands if you want."

I flash to an image of myself, stretching, hopelessly entangled, grasping for my phone so I can call for help. "No thanks," I say.

~

"Again!" Ben shouted, so I hit the reverse button on the CD player and the band rolled back into "Wagon Wheel."

~

And I'm sitting bedside, hospice care now, and Joy is struggling to memorize the numbers she needs for the forms they keep asking her to complete. She wants to prove she can continue to care for herself. She's practicing her social security number, but she can't get past the fifth digit. She starts mumbling about her garden, her tomato plants, the cherry tree, the pesky squirrels. She wants a big net to cover everything. She catches herself, pauses, and then quickly recites her phone number. Returns to her social security number. Stymied again. "I'm not sure how to do this," she says. "How are we going to do this, Gary?"

I regret my coaching answer even as I repeat the stock words. It's like I'm remembering the wrong prayer, but it's all that comes to me: "We'll get after it, Mom. We'll get after it."

∾

"One more time," Ben shouted out behind me and I was happy to let the kid keep singing, so I pressed the button again and waited for the guitar and fiddle to lead it off.

∾

Then it's near the end and the nurse is taking a bathroom break and I'm sitting bedside again. Joy's not reciting numbers anymore. Instead she's saying *No,* over and over.

I don't want that to be her last word. Where's her friend Erhard now? I ask if she'd like some water.

"No."

"Do you want the nurse?"

"No."

I've dreamed of having a different, less mysterious, long-lived father, but I never desired a different mother. My solution to the sadness I felt after my father died was to play more and more tennis, and that helped get me through the stepfather years. But what will the solution to this be? I know Laurie's answer: *Baby, baby, baby, let's have a baby.* It makes sense to me and we've been trying, but right now I wish my mother and I had talked more about precisely what to do with grief. I'd watched her find peace in her yoga practice and she'd watched me seek refuge on the tennis courts, but why hadn't we discussed it more? Why hadn't she insisted on preparing me for the next time and the times after that?

How are we going to do this?

Right back at you, Mom.

I look at her eyes, unsure if she can see me any longer. "Say something else," I beg her. "Please."

"No."

"The nurse is just down the hall."

"No."

"Is there anything I can get you, anything you'd like?"

"No, no, no."

Her breathing is slowing. I finger the bottle of pills on her nightstand. Is she watching me? "No," she says.

I twist off the lid. It's time for the next dose. It must be better than nothing. How many more doses will there be? But that's not the question I want to ask her. I set the bottle down and put my hand on hers. Squeeze. I lean over and plant a long kiss on the papery skin of her clammy forehead. "Does it hurt?" I ask.

She takes a deep breath. "Yes," she says.

$\sim$

Back in the apartment, Shannon was inside, waiting for us, and Ben rushed to her. I stepped into my bedroom and stretched a bit, still thinking of my mother. In her honor, I tried to focus on my breath as I banged out a few sets of push-ups and sit-ups. No substitute for a run, but better than nothing. I hit the shower and I could almost hear Joy saying, *No effort is wasted.* Like Paul and like the therapist, she would have encouraged me to start dating. She hadn't waited long. Alas. Wire-thin Morris stepped right in and tried to control our entire lives, from the water pitcher (always keep it full!) to the car's gas tank (always keep it full!). Rules, rules, rules, everywhere around the house. I couldn't get away to college fast enough. Then, after Morris, she was off to Big Sur. Good for her, but I'd always assumed she hadn't finished with men. When I asked her about it, she wouldn't answer directly. Instead, she'd smile and paraphrase guru Werner: *You don't have to worry about it working out for me. It has already worked out. This is the way it worked out.*

Whatever you say, Mom. And then I was toweling off, standing in front of the sink to shave. I studied myself in the mirror. I looked thinner everywhere, especially in my face. Laurie could stand in front of this mirror for ages, brushing her dark-brown hair, leaning in close to check her lipstick. I'd heard plenty of stories about people comforted by the spirits of their dead spouses. Maybe she'd chime in at last, stop by for a second to let me know everything was and would be okay. What would she say about how quickly my chest hair was going silver? Would she agree that my eyes seemed to be tunneling deeper into my face? Would she beg me again to resign from the TSA? Or maybe she had something to share about Diane? I heard nothing, but that didn't stop me from inventing a conversation while putting on the pricey jeans and bold-striped button-down shirt Laurie had once picked out for me:

How dare you, Gary!

But you always said you didn't want me to be alone. And you wanted someone to mother Ben.

You told me you'd die first. All that talk about actuarial tables? Remember?

Oh, I remembered, and as I walked into the kitchen I was remembering the half-jokes she'd make about Shannon:

What a sweet young competent energetic mother she would be! And wouldn't you love to be with someone even younger than me?

Just the thought of it is exhausting.

You're a grinder. You'd find a way to survive. She'd be good for your tennis game.

Maybe she's more your type.

But of course the fantasies sometimes swept through me. Shannon was around a lot and she was attractive in her bookish way and I knew what she could do on the court and she didn't seem unavailable. When I walked through the kitchen, shouting out "Have fun, you two," with one hand on the front door, trying for a no-drama exit, it did and didn't help that Shannon jumped up and rushed over to me. "Wait a second, Coach," she said, which is exactly what she called me in the most persistent fantasy, wearing only a towel, and not for very long. But in reality, she reached behind me and fiddled with my collar. I felt her warm breath on my neck. She rested an open hand between my shoulder blades and her touch tingled up and down my spine. Then she gently pushed me forward, as if I were another kid under her care, bound for recess. "You have fun, too," she said.

16

WHEN I PULLED UP AT THE STRAND mansion, Diane was sitting on the marble stairs that led to the front door. She twinkle-toed down the steps, trim, light on her feet, obviously happy to see me. She opened the door and started talking immediately about how she'd had a rough day at work and no one in the house was at all interested. "Let's get out of here," she said.

I wanted to ask about Alex's health and I also wanted to tell her about Paul and Vanessa to help her feel comfortable at the dinner. And what had drawn her to the Armed Ladies? I didn't know where to start.

"Where do you work?" I asked, even though I knew the answer.

"Upstate Animal Hospital," she said. "I'm a certified veterinarian technician, among other things."

"And what happened today?"

"Well, first an Irish wolfhound died."

I waited for her to go on, and she did, at length, and I realized my job was simply to listen. I didn't mind. It helped me relax.

She began by ripping into one of the privileged Haven College kids who claimed to want to become a veterinarian. "Spoiled-brat guy phoned in sick again," she said, and that left her responsible for a bunch of kennel cleaning in addition to everything else. She'd done that job regularly for years back when she was starting out, but today it felt more oppressive than she'd remembered. The shit and piss and vomit slowed for no one. Relentless. She wound up having to clean out the runs twice and repaper all the cages three times before noon. Then a high-strung beagle tried to nip off her nose. She was fighting back the temptation to slap the stupid dog's head when her boss, Dr. Block, called for her.

She described Block: late-fifties, effeminate, with long manicured fingers and a reclusive wife who rarely stepped into the hospital. I figured he wasn't competition.

"Thomas gets tired of my animal stories," she said. "He thinks I'm looking for sympathy and/or trying to charm away his father. Feel free to cut me off when you've had enough."

"I've got animal stories from work too. We can trade if you like."

She smiled and sank deeper into her seat. "It's so nice to talk to a regular, down-to-earth guy for a change," she said, and while I wondered whether or not it was a compliment, she went on with her story. In the exam room, the straggly Irish wolfhound was barely able to stand. She could see the whole rib cage. A young girl was petting the dog, and Diane guessed the girl and the dog were close to the same age, seven or eight. The girl had her whole life ahead of her. The dog would be lucky to get through the day.

The girl's father was there, too, and he explained that the dog's name was Van, as in Morrison, not Halen. "The dad reminded me of you a little," Diane said. "His daughter was crying and he was kissing away her tears as he told me that the girl and Van had grown up together."

"A baby and puppy in one house," I said. "Must have been crazy."

Diane put a leash on the dog and tried to lead it back toward the runs, where she could give it an ice bath, maybe get its temperature down, even though she sensed the dog was doomed. Irish wolfhounds rarely live more than nine years. Van took one step forward and then his back legs gave out and he dropped, toenails skittering against the floor before his body toppled over. The little girl knelt beside him, crying harder. The father was telling her everything would be okay. Diane lifted the dog up and carried him to the bath.

Ben used to yearn for a dog. One more year, Laurie and I would say, year after year. Maybe when you're a bit older, maybe when we get a bigger place, maybe when we have more free time. A dog is a big responsibility. We'd said those lines so often. But when was the last time Ben had asked about it? I couldn't remember.

I turned onto Madison Avenue. Probably ten minutes until we reached the restaurant. Diane kept talking. Could I request a fast-forward? I recognized the inevitable pattern. The wolfhound was too old. The aneurysm was beyond their reach. The cancer was too widespread. The bike was out of control. Could I say I preferred shaggy-dog stories to dead-dog stories?

And, of course, like karmic-wheel clockwork, along came the shimmering moment of hope. Diane set the dog in the bath and his temperature dropped. He seemed genuinely grateful, wagging his tail, licking her fingers. "He looked downright regal when he stood up on his own," she said. "He made the tub seem tiny. He was a dog for royalty, a dog that stood next to thrones. He shook himself off and soaked me. Then his whole body seized up. Some sort of massive stroke. I could barely keep him from sinking under the water. All of a sudden he was so heavy and there was shit everywhere. Dead in seconds."

"Holy hell," I said, surprised by the anger welling up. "What kind of story is that for a first date?"

Diane paused. Her eyes widened. She put her hands on the side of her face in mock shock and something about the lightness of her response charmed me. What did the therapist say? Life's a tragedy for those who feel, a comedy for those who think? He thought a little more comedy wouldn't hurt me.

"Sorry," she was saying, trying to hold back a grin. "It made me angry, too. Disappointed. After all that work. I can stop, if you want."

"It's okay," I said. "Didn't mean to overreact. Keep going. Please."

So she went on, though a bit faster. The daughter hugged the dog, the father led her out of the room, and Block went with them. Diane, alone with the damp, regal dog got to work with some towels and then a hair dryer. She pulled the long legs in tight before rigor mortis set in. She needed four extra-large trash bags to hold the body and she loaded it into a wheelbarrow and carted the poor thing to the freezer.

Was she macabre, tough, some combination of both? Was she thinking of her stepfather, almost dead in a different room? I didn't ask. Instead, I reached across and put a hand on her thigh. "Sounds awful," I said.

She rested a hand on top of mine. "Just another day," she said, "but it pushed me over the edge. After I shut the freezer, I walked to Block's office and told him I was quitting."

Quitting time. Maybe it would be contagious. I left my hand where it was. "How did it feel?"

"Terrific," she said. "Like I was finally free. I mean, I've been thinking about it for a while, making other plans."

"Such as?"

"We don't have to talk about it now. What I really wanted to tell you was that I thought about your son while I was watching that little girl. Like it might be nice for the two of them to talk. And I was thinking about his invitation and I decided I'd be happy to come to the birthday ceremony, if it's truly okay with you."

I turned onto Delaware Avenue. "It's okay with me."

We stayed silent for a few minutes after that. I stole a glance at my hand, there between her thigh and her palm, my skin a few shades darker than hers, that forever tennis tan, and I tried to remember how many days it had been—two? three?—since that same hand had been on her stepfather's chest, rigging up the AED. What a baffler time could be. I pulled into a spot in front of the restaurant and just as I was about to move my hand so I could shift into park, she pressed down harder. "By the way," she said, "is this really a first date?"

My impulse, as usual, was to be cautious. But, look, my hand was still where it was. And I was the one who'd used the words first, wasn't I? "Sure feels like it," I said.

She released my hand. "Sweet," she said.

17

THE ITALIAN-ASIAN FUSION restaurant was one of Albany's newest joints, a big part of the latest round of urban renewal buzz. I'd driven past the place, but it had only been open for a few months and I hadn't been dining out much, plus it looked expensive. The chef had moved Upstate from Brooklyn, won some sort of appetizer competition on a national TV show, and now she was a local celebrity, talking about transforming the blocks around her place into a "fine-dining corridor." Paul did marketing work for the restaurant and half-joked that before long the woman would either be homeless or running for mayor.

It was an unseasonably warm night, a sneak preview of summer, and people were decked out in hats, light hoodies, and short skirts. Had these diners and their stylish wardrobes been imported from Brooklyn too? Sure, if we walked a block in any direction we'd find aging brownstones in disrepair, sagging porches, car shells, broken glass, boarded-up windows, nothing even vaguely resembling a "fine-dining corridor," though there would be the occasional colorful garden plot, evidence that the hopeful hopeless struggle against the city's neglect and inherent inequality lived on. I moved closer to Diane as we strolled, aware that we were about to enter a far classier place than the pizza parlor we'd walked to with Ben. Diane looked splendid. Neffer could say whatever he wanted, but I saw the perfect balance of curvy and slender, and I liked the way her silky blouse hung loose around her neck, revealing the sharp lines of her clavicle, the black-lace straps of her bra. I glimpsed our reflection in the glass of the door and, for a second, I could believe we blended right in with this trendy scene. If I looked too long, though, I'd see my own weariness and worry, and then I'd be unable to avoid noting the many ways in which I differed from all these Brooklynish hipsters: my lack of ambition, vision, confidence, charisma. But, for now, I could open the door for my date, watch as she sashayed past me. If there happened to be a downtown booster on the other side with a tall glass of Albany Kool-Aid, I'd guzzle the stuff down.

While we waited to check in with the hostess, I was clueing Diane in about Paul and Vanessa—their history, the significance of this particular weekend for them. Then my phone vibrated. I fished it out and found a text from Paul: *Enjoying inside time. Staying in for more. Sorry not sorry. Have fun with your lady. Is she a tennis player? See you in the morning.*

I felt a flash of disappointment, but I had to be happy for the guy. And it wasn't difficult to see the no-show as a favor, really. I could focus on Diane, ask her questions, learn more about her and her family. I stuffed the phone back into my pocket and explained the change in plans. Her face brightened. It started in her eyes, and I would have sworn the green of them shifted toward blue. We were led to a table, we ordered drinks and food, and the drinks and food arrived. Such clear cause and effect proved there were well-established procedures here, SOP beyond the airport, and yet it remained mysterious to me, as if calling the night a date made it impossible for me to function. I had my questions, but I couldn't find a way to ask them. How could it be that I still couldn't puzzle out a simple thing like getting to know someone, like deciding it was all right to share stories—open and open and open?

Diane was doing her part, as she'd done in the car, now talking about reinventing herself, creating and embracing new opportunities. Maybe she'd do better as an animal hospital owner. She'd apply herself and she could have whatever career she wanted. She shouldn't have to defend herself to anyone, certainly not to bitter Thomas, though she understood how hard it must be for him to share the affection of his father. But, really, so what if her ambitions had changed? After all, what was she supposed to do if she wasn't driven in that direction any more, if she'd met too many miserable veterinarians, if Herriot was the only one who ever seemed remotely happy to her, and he'd lived in England and worked on farm animals and was dead now and Herriot wasn't even his real name? She wanted to have time for other things, and if there was truly money, there were other ways she could use it. It was time for her to have her own place, for instance, and if that made her more like her mother, a modern-day kept-ish woman, then so be it.

She paused for a moment, but I felt flummoxed, dazed, nervous, far too conscious of my own body, my own thoughts, my own quiet, the words I should say, the subjects I should bring up. "What about the family business?" I managed to ask. "They must have a good job for you."

She laughed. "The family business," she said. "It has its benefits, which I do seem to enjoy, but I don't think that particular path is open to me."

"Why not?"

"Kind of antithetical to who I am, for starters," she said.

"What do you mean?"

"Didn't I mention I was happy to get out of the house?" she said, lifting her glass of red wine. She took a drink and set the glass back on the table. "I bet we can find better things to talk about."

The nervousness returned, so I asked about tennis and, yes, she did play, though she claimed not to be good, but that was more than enough for me to begin imagining her on the court, a no-frills skirt, compression shorts, the muscles of her runner's calves. It would be easier to talk there, and even though I was out of practice, I could surely help her, and she'd probably be quick, like Ben said, like the way she'd zipped down the stairs, with great hand-eye coordination, good reflexes at the net. Maybe we could run together too. Then something like guilt washed over me and my head filled with the old touchstone memories, the greeting at the airport, the orange flowers on the passenger seat of her car, that birth in the bathtub, newborn Ben sleeping that first night against her chest while I watched and watched and watched, overwhelmed here, overwhelmed there, overwhelmed on the bike trail, overwhelmed by so much. Why couldn't I simply be whelmed? Being whelmed would be more than enough. Whelm me day in, day out, and I'd be fine. Instead, I wound up retreating into step-by-step forward movement, if that made any sense, or maybe there was nothing forward about it, maybe it was all backward, or merely all awkward and, as a result, clarity was only available in discrete spaces like courts and checkpoints. Forehand, forehand, backhand, crosscourt, crosscourt, down the line, approach, close it out at the net. Study the objects on the screen, follow the protocols, do what you're supposed to do. No threat, no threat, possible threat, radio the supervisor, resolve the situation.

Now, did I want dessert or not? What was the correct answer to that question? I'd follow her lead, so it was a no, as Neffer would have predicted, and then, all too quickly, it was time to drive her home. She had a CD in her bag she wanted to hear in the car, Van Morrison, in honor of that poor dead dog, and there on the CD cover she flashed at me was a picture of the singer with two Irish wolfhounds sitting beside him. Van crooned about fair play and someone stealing highlights, and we listened in near silence all the way to her mansion. I couldn't say who leaned across first, but as soon as I parked we were kissing in the car, like teenagers, the sensations as overwhelming as ever, and nothing like my time with Laurie, and I was at once aware of some differences—the bones of her face so close to her warm skin, a sweet desperation in how hard she pressed her lips against mine—and I was also aware of how much was escaping me since I kept closing my eyes, and it all seemed unworkable, even scary, and how could any of this be happening, on a public street, for god's sake? Then the music suddenly grew quieter and I opened my eyes to see her turning the stereo off. "Let's go inside," she said.

18

I WASN'T GOING TO STAY LONG. I could mention Shannon whenever I needed to and head home before everything got out of hand. Or more out of hand than it had already. Diane was waiting for me at the bottom of the marble stairs, glancing up at all the lighted windows. "Hope they weren't watching," she said.

"Should we take a walk or something?"

"Don't worry. They like you. They'll be glad to see you."

So I followed her up the stairs, abuzz with her, unable to take my eyes off her legs, her ass, the perfect tightness of those jeans and the looseness of her silky blouse.

Thomas opened the door, still in a suit and tie. He pulled out his earbuds and draped the cord around his neck. "Didn't expect you back so early," he said. "And you've brought along the hero. Must be a good sign."

Diane stepped right past him. "They get punchy when they work late," she said. "Especially when my mother isn't around. Don't take it personally."

I shook Thomas's hand. "How's your father doing?" I asked.

"I can't keep up with him," Thomas said. "I know he'll be happy to see you. I'll tell him you're here. You two grab a drink or something. Don't let her take advantage of you, though."

Diane let out a short laugh and led me back to the kitchen. Then, as if in response to Thomas's warning, she stood in front of the refrigerator and raised her arms above her head. "Officer," she said, "I believe I am in possession of some contraband."

When she smiled, her face looked rounder, more joyful. "I'm off-duty, Miss," I said.

"I'm still curious about how you do it," she said.

I would have been happy to pat her down, or at least start the procedure and see where it led. Laurie and I had gotten plenty of pleasure from role-playing like that, especially when my uniform was brand new. But I flashed to Nora Flint, her cold kitchen counter, the stack of pots and pans in her sink, everything happening too fast. Diane reached up higher for a moment, stretching out, rising onto her toes. Her belly button came into view. An innie. I could think of a million reasons not to rush. "You're supposed to put your arms up by your sides," I said. "Parallel to the floor. And men can't pat down women."

She kept her arms up and started humming something. Was it from that Van Morrison CD? She let her hips sway to the rhythm, like the start of a slow dance. She was gliding my way when I heard the footsteps coming down the stairs. Alex walked in wearing a leaf-green double-breasted blazer with matching slacks, a white button-down shirt, and a red-dominated paisley bowtie. "What do we have here?" he said.

Diane dropped her arms to her sides, but she kept humming. Alex began putting words to the song. It was about blossoms of snow blooming and growing.

Thomas was right behind him and soon after he joined in I recognized the song as "Edelweiss."

Diane switched from humming to singing in time for the final line: *Bless my home-land forever.*

I listened, surprised by how well their voices blended together, as if they'd practiced this tune before. A dapper, upper-crust trio. The Von Trapps of Albany. Thomas hit a high-falsetto final note, held it just right. They laughed when they stopped, playing their singing off as a joke.

"The hills are alive," Alex said, perching on a stool by the island. "Have a seat. How was dinner? I can't wait to dine out again. Did you try that new restaurant?"

"I know you have more work to do," Diane said.

"It often seems endless," Alex said.

Diane glanced my way. "Gary was wondering why I didn't work for the family business," she said. "That's one of the reasons."

"It can be exhausting," Alex said. "Almost enough to make me contemplate retirement."

We could all change careers together, I thought. Leave the animal hospital TSA real estate worlds behind. Find a better world for all of us. "How bad is it?" I asked.

Thomas jumped in to answer. "It's fine except for a few bad characters," he said. "Developers and some other select individuals trying to line their pockets. We spend so much time just trying to do it all the right way."

Alex nodded. "Your father would never have believed some of the transactions that are permitted now. Absolutely unethical. But we run our business the old-fashioned way. That's what keeps us working."

Diane walked over to stand beside me and she put a hand on my arm. "We'll go upstairs and get out of your hair," she said.

"Nights like this," Thomas said, "I bet you can't wait to get your own place."

It was a barbed comment and Alex glared at Thomas. Then he turned to Diane and said, "I like having you here. No one is pressuring you."

Nights like this. How many other men had stood where I was standing? And why was Diane living in this house? She wanted her own place. Thomas seemed to want her out. There seemed to be enough money to build more houses, apartment buildings, vacation villas. The kitchen appliances alone were probably worth a few years of my salary.

Alex went over to the refrigerator, pulled out three beers, and set them on the island. "Let's all visit for a little while longer," he said, sitting back down. "It's good for Thomas and me to take a break. Sometimes we forget."

Thomas grabbed three frosted mugs from the freezer and put them on the island by the beers. Then he poured a glass of water and put it in front of his father. "News flash," he said. "Doctor is thinking about lifting Dad's travel restrictions."

Alex sent him another glare. "That's enough about that," he said.

"Family secrets," Diane said. "My favorite."

I was so absorbed by the animosity between Diane and Thomas that I almost didn't notice when Alex turned to me. "Do you two have any plans for the weekend?"

Before I could answer, Diane said, "Tomorrow's the birthday of Gary's dead wife."

Alex stood back up. "I didn't realize," he said. "My first wife died almost twenty years ago." He looked at Thomas again and stared into his face, as if searching for traces of his dead wife there. "I still miss her," Alex went on. "She was an extraordinary painter. But that's talk for—"

"I was nineteen," Thomas said.

Diane picked up two beers from the island and handed one to me. She didn't bother with the mugs. "Now it's really time to go upstairs," she said.

The cold bottle felt good in my hand. I noticed two small black-and-white drawings on the wall across from the refrigerator. I turned to Thomas, the only one still sitting down. "Are those two your mother's?" I asked.

"No," Thomas said. "My mother worked on much larger canvases. They don't hang in the house anymore."

"Those two are Giacometti sketches," Diane said. "Do you like them?"

The name sounded familiar, but what came to mind was Pinocchio, especially since each sketch was of a thin, wire-like figure. Starved puppets. Men or women? I couldn't tell. I thought of Neffer again. "It's better than the airport art I see everyday," I said, "but they look anorexic."

Alex laughed. "Odd work to hang in a kitchen, right? Not the same as a photo of Buchenwald survivors, but not that different either." He pulled his phone from his pocket, checked something on the screen, and then offered his hand. "It really is good to see you," he said. "And, just so you're aware, I'm still thinking about that reward we discussed. I haven't lost sight of it."

I shook hands. "I'm glad to see you looking so much better," I said.

Thomas stayed in his seat. "Good night," he said, and then he reinserted his earbuds.

～

I sipped my beer and followed Diane up another stairway. There was more art to notice, but my eyes stayed on her body. Halfway to the second floor, she turned around and caught me looking. She grinned. "I've been meaning to ask you. What should I wear to the cemetery?"

"Ben and I have been talking about the same thing," I said. "We might go sport coat shopping in the morning, if we can squeeze it in."

Her laughter was like the sweet purr of a fine motor. It echoed in the stairwell and the sound made me almost certain she didn't deserve Thomas's bitterness. "That's funny," she said, and kept climbing.

"It wasn't supposed to be."

"You'll see why in a second. Follow me."

She led me down a hallway and paused before a large double-door. "We all have our foibles," she said. When she opened the thick wooden doors, there was a whoosh of air, as if the space had been vacuum-sealed, and the smell of cedar hit me. It was the smell of hers I'd noticed from the beginning. She stepped inside and flicked a few switches. The lights winked on, grew brighter. Two rows of suits hung on both sides of the closet. The back and front walls were mirrored, making the space seem even larger. I felt like the first customer, watching the owner open up shop. The long couch in front of the rear wall reflected back at me to infinity. "There's a story that goes with this," she said. "But I'll spare you for now." She walked deeper into the closet, sliding hangers, pausing, then sliding more hangers.

I struggled to take it in stride. The family hoards dress clothes in a closet that smells like a forest. It's a bunker, a bank, a walk-in safe deposit box. "Wow," I said. And then, trying to be more articulate, I added: "It's a bit overwhelming."

"Those two oafs have been wondering about a gift for you. They should have thought of clothes, but it never crossed their minds."

"Actually," I said, "it's all overwhelming. Not just this. The dinner. This house. Your stepfather. You."

"I don't know about me," she said, as she kept looking, "but this whole arrangement overwhelmed me for a while too. My mother and I didn't live like this before she met Alex, that's for sure."

"Where did you live before this?"

"We were down in Hudson. My mother ran a small gallery there. We lived in the apartment above the gallery. It was kind of hardscrabble until Alex walked in one afternoon. Then everything changed."

"How did you get used to the new life?"

"I guess it's easier to get used to having more than having less," she said. "Plus moving up is part of the Strand family history. Apparently, Alex's father was a tailor. He advanced slowly and then quickly, and he saved everything. Specialized in uniforms and made bank when he sold the business. Alex says money flowed to his father like water to a drain. My mother could say the same thing, I suppose." She stopped moving the hangers around and glanced back at me. "Now, something like this, dark blue and simple, that seems appropriate. I'm betting a forty-two regular?"

It had been a while since I'd been measured for a sport coat, but the one that hung in my closet was indeed a forty-two. "I think so," I said.

She walked to me with a blue jacket and held it open. "This is perfect for someone ordinary and exceptional like you," she said, somehow making ordinary sound sexy.

I didn't need to try the jacket on to know it was nicer than any clothing I'd ever owned. It had a surprising weight to it. The blue looked darker and deeper when I had it on.

"Is this Thomas's?" I asked. "Won't he mind?"

"He'll never notice," she said. "Besides, he owes me."

"He doesn't act like he owes you."

"He thinks I don't love his father as much as he does. It muddles his mind a bit. I know it's not about me."

"I was a stepchild for a while too," I said. "It wasn't easy."

"I knew we had a lot in common," she said.

I tried to think of some of the other things we had in common, but nothing jumped out at me. "Anyhow," I said, "you guys sound good together when you're singing."

"You're sweet," she said. Then she reached over, buttoned the sport coat's top button, smoothed the lapels, and kissed my cheek. "Congratulations," she said, her voice more serious. "You've been promoted to General Supervisor. Upper-echelon TSA, a leader in the Department of Homeland Security."

I smiled and brushed a hand down the sleeve. It felt like velvet. "Wow," I said, again.

"Your new position means you no longer need to feel overwhelmed."

"If it was only so easy—"

"Also, as you're no doubt aware, General Supervisors possess various extraordinary powers, including the authority to pat down both men and women. And I'm still in possession of contraband."

I shook my head. "It's really the worst part of the job," I said. I could have told her how, during my early days at the airport, the instructors explained that the body you pat down is like a canvas. You paint it and there shouldn't be any places you miss.

"Show me," she said, and this time she raised her arms correctly.

"It's not something I enjoy," I said. Another instructor had talked about making PB&J for lunch. You should use the same pressure on PAX bodies that you use when you're spreading peanut butter on the bread. Guidance like that was designed to make it sound like we were learning a simple household chore. Nothing to be disturbed about. Slide your hands up those inner thighs until you reach resistance. Keep it clinical. Impersonal.

Diane held herself remarkably still, waiting.

I'd asked Paul what he was afraid of. I must have wanted to hear about this kind of plunge. Kissing in a car was one thing, but there were so many ways this could go wrong. And then I felt ashamed of being afraid. I rubbed my forehead. The room was getting hotter.

Diane stepped closer. We were in a cedar forest together. "I'm waiting for my pat down, Officer."

"It's bad enough I have to do it on the job," I said. "We're having a nice night here."

"I'm trying to make it even nicer."

Laurie sometimes joked that it was her job to open me up. *We've all had our losses*, she'd say. *We don't need to let them shut us down*. It might have been the greatest gift she'd given me, with the notable exception of Ben. Then she'd knocked me to my knees with another crushing loss. And now Diane stood before me, arms spread, waiting. I was inside her mansion. I was the lifesaving family hero. I felt the warmth of the old handmade jacket on my shoulders and I knew what Laurie would want me to do.

"Come on," Diane said. "I've got a flight to catch. Let's go already."

It was a convincing impersonation of an impatient traveler, and the script kicked in almost automatically. "I'll get you on your way as soon as I can, Miss," I said. "Can you see your belongings, or would you like me to bring them over here?"

"I can see everything fine," she said. "Do it and get it over with."

"I have to follow the procedures, Miss. The precise language is for your protection and mine. I need to say the words."

"And what lovely words they are."

"I'm going to use my hands to pat down the clothed areas of your body. I'll use the backs of my hands on the sensitive areas, the buttocks, the zipper line, your breast area. I'll be clearing your collar and your waistline with two fingers. And I'll be clearing each inner thigh, sliding up until I reach resistance."

"Those hand gestures are a little unnerving, Officer."

I kept expecting her to drop the role. I stepped behind her. It was where I was supposed to be, but I thought it might also make it easier to go on. "Do you have any internal or external medical devices? Do you have any painful or tender areas on your body?"

"Get on with it," she said. She stepped back until her ass pressed right up against me.

I couldn't remember the last time I'd been so hard. I closed my eyes and inhaled. A cedar forest. A blanket. A picnic, just the two of us, slowly getting naked beneath the trees. And yet I did my best to continue the performance. "Do you have absolutely everything out of your pockets? Mints? Chapstick? Tissues?"

"Why don't you check my pockets for yourself?"

I stayed behind her, our bodies lightly touching. I spoke into her ear. "A private screening is available if you'd prefer. You can request one at any time."

"This is private enough, thank you."

"Place your feet shoulder-width apart and turn you palms up."

She followed my instructions. I wrapped my arms around her and pulled her tight, cupping her breasts, resting my chin on her shoulder. "Then I'd clear your collar and get to work on your arms, armpits, and back. You get the idea."

"Keep going," she said. "It's a learning experience. I like it." She pressed her ass back against me. "You like it too, apparently." Then she stepped forward again.

I wrapped my hands around her shoulders, moved them into her armpits, slid them down to the end of her jersey-length sleeves.

"What about my wrists, Officer?"

"I can clear them with my eyes," I said. "We don't touch bare skin."

She lifted her blouse off and dropped it to the floor. "I don't think that rule applies to someone of your rank," she said.

I kissed the side of her neck and wrapped my arms back around her. Could I lead her to the couch? I looked toward the mirrors. I couldn't make out the details of her body or my face, but the blue jacket looked even darker against her skin. Then the possibility of surveillance flashed across my mind. Wouldn't a mansion like this have security cameras everywhere?

She didn't seem concerned. "I believe you mentioned something about upper thighs," she said. "Something about resistance?"

I stepped around in front of her, adjusting myself so I'd be able to kneel and return to SOP, working my way down to her feet. I spent extra time on each leg, more massage than pat down now. I lingered at the top of each thigh.

"I appreciate your thoroughness, Officer," she said.

My phone vibrated again. Probably another nonapology progress report from Paul. But what if it was Shannon? "I'm sorry," I said, standing up, reaching into my pocket. "I have to look, just in case." And it *was* from Shannon: *Your brother-in-law is here. Says he needs to see you. Says he'll wait. Don't feel right leaving.*

"Shit," I said, as I texted back: *Be right there.*

"What?" Diane asked, crossing her arms beneath her breasts.

"Babysitter. Unexpected visitor. I need to get home."

"You can't leave a pat down unfinished, can you?"

I didn't want to make a mistake and ruin whatever this was, but just as Laurie had told me to play along and open myself up, she was now telling me to get home. Even though Hank was her brother, that didn't explain a late-night drop-in, birthday or no birthday. What could I do? "I guess you could come with me," I said. "It's my brother-in-law. He didn't tell me he'd be stopping by."

Diane reached down and picked up her blouse. She didn't put it back on right away.

"You're beautiful," I said. "I haven't had a night like this in a long time, if ever. I'm sorry."

She pulled the blouse on. She seemed to be taking it better than I expected and that was a relief. "It's okay," she said.

"It must have something to do with the birthday tomorrow."

"I'm still planning to be there, unless this abrupt departure means something else."

"It doesn't mean anything else," I said. "I want you there. And, for what it's worth, Ben hasn't stopped asking about you."

"That reminds me," she said, and then she wandered deeper into the closet again, back near the mirror. She moved a few more hangers. They clattered and slid. "What color does he like?"

"He used to have a seersucker jacket, but he outgrew it."

"Easy enough," she said, walking back with a jacket. "I bet this will fit."

"Are you sure it's okay?"

"Yes."

"We'll take good care of them," I said. "We'll get them dry-cleaned."

She shook her head. "You're a sweet odd man," she said. "This isn't a loan."

"They really won't mind?"

"You do remember that you saved my stepfather's life, right? Plus, I do things for them. Like I said, those busy-bee businessmen owe me, too. We're nowhere close to even, though they tend to forget that fact. Now let's try to make it downstairs without getting their attention."

19

IN THE CAR, SPEEDING BACK across town, I worried about Hank and whatever it was he wanted. Had something happened at the airport? Had one of the so-called Stooges been spotted? At the same time, I couldn't get Diane out of my head. I was kneeling before her in that preposterous closet and she was looking down at me, appreciating my touch. I told myself it was good and wise to delay getting naked with her. There was no rush. It would be better for everyone not to rush.

Meanwhile, the CD played on and I cranked it up. Van was shouting about pulling punches and pushing rivers when I parked in front of the apartment building. Hank was waiting on the stoop and quick-stepped over to meet me on the sidewalk. He was wearing the same suit, as pressed and creased as ever.

"Bet you didn't expect to see me again so soon," he said. "Walk me to my car. I can't hang out."

I tried to get some steady eye contact with him, but he kept glancing around. "Is everything all right?" I asked. "Something happen at the airport?"

He shook his head, like I'd disappointed him again. "I didn't come over to talk about work," he said.

I'd made the same old mistake. He'd never really confided in me about his work and that wasn't about to change now. Still, he seemed slightly shaken. And, just a moment ago, he'd been sitting on my stoop in the middle of the night. "Then why—"

"It's harder to spend time here than I thought," he said. "I don't know how you do it. Does she haunt your dreams too?"

He looked exactly the same, but I'd never heard his voice like this. He sounded younger, confused. I almost had to jog to stay beside him. "What do you mean?"

"I'm not known as a good sleeper, but it's been ridiculous lately. Laurie keeps waking me up."

I wasn't sure what to tell him. "I keep waiting for her to appear," I said. "I talk with her sometimes, but I haven't seen her."

Hank beeped his car unlocked. "Tonight she was just standing there, watching me. *Talk to me*, I said. *Please say something*. But she always refuses to speak. She closes her eyes and then she's gone."

I glanced up and down the empty street. A few of the row houses were brightly lit, but it looked like most of the neighborhood was asleep. And here was my brother-in-law, drawn out of his bed by some ghostly vision of Laurie. He'd come to share it with me. "You know," I said, "I haven't thought enough about how difficult this has been for you. I've been so focused on myself."

"Thanks for saying that," he said. "And right back at you. A birthday without her. It's getting to me."

"What do you think she wants?"

"You think she wants something?"

"I don't know. Isn't that why ghosts appear?"

Hank opened the car door. "She's just in my dreams. Did I say I'd seen a ghost?"

"I wouldn't mind a ghost of her," I said.

"Careful what you wish for," he said. "I wouldn't mind a full night's sleep. Where were you, by the way?"

I wasn't going to lie to him, not after he'd been more open with me than ever before. "I was spending a little more time with Diane Percy Strand."

"I see," Hank said, smiling. "Maybe Laurie wants me to put a stop to that."

Hank remained difficult to read. Was he serious? "Well," I began.

"I'm joking," he said. "We both know it's what she would want. She wouldn't want you to be alone. She never wanted me to be alone either." And then he was behind the wheel. "Might as well get back to work now since I'm awake. You get some sleep, if you can."

He shut the door and, as the Charger sped away, he didn't lower his window to say goodbye. Just like old times.

~

Inside the apartment, I found Shannon sitting on the living room sofa. I sat next to her and tried to create calm. "Sorry about that," I said.

She was tough, a gritty player, fearless at net, but I could tell she'd been caught way off-guard. She was still shaky, clasping her hands together in her lap. "I was fixing a snack in the kitchen when he showed up," she said. "He was nice enough. Might even have been flirting with me. Told me it would be fine if I left, but I couldn't bring myself to do that."

"I'm glad you didn't."

"I guess I don't like him," she said. "And you know how much I loved Laurie. But there's something off with him."

Tell me about it, I thought. My phone buzzed with a text from Diane: *Everything ok? Still thinking of u.*

I wrote back as quickly as I could: *All's well. Thx. U = wow.* I tried my best to keep talking to Shannon. "I wish I understood him better," I said. "Seems like the birthday is hitting him hard."

She leaned in closer. My body hadn't quite stopped thrumming from Diane. And yet it was apparently happy to respond to the woman I'd often fantasized about. Why not comfort her? Probably wiser to move away from her.

"Are you all right?" I asked.

She tilted her head against my shoulder. "Much better now, Coach," she said. "How was your night out?"

"Can't complain," I said. "But tell me how things were here, before the surprise guest."

"Ben and I worked on some surprises of our own," she said. "Pleasant ones, I hope."

Often, when Shannon babysat late into the night, I walked in the door and found her half asleep and I'd tell her she could crash on the sofa if that was easier than heading home. She always said no. So it was just a formality when, as I stood up, I made the same offer again.

"You know what," she said, "I think I will tonight, if you really don't mind. We can all drive over to the cemetery tomorrow."

"Excellent idea," I said. I grabbed some extra sheets and a pillow for her, trying to act like it was nothing. Then I went to check on Ben.

"By the way," she said, as I walked out of the room, "is that a new sport coat? It looks great."

It fit so well I'd forgotten I still had it on. I nodded and thanked her. I smelled the cedar all around me when I took it off.

~

As soon as I tiptoed into Ben's room, he sat up, eyes open wide. How much of the night had he heard? How much of the year? Impossible to tell, as usual. "Dad," he said, "is she coming?"

"Yes," I answered, assuming at first the question was about Diane. But maybe the kid had been in the middle of his own Laurie dream. "Now back to sleep. Head on pillow. I love you."

"Stay with me."

I stretched out beside my son, watching those eyes close again, open for a second, close. I could hear Mickey Mouse ticking and our breathing slipped into time with the old watch. As I breathed and waited, my eyes slowly adjusted to the dark, and various versions of the room drifted in and out of focus. I could see the space as it had been when we first moved in, empty, and I'd made it into a TV-room-slash-guest-room with a drab futon couch. Then Laurie moved in and the room became a yoga spot for her, complete with mats, foam blocks, a Buddha head, bells on the mantel, the smell of incense. Then came the nursery—crib, changing table, bouncy chairs, musical mobile screwed into the ceiling—and now it was Ben's current room, with a big-boy bed, an early Bob Dylan poster, baskets of dinosaurs, cars, costumes. A fine, safe place to close your eyes, just for a moment, just for a quick rest, and who knew, the place could keep transforming while I slept. Who could say what I'd find when I woke up?

20

AT ONE POINT, THE THERAPIST had floated the idea of a dream journal, something I could keep by the bed to record whatever lingered in my brain each time I awoke. Confront and thereby control the demons, or at least be less controlled by them. See it so you can handle it. Call it a corollary to *What you don't see is what you get.* But I didn't want to be sitting up in the middle of the night, struggling to capture hazy memories of the terrible images that had woken me.

This time I was convinced it was Ben having the nightmare, his thin arms flapping against the mattress, the watch almost hitting me in the face. *Ben, Ben, what is it?* I said, but my son wouldn't wake up. Shannon came to the bed, but she couldn't wake him either. She shook her head slowly and stepped back. Even in the darkness, I could see her breasts pressing against her thin, tight T-shirt. *I need to be going,* she said, but before she could leave, Hank was in the doorway. *I knew he needed me,* he said. He had an AED with him in a bright-blue briefcase, but it was far too big, it would never have fit as a carry-on, and when he opened the case, I could see that the machine was all wrong, some kind of explosive device stuffed with bullets and knife blades. *It's not mine,* Hank was saying. *It doesn't belong to me.*

I was grabbing at the briefcase handle when I woke, heart racing, cold sweat on my forehead. Ben was sound asleep. I stood up and started walking quietly out of the room, catching my breath. It was five thirty. It was the weekend. I could hit the bathroom, get back to sleep, and grab a few more hours. I didn't have to worry about last-second clothes shopping anymore. After the bathroom, I shuffled to the kitchen for a glass of water. I almost walked right into Shannon at the sink. I'd forgotten she'd actually stayed over this time. "Hey," I said.

"Trouble sleeping?" she asked.

"Lousy dream," I said. "That's all." I tried to move past her to get a glass from the dish rack, but she was blocking my way. The matching Haven College shorts and tank top she was wearing couldn't be Laurie's—I'd boxed all that stuff up and lugged it into the basement—but Laurie had liked that same light-green-and-white gear.

"Do you remember what you used to say before we hit the courts?" she asked.

Of course I remembered. I'd said it almost every day for years and, before that, I'd heard others say it. I'd borrowed it from my high school coach. *One more thing, people*, Coach Dorley would say. *Don't forget to have fun out there!*

Shannon clamped a hand onto my bicep. "*Have fun out there!*" she said, doing her best imitation of my voice. "I've been thinking about that and about Laurie's birthday and about you."

We'd touched before. There'd been plenty of quick embraces and pecked cheeks. It had always felt chaste, a shorthand way of communicating around our shared loss. Hello, goodbye, thanks for all of your help. But her hand tight around my arm now felt different. I put my hand over hers, patted it, and moved toward the cabinet for a glass. "It's an intense time for all of us," I said.

She didn't loosen her grip. "Everyone has their checklist, don't they?" she asked, chasing my eyes with hers.

"I guess so, but maybe—"

"You're kind of what I want," she said. "I've been trying not to think that way while you've been mourning. While we've both been mourning. How you fit my profile. Your steadiness. Your solidness. I want to be here for Ben, and for you, and that should be enough—"

"I don't know what we would have done without you, Shannon, but—"

She put her other hand over my mouth. Her palm felt soft against my lips. Salty. "I need to say it," she said. "When Hank came in here, he really wanted me to leave, but I couldn't. I needed to stay with Ben until you got back. And while I waited, I tried to figure out what that means."

I kissed her palm and then lifted her hand from my mouth. "It means you're a good person," I said. "It means we're fortunate to have you in our lives."

"You're such a sweet father to him," she said, her other hand still gripping my arm. "My own father, well, that's not what I want to talk about. Let me finish what I was saying first." She tried to pull me closer as she leaned in and pressed a kiss against my lips. "We both woke up in the middle of the night," she said. "Tell me you haven't thought about it."

Oh, I was tempted. I could have told her that. I could have described a detailed fantasy or two. I could have returned the kiss with interest and made it all clear. But what filled my mind was the absurdity of the situation. A divine joke dreamed up by a god with too much free time and a twisted sense of humor. I'd lived through years of solitude, a wasteland of loneliness, lusting after various women from afar, yearning to touch and be touched in return. For so long I'd channeled as much of that desperate energy as I could onto the courts. Now, my dead wife's birthday comes along, my brother-in-law brings his chaos to town, and for no discernible reason two women reach out for me at once. "Shannon," I said. "We're so grateful—"

"Don't say no."

I imagined Ben walking out and finding us. "It just doesn't feel right," I said.

"It feels right to me."

I held her gaze and told myself I was looking at my ex-player, my son's babysitter, my dead wife's friend. I didn't and shouldn't and wouldn't want her to be anything more than that. "I'm sorry," I said.

She turned away and the quick swivel of her neck reminded me of Ben, his precise body language when he didn't get what he wanted. She went back to the couch and picked up her sweatshirt and sweatpants. "I can't believe you're really going to say no," she said.

"It's been a crazy day," I said, following her into the living room. "If you knew everything else going on right—"

"It's okay," she said. "Don't worry. I get it."

"Let's sit down. We can talk more—"

"If we talk more, I'll say what I shouldn't say."

"You can say anything."

"Really? Anything? How about this: Laurie used to tell me you had trouble believing in yourself. *He struggles with his confidence*, she'd say. *And that leads to bad choices.*"

I'd refused her and now she was trying to hurt me. It would be a mistake to take it personally. Even if what she was saying was true, vouched for by my dead wife, my therapist, and my friend.

She snapped her sweatshirt and sweatpants like towels. She kept talking as she pulled them on. "She told me you were wasting a chunk of your life. *Frittering it away*, that's what she said."

The therapist had liked to talk about the different legacies of my father and stepfather. He said my father's early death was a devastation, a deprivation that left me unprotected. My stepfather, with all his nonsense rules and cruel control, was the one who went after my confidence and self-esteem. "There's a technical term for this," he'd said. "We call it a real double whammy."

I sat down on the chair across from the couch. "Shannon," I said, "I think I have to—"

"You have to stop punishing yourself," she said. "The dead-end job. The stupid moratorium on tennis—"

Let her say whatever she wanted to say, but then I was interrupting her. "I don't want to compete anymore," I said. "If I hadn't been racing her down that hill—"

She was standing in front of me now, looking at me, red-faced, angrier than I'd ever seen her, and yet I could still hear kindness in her voice. "It wasn't your fault, you idiot. You're the only one who thinks it was your fault. She would have tried to beat you down that hill whether you were racing or not. You know that. And who says you need to compete when you play tennis? Hit the ball. Enjoy being on the court. Enjoy being alive."

"I get it," I said. "I believe you. But I just need—"

She shook her head as she cut me off again. "Excuse me if I don't want to focus on your needs anymore right now. I need to take a walk. A walk will do me good." She slipped on her sneakers and rushed out the door. I could hear her chanting, "Idiot, idiot, idiot," as she went down the steps.

The building's front door banged shut and then it was dawn quiet. Sleep didn't seem very likely. I could call Hank and tell him to come back over, do his work from here. We could both stay up all night. Instead, I wandered to the kitchen, drank my glass of water, and began making coffee. How many things should I have done differently? Starting when, exactly?

I didn't need to run through the list. Instead, I walked down the hallway to check on Ben, but after a few steps my phone buzzed again. It wasn't a familiar number. I answered anyway. Maybe Shannon was calling from a payphone. I didn't recognize the voice. It sounded like a woman and she wanted to make sure I was Gary Waldman. I wasn't sure of much else, but I was sure of that. I waited for the random sales pitch or survey request. Might be relaxing to hear some sales patter after what had just happened. "This is Elizabeth," the woman said. "I know this must be a difficult day for you and I'm sorry for calling so early. Is Hank there?"

I pieced it together as best I could. This was the woman Hank had been seeing, the woman he'd called an overcorrection. "I'm sorry," I said. "You're looking for Hank?"

"I thought he might be with you."

"He was," I said, "but he took off a little while ago. Do you have a message for him or—"

"Listen. Does he seem like himself?"

"I don't know him that well, but he seems pretty much like himself to me, given the circumstances."

"Well, you should know he might be reeling a bit. We decided to take a break and he didn't welcome the idea."

"I see," I said. Was I supposed to offer sympathy? She kept quiet so I kept talking. "Not his choice, I'm guessing."

"You didn't hear anything from me. He'll tell you what he wants to tell you."

"Is there anything else you think I should know?"

"He's upset, that's all I'll say. I need to go. Look after him, if he'll let you."

"Thanks for the heads-up. Where are you calling from, by the way?"

"I'm in Los Angeles. I'll tell you that much, since I'm leaving town for a while."

I poured a mug of coffee and took a sip. It was a relief to have something else to puzzle over. Maybe this was a chance to pin down some facts about the guy. "Has Hank ever talked to you about doing something else with his life?"

She squawked out a crowlike laugh. "Of course he has. All the time."

"Do you think he'll change?"

She laughed again. "What do you think?"

"I don't even know exactly what he does now."

"That's my Hank," she said. "Good luck."

"Wait," I said, but she was gone.

Had I ever heard anything in particular about Elizabeth? Maybe she was a lawyer? Hank had never brought her around and Laurie had never spoken of her. I had no image of her. Didn't know her last name. I could try to talk with Hank about her some more, but how far would that go?

I put the phone back in my pocket. I was still wearing the jeans. Ben would be up soon. I wanted to be wearing different clothes. I drank a little more coffee and carried the mug into my bedroom. It wasn't even six thirty yet. Ben might give me until eight. Maybe nine. That was the weekend tradition. I set the coffee on the nightstand and stretched out on the bed. The dawn light was brightening the room and the caffeine was coursing through my body, but my eyes were closing anyhow. The night could have gone in very different directions. I could have spent some quality time on that closet couch with a thoroughly patted-down Diane. I could have been sleeping beside Shannon in this very bed at this very moment. And then, somehow, I was going to see them both in a few hours at Laurie's grave, with Hank looking on. Was this all happening to me or was I, in Gallwey/Erhard fashion, letting it happen to myself? *It has already worked out. This is the way it worked out. You don't like it? Too bad.*

21

DAWN OR NO DAWN, CAFFEINE or no caffeine, I was so sound asleep that when Ben called to me I was certain I'd zonked out for hours. I'd missed the ceremony. I'd disappointed Shannon again, lost another chance with Diane, and pissed off Hank. I'd betrayed Laurie. I'd failed my son. The whole day had passed me by and I'd never get it back. More of my life frittered away.

"Let's go," Ben said.

I was ready to rush, undo as much damage as I could. Then I checked the clock. 8:01. I rubbed at my eyes and reached for the coffee on the nightstand. It was cold. I took a small sip anyway. "I'll need something fresher than this," I said, grimacing for Ben's benefit before spitting the bitter swill back into the cup.

Ben laughed, and the morning filled with promise again. "I'll get dressed," he said.

Our weekend morning ritual usually included a neighborhood stroll. Ben would scooter or ride his training-wheeled bike and I would jog slowly alongside. We'd cut through Washington Park and wind up at Stack's Coffee on Lark Street, where the baristas knew to serve Ben a warmed-up croissant and a steamer. We'd sit on the stools by the window, watch the world go by, and plan the rest of the day.

Ben rushed back, all dressed. "We need to hurry, Dad," he said. "Shannon promised to be here for brunch."

I didn't think Shannon would cancel on Ben, no matter how badly things had gone last night. "Almost ready," I said.

"And what did Diane say? Is she coming?"

I needed more sleep. And I was going to have to guard against crankiness. It wouldn't be helpful, for instance, to ask my son why he was so interested in Diane and Shannon. *Aren't I enough?* Of course I wasn't enough. "She'll be there," I said. "Also, she gave me something for you. I left it in the car."

Ben started clapping. He'd clearly slept fine.

"It's not a toy," I said, to avoid disappointment, but also to stop the clapping, which was far too loud.

"What is it?"

"Follow me."

We went out to the car and as soon as Ben saw the seersucker jacket, he wanted to try it on. I helped him button the top button. I smoothed the lapels, like Diane had done for me, and then I kissed the top of his head. While he stood by the side-view mirror, grinning at himself, I snapped a quick photo and texted it to Diane. Then I said, "All right. Let's hit it, handsome." I had the hanger in one hand and I held out my other hand for the jacket. "We can leave it in the car for now."

"I want to keep it on," he said.

So he wore the jacket throughout our morning ritual, on the bike and in the café. Afterward, when we were almost back at the apartment, he caught sight of Shannon waiting for us on the stoop and raced ahead, the jacket flapping up behind him like a cape. There were training wheels and Ben's helmet was securely fastened, but I still almost shouted *Slow down!* Instead, I picked up my own pace, staying close.

Shannon stood up and Ben rushed into her arms. "It's good to see you," I said.

"You could have seen more," she said.

She was smiling, putting on a brave front, which was fine by me. Hadn't I actually done the right, respectable, decent thing? It was better for everyone. "Shannon," I said, "I—"

"I was promised brunch," she said. "Plus this seer-suckered gentleman and I have a few things to prepare."

"Can we have brunch at the cemetery?" Ben asked.

"A picnic," Shannon said, weighing the idea. "Sounds good to me, but it's up to your dad."

They both gave me their sad-eyed beseeching look and I wasn't about to say no. The truth was I still didn't have a plan for the imminent ceremony. When could I have made a plan? I hadn't even bought a cake. "I'm in," I said, and then I went to shower and shave.

~

Since the funeral, I'd visited the cemetery just once, on our wedding anniversary. Ben was still five and I'd decided not to mention the loaded occasion. Instead, I'd left Shannon at the apartment that night so I could visit the cemetery by myself. I sat by the grassy grave, highly aware of the softness of my aching head. The tombstone was more than hard enough to get the job done. All I required was the willpower. If I didn't like that way, there were others. Punch the accelerator, point the car, close my eyes, hold the line. If it hadn't been for Ben, sleeping soundly, oblivious, I might never had made it back home.

Now, months later, I let the hot water beat down on my back until steam clouded the room. What better place for a ghostly Laurie visit? I waited for her, ready to remind her that I loved her. I should have reminded her more often, though I did tell her a lot, didn't I? *Come back*, I could say, or *Take me with you. At least tell me what to do. Please. Am I doing everything wrong? How should I go on?* But she didn't appear and by the time I turned the water off and wrapped myself in a towel, my thoughts had drifted, for better or worse, toward other concerns, other people. Ben, first of all, but there was a list now, and it was growing: Alex, Neffer, Shannon, Hank, Diane.

"Grief can alter your brain," the therapist had said. "However," he'd added, "it's not all permanent. Naturally, there will be scars, but there will also be healing. Believe it or not, your brain will eventually make room for more life."

I wiped the steam from the mirror, lathered up, shaved, watched my tired face reemerge. Was my concern for others a sign of healing or giving up, or both, and more?

~

Back in the kitchen, I found Shannon stuffing a bunch of things into a Haven College canvas bag. I couldn't see what she was putting in there, but her yellow-and-white summer dress resembled a tunic.

Her leather sandals laced up above her ankles. She might have fit in at an ancient Greco-Roman temple. Or over at Mary's monument. Meanwhile, Ben looked spiffy in his seersucker, the perfect attire for a day at the races up in Saratoga. He'd somehow buffed his shoes to a deep shine. All he needed was a straw boater. "Is there anything we should pick up on the way?" I asked, fidgeting with the buttons of my own "new" jacket, waiting for Ben to take note, but he was busy whispering to Shannon, peering into the canvas bag.

"I think we're all set," Shannon said.

We went outside and climbed into the car. I drove north on the thruway and I kept my eyes on the road as we passed the exit for the airport. It was the weekend. I wasn't going to be the one to bring up work, though I did check my watch, tried to guess where I might be on my shift. Closing in on break time. Made me wish I'd brought some coffee for the road. Traffic bunched up around some bridge repairs but then there were three lanes open, plenty of room, the High Peaks of the Adirondacks less than two hours away, Montreal waiting on the other side.

"I told Ben today would be a good day to talk about Laurie," Shannon said. "I told him we'd do our best to answer whatever questions he might be carrying around."

"Fine by me," I said, even though I wasn't sure I could handle it. I almost shared the fact that Laurie and I had always planned to spend a long weekend in Montreal. But what question would that answer?

"Go ahead, Ben," Shannon said.

"What did Mommy want me to be when I grew up?"

Shannon laughed and I noticed how tightly I was gripping the steering wheel. Relax. I could handle this question and, with any kind of luck, a few more. The cemetery was about fifteen minutes away. Maybe this kind of Q&A would help me figure out what to say when I had to speak at the grave.

"Well," I began, "you know your mother and I met while we were working at Haven College and, even before you were born, when I stopped coaching and started at the airport, I used to think if she kept her job at Haven, you might be able to go there for free. But your mother would say, *College is great. He could also be a farmer and help feed the world. He could be a potter or a carpenter or a mason. I just want him to do what he loves."*

"Do you love work, Dad?"

I wasn't ready to get into that. Could I honestly say I loved my work?

"I remember watching your father coach tennis," Shannon said. "There was no doubt he loved being out there. I remember how—"

"I thought we were talking about Laurie," I said, my grip on the wheel tightening again.

"What were her favorite things about me?"

"Sweetheart," I said, reaching up to rub a palm into my right eye. "How much time do we have?"

Shannon was looking over at me, pleased with her plan, whatever it was. Despite the awkward night, she remained eager to help. "Your mother loved everything about you," I said, rubbing at my other eye, buying time to bring order to the list lining up in my mind, starting with how soft his new skin felt against hers, the gift of his wide open eyes, the complete trust he showed when he allowed her to file down his tiny sharp fingernails on the first morning of his life.

I was just getting warmed up, but Ben was already on to the next question: "What did I do to make her laugh?"

"She loved to laugh," I said, turning around for a second, trying to catch his eyes. "You made it easy for her. You farted. You burped. You made noises we could barely understand. You had your own sounds for everything. You'd sit on the floor in your bouncy chair and you'd blurt all those noises at the world and your mother would laugh and laugh. She laughed when you clapped, when you pooped, when you crawled, when you walked, when you fell down, and then when you laughed, you know what she did?"

"What?"

"She totally cracked up."

"It's true," Shannon chimed in. "Even when your mother was upset with you—when you wouldn't nap, for instance, which was almost everyday for a long, long time—she couldn't help cracking up when you laughed."

Ben was the one laughing now, and I listened as I took the exit that led to the cemetery. If the place had been within walking distance, or somewhere within running range, or even along my commute route, I might have developed a habit of stopping by. But it was farther north, near the retirement community where Laurie's parents had died, across the highway from a shuttered, deteriorating shopping mall. Before the mall, the land had belonged to the Stuyvesant Country Club. Now those acres would most likely be sold to the expanding cemetery. That was the kind of real estate "development" ignored by the Albany boosters. They were happy to talk about the nanotech boom, but they had no desire to advertise death as one of the region's growth industries.

I didn't dwell on that downward trend. Instead, I remembered that I needed to make a will. Laurie and I had discussed cremation once or twice. I'd joked about her wearing my ashes in a locket and she'd promised to use them for cooking whenever she missed me. But we'd never actually written anything down. The last time the subject had come up she'd said she wanted to be in the plot with her parents, and so she was.

I wanted to be cremated and I wanted Ben to have the ashes. And who would take care of Ben? If I didn't name someone in a will, what would happen? Would the state award custody to Hank?

I was passing through the cemetery's tall wrought-iron gates when Ben asked his next question: "What did I do when you told me Mommy was dead?"

I should have seen the familiar question coming. Another part of Shannon's plan. I knew what she wanted me to do, what I should have done already, but there I was, offering my usual answer right away. "You stared at me," I said. "Even before you knew, you were in shock. You'd been waiting on the stoop for me with Shannon. You stood up, staring. I shook you a little and hugged you and told you again and then you cried and cried."

No one was laughing now. Shannon was glaring at me. I wouldn't meet her eyes. I pulled into the parking lot, picked a spot, yanked on the emergency brake, and switched off the car.

"I remember," Ben said, as if trying to convince himself. "I remember."

I stepped out of the car and walked a few steps away, gazing toward hillsides and fields full of graves. Shannon had glared at me because we'd discussed setting the record straight and I'd just failed to do so. Again. She didn't think it was fair to Ben. Of course it wasn't fair to Ben. But what could I do? I hadn't managed to turn the clock back before. Wasn't likely to manage it now.

I started walking in what I thought was the right direction. Then I saw Ben chasing after Shannon as she jogged up the hill off to my left, the bag swaying on her shoulder. Maybe she'd visited more than I had. I followed along behind. The place needed more trees. The dead deserved seclusion and shade. And quiet. Even on a Saturday morning, the whoosh of highway traffic was nonstop. The air smelled of truck exhaust.

I walked slowly, wondering if anyone else had already arrived, wondering what on earth I was going to say. I'd never been a public speaker. Even as a coach, I wasn't the type to give motivational speeches. I'd shout my trusty phrases to the whole team: *Have fun out there. Show interest in the ball. Be aware of your racket. Find your quiet mind. Let it happen.* But whenever I needed to say more than that, I tended to do it one-on-one.

Now I watched my kid and babysitter crest the hill. Closer by, a small brown rabbit hopped out from under a bush. I crouched down slowly. Maybe I could tear off a few blades of grass, lure it closer. The rabbit sniffed the air. Its whole body quivered along with its whiskers. Then it jumped away, darting beneath another bush. I waited to see if it would reemerge. It did not. Then something white, dimpled, and round caught my eye. An egg? Rabbits didn't lay eggs. I took a few steps. It was a golf ball and I knelt down to pick it up.

In the palm of my hand it felt cold and unbreakable, not at all egglike. I buffed it on my jeans. A Titleist. Relatively new. Not a remnant of the old country club. Someone was driving balls in the cemetery. Or maybe it had been an offering left by the grave of a dead golfer. Washed downhill by heavy rain. I walked on, tossing the shiny ball up, catching it, enjoying the way it smacked lightly into my palm. But where was my offering? Shannon was carrying that stuffed canvas bag, full of who-knew-what; I was empty-handed.

I had no speech. Worse than that, I'd failed once again to tell my son the truth.

You want to know what you did when I told you? You laughed. You couldn't stop laughing, even after I shook you. You were in shock, that part is true. And you did eventually cry and cry. But first you laughed. Maybe I should have told you that from the start. I don't know. I'm sorry.

Why couldn't I say that? Why hadn't I said it?

I squeezed the golf ball tighter and walked up to the grave. The crowd was bigger than I'd expected. Diane was there, with Alex. Hank was there. As were Paul and Vanessa. And Neffer, with a woman standing close beside him. I had no idea how Neffer knew the details of the plan. Could Shannon have invited him? More likely it was Hank. "Nice to see you here," I said.

Neffer was maintaining his spiffed-up look, freshly shaved again, sporting the new glasses, suit and tie. "Team spirit," he said. "The words mean something to me, you know that." Then he introduced his wife, Chloe. She looked like she was from the Caribbean. I guessed Haiti and put out my hand. Chloe wrapped her two hands around it. The crow's-feet near her eyes and worry lines on her forehead made me think she was a few years older than Neffer. Maybe she was a smoker too. Her hands were warm and soft. "You have our sympathy," she said.

I looked for Ben, ready to introduce him, but he was with Diane and Hank, an unlikely pair, though they seemed to be getting along. They were squatting in front of Ben, fawning over his jacket and his watch. What sort of questions was Hank asking her? Alex was near them, leaning against a tree, wearing another fantastic suit, this time with a shiny black tie. When Hank stood up, he moved closer to Alex. I thanked Chloe, excused myself, and started walking toward my son and brother-in-law. What sort of greeting would I get from Diane? Then I felt guilty for being curious. Hank was nodding, about to say something, and I wanted to hear, but Shannon took my arm and began tugging me away. "I'm still upset with you," she said, "but we'll work it out later. It's going to be fine. Now we need to get started." She stopped right next to the plain tombstone. *Laurie Bell Waldman. In loving memory.* "You speak and then Ben and I will do a little something, okay?"

I nodded, even though I felt dizzy. I was still holding the golf ball. I squeezed it again and then tried to slip it into my jacket pocket, but the pockets were sewn shut. The inside pocket was open, so I dropped it in there and I felt it against my chest as I buttoned the top button. Then I was speaking, thanking everyone for coming out, and telling them I wanted to share a story and they grew quiet and this story takes me back to those early weeks with Laurie and I try to keep it all straight and it's almost two months since she met me at the airport with those lilies and we've been spending three or four nights a week together, and it seems inevitable that someone will eventually at least mention the possibility of a more permanent arrangement, but whenever the idea crosses my mind, I push it away. I want to enjoy what's happening without clutching it too hard. And along comes an empty afternoon, we're blissful in her sleigh bed, basking. She sits up, stuffs a pillow behind her back, glances out the window, and says, "Nice day for minigolf."

I roll onto my side, gaze up at her, enthralled as ever. "I was thinking the same thing," I say, though I can't even remember the last time I held any kind of golf club at all.

It's been, in many ways, an athletic courtship and we're still discovering how we like to spend our time together. In bed. Walking up and back to Mary's monument. Playing tennis. Mountain biking. I like how enthusiastic she is. She works hard on the bike and on the court, a good listener, trying to improve, raise her game. She doesn't seem to mind that I'm better than she is, faster than she is. She's motivated, excited by trying to keep up.

At the minigolf course, I see quickly that she's led me into a trap. She takes her putting seriously. Here's a game where her skills eclipse mine. Her first putt is a bank shot off a cinderblock corner, up and down a slight hill, right into the cup for a hole-in-one. We high-five, but she doesn't put much joy into it. She's on to the second hole, studying it, even though I suspect she's played this course many times.

"I thought minigolf would be relaxing," I say.

"You can relax if you like."

And I do relax, content to watch her, learn from her form for a change. But something gives me pause. I know what she looks like when she's having fun and this is not it. She's unstoppable, though.

"What else have you been hiding from me?" I ask.

"Let's drive a basket of balls," she says.

And then there's the first hitch to the story, one particular fear: did I truly know her? Best not to dwell on that now. These people here want me to keep talking. And of course I knew her. Yes. But did I have enough time to get to know her? The answer to that question has to be no. Not nearly enough time.

Better to attend to the surprise of her beauty. That's what I'm talking about. The way she held those flowers out to me. The way her body smoothly turns and uncoils, the slow motion precision of it, and then the ball rockets off, the smack of perfect contact echoing as I track the shot. I think of my father on the tennis court, that one-handed backhand. There's a gigantic round wooden target, painted to resemble an enormous golf ball, 150 yards away. Laurie plunks it and then clears it, at will, and now she's having fun. How does she do it? Why wasn't she enjoying it at first?

I learn about that later. It connects to brother Hank, his persistent taunting, the mean streak he's wrestled with his whole life, but no need to mention that here. Take the high road, for Ben's sake. Besides, what she says is: "That doesn't matter. What matters is I'm enjoying it with you."

And, in the months to come, as our lives wind tighter and tighter together, I'll also learn she's a dynamite swimmer. She's got a sweet set shot, and a strong left hand when she drives to the basket. But, in that moment, during that first trip to the minigolf course, seeing her enjoy afresh a talent she'd been blessed with, I feel more confident than I have in years, certain I have something to give her and certain her surprising beauty will fill my life.

We will help each other enjoy afresh our god-given talents.

I grin at all this new knowledge and I'm overcome with the desire to get her back into bed. We will fuck even better now, I'm sure of it. And we've already been fucking just fine. And then I do get her back into that bed and that's when we begin to talk about marriage.

And I'm pretty sure I'm speaking most of this in some way, hitting the highlights, leaving out what's inappropriate, celebrating this birthday as best I can, but the more I talk, the more uncertain

I become, and it grows difficult to tell the difference among what I'm saying, what I'd like to say, and what I'd never say. I'm almost sure I'm doing a good job, moving along, finding the words, even though I've also entered some odd zone—not quite present and not quite past—where I can share part of the truth, but not all of the truth, and then I feel it all veer out of control because I recognize the memory of the way we were in bed the night before the bike ride, and I try to bring a stop to it, but my thoughts are rushing into it, preparing to speed downhill.

It's misty and we're climbing into thick fog that breaks open and then closes up again near the top of the hill. We've already biked this hill more than a hundred times during the eight years of our courtship and marriage. On this particular morning we're not talking much because we're avoiding some big-ticket items. Plans for an upcoming vacation. The possibility of trying harder to have another child. The idea that I should quit the TSA, return to school for a graduate degree in physical education, find my way back to coaching college tennis. Also, shouldn't we at least try to live somewhere else for part of our lives while we're young enough to pack up and go? Nothing against life in beautiful Upstate New York, but there are other places in the world.

Those issues aren't going anywhere and we both decide to celebrate how good it feels to be outside, on our bikes, picking up speed. Do we have a little extra time to head down to the Hudson for a riverside sprint? If we push it we can make it, can't we? She says, "Sure," and I say, "Then let's hit it," and I laugh as she stands up, accelerating into the downhill, trying to get a jump on me, but I'm faster and I stay even with her. "Not today you don't," I say, as I begin to pull in front. She's a week from turning thirty-two and she looks as strong as ever. I can see it in her triceps, her calves, how taut they are. She's in even better shape than she was before pregnancy. I can smell the miles we've put in already, the scent of the pine needles and grass and mud we've churned through. I'm not cutting her off. I leave her plenty of room. She'll probably overtake me before long and then we'll trade the lead all the way down the hill.

I'm not that worried when she goes airborne. I've seen her crash before. She's far tougher than I am and I know what she'll say when I rush over to help her. She'll tell me I'm in trouble now, and then she'll hop back up on the bike and speed away. In fact, I'm almost sure she's looking at me before she hits the ground and she's smiling, laughing it off before it's over, and I can hear the familiar sound of her laughter, imagine it echoing outward, breaking up more of the surrounding mist, and she doesn't see the rock and neither do I, so how can I warn her and how can she avoid it? She's not in control and neither am I. There's the joyous burst of her laugh and the thud of contact.

A breath of silence and then everything is so far from quiet. The rattle of her bike, my bike thrown down, my footsteps, my breathing, my shouting. It's just her body that's quiet, as if something snapped off, and I can hear the mist moving through the branches of the trees, the birds twittering on as if nothing has happened, and yet there's the feeling that other animals are watching me, observing, and I can hear the clouds above the mist, and she's not moving and not moving, but she is breathing, at least I can feel her breath. I'm afraid to shake her, her eyes are closed, and then, believe it or not—*bam!*—her eyes are open again, and she gets up, touches her left side, doesn't laugh, but does smile, and says, "Oh yeah, there's gonna be a bruise," and she begins to climb back onto her bike, and, relieved, amazed, unsteady, I'm heading to get my bike when I hear her hit the ground again, and this time her eyes stay closed.

I can't see the spleen torn from its pedicle, I don't even know what a pedicle is, but that's what has happened, a grade-five ruptured spleen and the internal bleeding is alarmingly fast. Maybe there would have been time if she had been in a hospital and someone had seen it happen, but not here, where no one can see inside her. I can't leave her, but how will anyone get to us, I'm shouting to the woman on the phone now and I want her to tell me what to do but she keeps asking questions and she can't see that Laurie's breathing is slowing and slowing, so I have to lift her up, what choice do I have, I have to get her down the hill, away from Mary and that damn monument, and she's warm, she's warm against me, and I'm certain she's alive, but that's not what I see in the eyes of the EMTs when they finally arrive, going as fast as they can along the gravel, brown clouds swirling into white.

Sometime I'll have to tell all of this to Ben, won't I, all I haven't told and more, but not here, not now, not yet, and there's Ben's face, leaning forward, expectant, worried, frozen, like my own, and I want to tell him that everything will be okay, everything is okay, even if it doesn't look that way right now.

Do I say that aloud? I'm not sure, but I say that she left behind her smile and laughter and her hidden powers, and I'll keep learning more, and I'll share it all, and I'll never forget how she rose back up, how she was climbing back onto her bike.

~

And then Shannon was walking up to me, and Neffer was there too, that big arm around my back, and they were leading me away from the stone when Neffer said, "That was a beautiful tribute, Officer. You had my wife in tears and she's no softy, I'll tell you that."

I heard that familiar voice and I felt eager to get back to work, where I'd have a better idea of what the hell was going on. I needed to eat something. Weren't we going to have a picnic? There was the blanket and Shannon told me to sit down on it. Neffer and his wife sat beside me. Diane and Alex were standing nearby, as was Hank.

In front of us all, Shannon and Ben stood and began removing items from the canvas bag. There were boxes of Band-Aids and a spray bottle of the Wound Wash from CVS. It wasn't something I'd wanted to buy. Couldn't I control even that much? I was about to walk up and take it away, but Shannon was already talking. "This next part is Ben's idea," she said.

Ben stood behind her. "You tell it," he said.

"I don't remember what you want," she said. "Hands out, or something like that, right?"

Ben held up the bottle and began to explain what he wanted everyone to do. "Spray a little of this on your body somewhere and then put on one of these Band-Aids."

"Tell them why," Shannon said.

"They know," Ben said.

"They might," Shannon said, "but tell them anyhow, just to be sure."

Ben talked quickly. "When my mom crashed, she got hurt inside. She didn't know how bad it was. No one did. Now we're all hurt inside. That's all."

Ben pushed up the sleeve of his jacket and sprayed the Wound Wash on his forearm, near his watch. He rubbed it in and put on a Band-Aid. Shannon did the same thing.

Watching my son brought me slowly back to myself. Why should I be upset about the Wound Wash? Shannon must have seen annoyance on my face, though. "Try to relax," she said, as she offered me the bottle and the box of Band-Aids.

I kept my eyes on Ben, marveling. I'd done nothing as thoughtful or compassionate at either one of my parents' funerals. All of my meandering talk was nothing compared to this ritual Ben had concocted. I unbuttoned my shirt and pulled down the collar of my T-shirt. I sprayed the stuff on my chest and rubbed it in above my heart. It smelled like the ocean, though it was stickier than seawater. I pressed on the bright Band-Aid.

Ben went from Hank to Paul to Vanessa to Diane to Alex to Neffer, who had Chloe spray the back of his neck so he could apply the Band-Aid there. Then Hank took a piece of paper out of his suit jacket pocket. "I'd like to read a poem," he said. "I heard it recited on the anniversary of 9/11 a few years back, but it seems appropriate here too on this April morning. It's called 'April Orchard' and it's by Franz Wright. I don't know much about him, but I feel like he knows something about me. I feel like he knows about what nephew Ben just called the hurt inside us." Hank paused to clear his throat. He stood up taller. The paper shook in his hands. "Here we go," he said, and he began reading.

I tried to follow the poem. There were lines about existence, birth, and death, and talking with a son. Then I drifted away for a few lines and stared at my son, thinking of the talks to come. Maybe this very April afternoon. We could walk in the park and talk and talk.

Meanwhile, Hank was still reading, and now there was a sun shining, rising, not rising. I looked up into the sky. The poem was talking about the sun, not my son. We all make mistakes. The sun was bright and my forehead was hot. Maybe there would be no more talk of snow. I remembered the sound of Elizabeth's voice and

I wondered if Hank was reading the poem in part for her, hoping to get her back. A prayer of forgiveness for whatever he'd done. A prayer of peace for his departed sister.

I tuned back into the reading. "In deep sleep sometimes even we get well," Hank said.

I missed some of the words that came after that because, a few steps behind me, Diane and Alex were whispering. I saw Alex hand over his phone and Diane stepped away, pecking at the device as she walked.

"We are all going to be perfectly all right," Hank said. And then the poem was over.

Perfectly all right sounded good to me, but Laurie was the one in the deepest sleep. Still, Hank and I would both surely settle for some deep sleep while we got well. Or maybe this had been a year of deep sleep and the getting well was already happening. Hank folded up his paper and slipped it into his back pocket. I still couldn't believe that he'd spoken, let alone read a poem. I walked over to him and said, "Thank you for that."

"Don't thank me for trying to be a decent human being," he said, clearly uncomfortable. "I'll be back in a second."

I watched him walk over and hug Ben. Then Neffer and Chloe were at my side. "Thank you again for coming," I said.

"I wish we could stay longer," Neffer said, his arm tight around Chloe. "But now a different duty calls. See you Monday morning. Don't be late. Your brother-in-law and I agree: it's shaping up to be a doozy of a week."

They walked away, hip-to-hip. The Band-Aid looked tiny on the back of Neffer's big neck. Then a hug from Diane caught me by surprise and it was over before I could really feel it. "I wish I could stay," she said, "but Alex needs me to get him home. Thomas has questions, or more phone calls, or something. He sends his sympathy, for what that's worth."

"I'm glad you were here," I said.

"Me too," she said. "Your brother-in-law, though. Creepy."

"What do you mean?"

"The way he read that sweet poem gave me the chills. It was like he kind of hated poetry."

I considered defending Hank. But what could I say? It was good to hear her sense of him.

"I really have to run," she said. "You stay strong, if you can. I can't imagine what this day must be like for you. I'll check in with you later, okay?"

I wanted to talk more with her, but I thought I could feel Laurie watching. And Shannon. "Okay," I said, sticking to my script. "Thanks again for coming."

Alex stepped up and shook my hand. "Ceremonies like this are too much for me," he said. "Too many memories. My heart goes out to you." Then he rubbed the sleeve of my jacket for a moment. "Nice threads," he said, winking. His skin had good color, but he leaned on Diane as they walked away.

Ben and Shannon were back by the canvas bag, getting out some fruit and muffins and juice. Paul and Vanessa were helping set the food on the blanket. I started toward them, but once again my path was blocked. Hank was back, standing in front of me. "There's more I want to mention," he said. "Laurie would want me to, if you don't mind."

"It's okay," I said. "You can say whatever you want."

"I should have been here more often," he said. "That's part of it. And I want you to know I think you've done a good job with the boy. I've been hard on you for far too long. I should have been more helpful. I should have made more of an effort. I want to apologize for that."

I tried to be open to Hank's sudden kindness, the thoughtfulness of it, but I couldn't stop thinking about what Diane had said. I also thought about leakage. That was the word we used on the job. One of the instructors had told our training class about physical responses most human beings could not conceal. "Our bodies betray us," the guy, an ex-Best Buy salesman, said. He went on to mention sweat, twitches, tics, stutters, and more. I must have done plenty of leaking during my rambling speech. Hank had seemed nervous before. Now he was extremely calm. He didn't have the lines written down, but it all seemed rehearsed.

Laurie used to apologize so sweetly. She'd taught me the importance of apologizing. Admit your mistake. Own it. Be real about it. Then move on. I found it brave and heartwarming. Yet another thing that had deepened my love for her. I'd always assumed it was part of what she'd grown up with, which made it all the more telling that Hank seemed to struggle with it. His words seemed forced. The absence of leakage felt like leakage somehow.

Still, I knew what I needed to say. "Apology accepted."

"Thank you," Hank said.

"Come on over, you two," Shannon called. "We're waiting for you."

Hank put an arm around my shoulder and walked me toward the blanket. "By the way," he said, "I'm free for the next few hours. I was hoping I could roll with you and Ben. What do you think?"

More than anything, I wanted one-on-one time with my son. We had a lot to talk about. But how could I possibly say no?

I sat next to Paul on the blanket. "You did a great job up there," he said. "Inspirational, as you say."

I looked over at Vanessa, who was chatting happily with Shannon. I lowered my voice. "How are things going in your world?"

"Better than expected," he said.

Shannon handed a plate of food to Ben and told him to pass it to me. "Eat some food already," she said. "You look like you're about to pass out."

Ben gave me the plate. I suddenly remembered how hungry I was and dug in.

22

AFTER WE ATE, I WOUND UP IN the Subaru with Shannon and, though I didn't like it, my brother-in-law sped off in his Charger with Ben. I kept them in sight until they hit the thruway. Then Hank stomped on the gas, slid the Charger into the left lane, and kept on accelerating. Ben waved back at us. The Subaru didn't have a prayer.

The possibility of Hank kidnapping Ben lodged itself in my mind. The guy could make himself disappear. He could easily make Ben disappear with him. His whole oddly flat apology could have been a distraction, a way to keep me, once again, off guard. Diane had sensed something too. Maybe this is what he really came here to do. He would punish me and take away the only thing left in my life that mattered. When he called in from some undisclosed location to explain it to me, he'd tell me that Laurie had told him to do it.

I took a deep breath and tried to move those thoughts along. I thought back to that poem Hank had read, the "perfectly all right" of its ending. He was a professional. No professional would kidnap his nephew.

Meanwhile, Shannon leaned back in the passenger seat with her arms crossed, staring into the side of my face, reminding me that I had other worries. I began to apologize. Get out in front of it, if I could.

"I'm sorry," I said. "I should have told him."

"You understand he already knows, right? He needs you to tell him what really happened and that it's okay it happened. He's basically begging you to tell him. *Not* telling him only makes it worse. And telling him something different, well, that—"

I knew she wouldn't stop glaring at me until I looked over at her. I'd lost sight of the Charger anyhow. I turned and met her eyes. "I'll tell him," I said.

"When?"

"Today. I promise."

"I want you to call me after you do it."

"You can come watch, if you want. Spend some more time with Hank."

She uncrossed her arms. "That guy looks better in daylight," she said. "Seemed like he was really hurting. And the poem was a surprise."

It was interesting to get a different take on Hank. I was tempted to ask for her take on Diane. Asking would help keep our boundaries straight. But it wouldn't be very kind. "About last night," I began.

"I don't want to discuss that right now."

"Okay, but I just want to—"

"There's something else I'd rather discuss," she said, "now that I'm done scolding you."

"You're done? Forever?"

"Listen," she said, "you did a nice job up there. It couldn't have been easy."

Her approval made my face grow warm. "I felt like a fool," I said.

"I thought you were brave."

"Sure. It takes real bravery to be incoherent in public. A special kind of—"

"You don't need to mock it, Gary. It was moving. Laurie would have been proud."

I scratched at the Band-Aid above my heart. It was tangled up in my chest hair. Peeling it off wouldn't be much fun. I looked over and saw the T-Rex Band-Aid that Shannon had pressed tight to the underside of her wrist. "She'd be proud of you, too," I said.

She nodded slowly. "I really do miss her."

I kept driving, feeling closer to my ex-player/babysitter/family friend than ever before. Even closer than when she was offering herself in the middle of the night.

"I'm sorry I got so upset," she said. "My own father almost never told me the truth. Even about small, stupid things."

"My father didn't tell me he was walking around with an aneurysm in his brain," I said.

"Laurie told me about that," Shannon said. "She told me you've been on guard ever since. I know that's connected to everything I said last night. I'm sorry about that, too." She reached across and rested a hand on my shoulder. She applied almost no pressure, but heat radiated outward from each fingertip.

"Your father was protecting you, though," she went on. "That's different from lying. My father would say he'd be somewhere and not show up. He'd say he'd bring something home, but then he wouldn't even come home and when he did, he'd forgotten to bring whatever he'd promised."

"I want to protect Ben," I said, "but I don't want to lie to him. I won't lie to him. I just need to know where the line is between protecting and lying."

"The ball's in or the ball's out, Coach. Watch where it lands and make the call."

"I wish it were that simple."

"Of course you do," she said, kneading my shoulder a little. If I hadn't been driving, I would have shut my eyes and leaned back into it. "Do you know what my father said to me the last time I saw him?" she said.

"How old were you?"

"It was when I was at Haven," she said. "He'd left my mother again almost right after I graduated high school. He was living in Vermont, doing something with solar energy. When I made the tennis team, he said he couldn't wait to see me play. He didn't come to a match until junior year. We were playing against Buffalo. They wiped us off the court. But he didn't show up until the match was over. The Buffalo players were climbing on their bus. You were leading us back to the locker room. Remember?"

I tried to remember. I could picture Shannon on the court. She had a speedy flat serve and her net game improved every year. Went undefeated as a senior. But I had no memory of her father. I shook my head.

"I was so happy to see him. I wasn't even angry. I hadn't played well anyhow, though maybe that was because I kept looking back at the bleachers. I wanted to introduce him to you, but he said he couldn't stay around."

More and more, those years at Haven blurred together in my mind. I could see the courts, the team hard at work beneath the blue sky, surrounded by green hills. I'd wanted to keep that job forever.

"I was sweaty and cold," Shannon said. "I was shivering while my father stood there and told me he was going to try again with my mother. He couldn't bear to lose our family. He'd never done anything better than marry my mother and become a father to me. Nothing in his life was more important. He hugged me and I believed him."

"Then what happened?"

"A week later, my mother called to tell me he'd moved out to Idaho. I never heard from him again."

"You deserved much better than that," I said.

"I'm not asking for sympathy. I'm just saying that kind of behavior didn't protect me at all."

"He should have watched you play. It was a pleasure."

I drove on, thinking about how she and I had been sharing sadness since Laurie's death and maybe even longer, back to our histories of lost fathers and tennis courts. When I pulled up in front of her apartment building I said, "I don't know what we would have done without you this year. Laurie always knew you were good for Ben."

Shannon unbuckled her seat belt and pushed her door open. "She probably thought I'd be good for you, too."

"You are."

"I bet she'd tell you I could help lead you back."

I kept my hands on the wheel. "Back where?"

"I don't know. Out of the airport. Onto the courts. Something like that."

I looked straight ahead, down the street lined with row houses and budding trees. How much time had passed since I'd been standing at Laurie's grave, blathering away? It felt like a different day. "I never thought she'd die before me," I said.

Shannon leaned across and pecked my cheek. I hugged her, but my seat belt was still on, which made it more awkward than it already was. Then she was out of the car, resting a hand on the door. "You should catch up to Hank and Ben," she said. "They must be waiting for you by now."

"I'll call you after the talk."

"I'll be waiting."

She closed the door and walked up to her building. I watched her unlock the front door. Ex-player. Babysitter. Laurie's friend.

∽

When I pulled up in front of my building, I didn't see the Charger anywhere. I got out and sat on the stoop, watching cars drive down the street. I checked my phone. I listened for sirens and tried not to picture accidents. The kidnapping thoughts flashed back at me. The late-night phone conversation with Elizabeth ran through my mind. Hank was *reeling*. Yes, he'd read that poem, but the woman he'd been seeing didn't want him to know where she was.

I needed a break from thinking about threats. They'd probably stopped off somewhere for a snack.

Then the text came in: *Picking something up for Ben. Be there in 5.*

And when the Charger roared up, I could see Ben and Hank yakking away. Ben was still talking when they stepped out of the car. "How old was she when she got it?"

"That's a good question," Hank said, more like a caring teacher than a drill sergeant. "Let me think for a second. I was nine, so she must have been right around your age, six or seven."

"What took you guys so long?" I asked.

"You'll see," Ben said.

Hank popped the trunk of the car and lifted out an old neon green Schwinn with a banana seat and glittery tassels dangling from the chopper-style handlebars. I'd never seen it before, but there were photos in old albums. It was Laurie's. The reflectors caught the light. There were no training wheels on it.

"Hey," I said. "I don't think—"

"I've had it forever," Hank said. "I figured it was time to pass it along."

"No," I said. "No, thank you."

"I like it, Dad," Ben said. "I want to keep it."

I spoke directly to Hank. This was something I could control, wasn't it? I didn't look at Ben because I didn't want to waver. "It's thoughtful of you, but we'll get a new bike when it's time."

"I should have talked it over with you first. I get that, but—"

"Hank, please put the bike back in your trunk."

"Dad," Ben said. "I want the bike."

"We'll talk about it later, son."

"I can see you're upset," Hank said.

"Yes, I'm upset," I said. "And, yes, you should have asked me about it. I mean, enough already. I don't want that bike. I don't have the other bike and I don't want that bike."

"You don't have to decide right now," Hank said. "Think it over, how about that?"

I was overreacting, but I'd come too far to stop. I was close to shouting. "Let me handle bikes. How about that? Of all the things to bring over here today. You had to zoom off to get her old bike?"

"Dad—"

"Not now," I said. "Please."

"I should have asked you," Hank said. "I'm sorry. But I didn't pick the bike. There was a bunch of stuff in my dad's old storage space. Ben picked the bike. It was his choice."

Ben. The audience for this whole show. And I couldn't help playing it to the end. "Do you need me to put it back in your trunk myself?"

Hank silently set the bike back in the car. Ben began to cry and then rushed inside, slamming the door to the building behind him. Hank banged the trunk shut, walked around to the driver's side, and leaned against the Charger, his thick arms stretched out on the roof. "I'm sorry," he said. "I'm overloading you, aren't I? I can do that, I've been told. I've been driving all over Upstate New York. The whole new-leaf thing isn't easy for me."

The guy really was trying. I could almost believe it. And, as Shannon had suggested, on some level he was really hurting too. Still, I pressed on. I wanted him, and all the threats that circled around him, out of my life. Ben was in the building's entryway, crying. "I need to get inside," I said.

"I'll come by another time."

"Sure," I said. "But call first, like normal people do, okay?"

~

I did my best to calm down as I walked up the steps. I was supposed to be making things better. I was supposed to have an overdue talk. Ben was waiting, breathing hard by the locked door. He followed me up to the apartment and then as soon as we were inside, he ran into the bathroom and locked himself in. "I'm not coming out until you get Mom's bike back," he said.

The bathroom door was the one door inside the apartment that locked. I'd considered switching out the doorknob when I childproofed the place years ago, but all I needed was a paper clip to get in, so I'd left it alone. "Hank's gone," I said. "I can't get the bike back right now."

I was tempted to pop the lock. It seemed silly to talk through the door. I could bang my head against the door, open it like that. It was that kind of day. And, before I thought it through, I was banging my head against the door. Once. Twice. A third time. A more visceral do-it-yourself home version of the "Clobber" sculpture.

"I'm not coming out," Ben said.

My son's voice brought me around. Plus, though the door was hollow, my head ached a bit. I went to the fridge for an ice pack. Maybe I'd need another shot of Wound Wash. Had I really just banged my own head? It reminded me of those early weeks and months after Laurie's death, how difficult it had been to keep it all together. Shannon had been there, in ways I didn't often allow myself to recall. How she'd held me and held me. Now I wanted to hug Ben. Try to explain why I'd overreacted. Do some more apologizing. There were paper clips in the top kitchen drawer next to the fridge. But I sat down by the bathroom door, ice pack on and off my forehead. It would be better for everyone if Ben opened the door by himself.

"Look," I said, "I made a mistake. I was upset about other things. The bike felt like the last straw. I'll talk to Hank and get it back."

I imagined Ben sitting on the closed toilet seat, or perched on the edge of the tub, hunched over. I hoped he wasn't still crying.

"I promise," I said. I put my hand against the door. "I'll call Hank as soon as you open up. We can talk to him together if you want."

Ben stayed quiet.

"Can I tell you something else?"

Nothing.

"At least let me know you can hear me."

"I hear you."

"I made a mistake. I made more than one mistake. But you know what?"

I waited.

"What?"

"You did a great job today. The plan you made with Shannon was perfect. I was wrong about the Wound Wash."

"Another mistake," Ben said.

He didn't seem to be crying anymore. "Open the door and I'll tell you about an even bigger mistake."

"Why did the bike make you so upset?"

"What's your guess?"

"It made you think of the other bike, the one she crashed."

"Come on, Ben. Open the door. It's hard to talk about this without seeing you."

"But she didn't crash this bike. It didn't even have a scratch on it."

"I'm sorry, Ben."

"I'll be fine on this bike, Dad. I know just how to ride it."

"Of course you'll be fine on it. I made a mistake. I wasn't thinking about you. I was frustrated. It was nice of Hank to offer you the bike. I made the wrong decision, but I'll make it right, okay? What else can I do? Please open the door."

"What's the other mistake you were going to tell me about?"

"I can't tell you until you open the door. Shannon said I had to look you in the eyes and tell you."

"You promise you'll call Uncle Hank and get the bike back?"

If Ben needed to hear it over and over, it was the least I could do. Surrender. Apologize. Repeat. "I promise."

The doorknob twisted and the lock popped. I stayed where I was. "Have a seat," I said, patting the space next to me. "I don't think we've ever sat here together."

Ben plopped down by my side. "Tell me the mistake," he said.

I put an arm around my son, so warm, as if he'd run a few miles. I pulled him a little closer. "Look," I said. "I'm sorry for confusing and misleading you. Here's what I need to tell you." I started talking faster, just to make sure I didn't stop. "I think you remember what happened when I told you about Mom's accident. I keep saying that you cried, and you did cry, but the truth is that you laughed first. Not because it was funny."

Ben fiddled with the buttons on his seersucker. There were tears in his eyes. "I must be bad," he whispered.

I couldn't believe what I'd heard. I leaned down and wiped away his tears. "You are not bad at all," I said. Then I leaned down farther and kissed a few more tears away. "You are so good. So good."

"Then why did I do that?"

"It was shock. Sometimes we do strange things when we're overwhelmed."

"Have you ever been overwhelmed?"

"I'm overwhelmed right now. It can be an overwhelming world. That's why I'm holding this ice pack against my head."

"Have you ever done strange things when you didn't know what to do?"

"Too many times to count."

"Do you laugh too?"

"I get quiet," I said. "I've been too quiet for years. And sometimes I get angry when I shouldn't."

"Like when you saw Mom's old green bike—"

"Maybe I should have laughed. Or maybe I'm bad too."

Ben looked at me, smiling, and said, "You're not that bad."

"I could be better," I said, but I was smiling too. I kissed his cheek again. I glanced down the hallway to the bedrooms, then down the hallway to the kitchen and the living room. The floors were dirty, dust all along the moldings. When I looked up, I saw a few cobwebs.

I wiped a finger through the dust. If we weren't going to move, at least we could clean the place up. Maybe do some repainting. "This place is filthy," I said.

Ben wasn't ready to change the subject just yet. "Why didn't you want to tell me the truth?" he asked.

"I've been asking myself the same question. I think I didn't want you to blame yourself for anything. But, really, I didn't want to blame myself. I told myself I was protecting you."

"Shannon says you can't always protect someone, no matter how hard you try. Like you couldn't protect Mom."

I could have started talking about my father, aneurysms, cancer of various kinds. I could have shared more senseless losses in the spirit of openness, in the spirit of not protecting. I pressed the ice pack back against my head. "Well, speaking of Shannon," I said, "let's give her a call. You can tell her I finally told you the truth. She thought you should know. She was right."

She didn't answer, so we left her a message, both of us talking at once. Then we called Hank and left another message together.

I stood and reached a hand down to help pull Ben up. "Now," I said, "how about we ditch our fancy clothes, have a snack, and take your old bike out for one last training wheel ride?"

Ben grabbed my hand and hopped right up. "Plan!" he said.

$\sim$

The afternoon had grown warmer, the sky was clear blue, and the park was a thrumming public space, just the way the Albany boosters liked it, filled with picnickers and Frisbee players, dog walkers and kite fliers, skateboarders, drummers, and a few brave sunbathers. Fishermen and fisher children were scattered around the dingy lake. Ben buzzed along on the bike and I followed behind, jogging every now and then to keep pace. Maybe I'd managed to pass another test. Not with flying colors, but a pass was a pass. We could take our time in the park, skim stones away from the fisher people, run around the playground, and then coast in for another round of pizza, frozen yogurt, and good night.

Ben accelerated up a hill on the bike and I was proud to see how smoothly he rose from his seat, kept his balance, pumped the pedals faster. I needed to accept that he'd be fine without the training wheels. I was jogging again to catch up when I heard a familiar voice call, "Hey, Waldman!"

It was easy to recognize Kevin, even out of uniform, strolling along with his family. He introduced his wife, Tanya, and their kids, Sofia, Franklin, and Ronda, ages five, seven, and ten. The kids had a soccer ball and they ran off to kick it around. Kevin kept talking to his wife: "I've told you about Waldman. He's the one who taught me how to do pat downs—"

"You already knew all about that," she said.

"I'm serious," he said. "This guy helped me through."

Ben came zipping back down the hill to say hello and then he was chasing after the soccer ball with the other kids. Before long, we decided to grab pizza together on Lark Street. While we ate, Kevin began talking about the latest from Sanchez and August. "They're pretending to be excited, but I think they're worried too," he said. "Also, their latest theory is Neffer might not be going for a promotion after all."

"What do you mean?"

"They think he might be leaving because he's lost faith in the TSA."

Before I could respond, Tanya chimed in. "Does anyone really have faith in the TSA?" she said, laughing. "Don't get me wrong. I'm a fan. Before this, Kevin had a bunch of jobs, always tried to work his way up, kept getting downsized. My father worked for a GE affiliate outside of Schenectady for thirty-four years. Retired with a solid pension. Where's that steady work now?"

"There's always the military," I said. "FBI."

"Prisons," Kevin said. "Correction Officers."

"Sad but true," Tanya said. "And the TSA. You've been promoted, what, twice in three years, right?"

"That's correct."

"And the benefits are getting stronger," she said. "I might apply once I get some of these kids out of the house."

Kevin placed a hand on her belly. "We might have some more years to think about that."

"Shh," Tanya said. "We don't know what's going to happen." She turned to me. "We're waiting and seeing," she said.

"I won't breathe a word," I said.

"Whenever the time comes," Tanya said, "I think it might be good work for me."

I couldn't imagine Laurie ever applying to become a TSO. Shannon wouldn't ever try it either. But despite her Question Authority T-shirt, Diane could have the skill set and the temperament. There was that pat down, after all, and whatever the Armed Lady story was.

Ben was finishing up his second slice of pepperoni, racing Franklin to the crust. All four kids seemed happy. A reminder that if I couldn't provide siblings, at least I could work harder to arrange playdates.

Tanya and the kids walked out of the pizza place first, leaving me and Kevin behind to pay. "Well," Kevin said, "any real news from Neffer or your brother-in-law?"

I didn't know where to start. "They're both so professional. I don't think we'll get any more than those Three Stooges photos."

Kevin nodded, like he'd seen it coming. "I'm looking around for those guys even when I'm not at work. Did you hear how Rodgers shut all the lines down because she thought she'd found one of them?"

I shook my head, so he kept going.

"This guy had a neck tattoo that said I VOTED. She was sure it had been altered from DEVOTED. But nothing else matched up and he looked nothing like the guy in the photo. Neffer went easy on her afterwards."

I felt like I had those faces from the photos memorized, but now I felt like I hadn't been thinking about them enough when I was off-duty. Too many other things on my mind. Would I recognize them if they'd managed to change their appearance somehow? What had it felt like to Rodgers, certain she had someone from an ISIS cell standing right in front of her? "Crazy times," I said.

Kevin shrugged it off and drifted back to lighter topics. "What do you think of the Neffer's new look?"

"Sharp," I said.

"Are you chasing after another job?"

"The thought crosses my mind more often these days. What about you?"

Kevin gazed out toward his kids. "I hope I don't have to," he said. "I want the TSA to be my GE."

"Well, let's see if we can make it through the week. One step at a time, I guess."

"Maintain focused attention," Kevin said, grinning, and then we stepped back outside.

~

Later that night, after Ben was sound asleep, after I'd left another round of messages for Shannon and Hank, I burrowed into my bedroom closet and pulled out my tennis bag. I grabbed one of the rackets, wrapped my hand around the grip—a little dried out, but more than fine—and it was like shaking hands with an old friend, wondering why you'd let so much time pass between meetings. Why exactly had I decided to take a break from playing? Punishment? Mourning? The therapist had pushed me on it and I had to agree that Laurie would have wanted me to play more, not less. "And playing tennis would probably make you feel better," he said. "At least it almost always has. So, why stop playing?"

"I guess I don't want to feel better."

"You guess?"

"I'm not ready to feel better."

Now, with the racket back in my hand, I still wasn't sure I was ready. I needed to channel Paul, his determination to be ready for Vanessa. Surrender everything, including expectations. After all, whatever Paul had done, it seemed to be working. I'd rib him about it in the morning. And it might be fun to see what Diane was like on the courts. Maybe Ben would start getting excited about the game.

I was about to carry the bag to the front door, leave it where I used to leave it every night, but the racket felt right in my hand. I set the bag on the bed and took the racket into the bathroom with me, leaned it against the wall while I pissed and washed up. Then I brought it back to the bed and kept it in my hand while my head sank into my pillow. It was still in my hand when my phone buzzed me awake. I checked the time. About an hour had passed.

"Want some company?" Diane asked.

I didn't think about the birthday. I didn't think about my son asleep in the next room. I didn't think about the ridiculously long day. I didn't think about the condition of the apartment or of myself.

"Yes," I said.

~

As soon as I was off the phone, I started thinking again. I looked in on Ben—sleeping peacefully, despite the ticktocking of the watch—and closed his bedroom door. I waited to hear from Laurie as I quickly cleaned the apartment. I heard nothing. I went after the dust in the hallway with a few damp dish towels. I swept. Put the dirty dishes in the dishwasher. Did what I could with the bathroom, washed up, slapped on a little aftershave. Still nothing from Laurie. If she didn't want me to go ahead, there'd be a sign, right?

For laughs, I put the Strand sport coat back on.

Diane smiled when she saw it and then wrapped her arms around me. The golf ball, still in the inside pocket, pressed against my chest. Was that a sign? It didn't hurt. Just got my attention and made me stand up straighter. I waited for Diane to say something about it, but she was already stepping back from me, kicking off her shoes. One of them banged against the door. "Oops," she said. "Mustn't wake the child."

"He's a good sleeper," I said.

"Shh," she said. "You must be all talked out after a day like today."

"Can I get you a drink or anything?"

"Shh," she said, a little more forcefully. "I'm just here to seal the deal. We have unfinished business, as they say. Let's get the beautiful sport coat off, shall we?"

We stripped right by the front door, lit only by the streetlights hazing through the window. She looked taller naked, and she seemed completely comfortable, unashamed. I felt ridiculously hard. I tried to think of taxes, ice, that poor dead Irish wolfhound, SOP, anything to create just a little calm. She reached over and tugged the Band-

Aid off my chest. "You've got a nice body for such an ordinary guy," she said, pressing the Band-Aid between her breasts. "More proof I was right about needing someone more down-to-earth. I wonder what other surprises I'll find."

If anything, I grew harder. And that didn't change when she wrapped a hand around me and started leading me down the hallway. "Point me toward the bedroom," she said.

I put my hands on her warm, round shoulders and we shuffled forward. I steered her into the room. She stopped in front of the bed and took in the racket and tennis bag, which had somehow escaped my quick cleanup. "Is this part of a special tennis training regimen?" she asked. "Or is it some odd kink of the ordinary man?"

"I was getting ready for tomorrow," I said. "I haven't played in a while and—"

"Shh," she said, squeezing me tighter. It was almost painful. She lifted the racket up in her other hand. "Nice equipment," she said, squeezing me again. Then she swung the racket slowly from side to side. Even in my current state, I tried to assess her form. I saw potential.

I also couldn't quite believe it. It seemed too good to be true. But it wasn't easy to follow those thoughts. She tossed the racket onto the other side of the bed, sat down, and guided me into her mouth. I put my hands in her hair. It felt softer than it looked, downy instead of spiky. She paused. "You seem excited," she said.

"It would be good for me to talk and slow things down," I said.

"What if I don't want to slow things down?"

I flashed to the silent moments in Nora Flint's dirty kitchen. How unsatisfying and demoralizing that had been. The memory cooled me off. "It's been a while for me," I said.

She paused again. "So you'll appreciate this more," she said. She blew onto my cock before putting it back in her mouth.

Everything started happening too fast again. I backed away. "There might be benefits to taking our time," I said. I pushed her onto the bed, knelt by the edge, and slowly began to explore her.

"If you put it that way," she said, sliding herself forward to make it easier, resting her hands in my hair. "I guess we don't have to rush."

I wanted to keep talking. Maybe this would be a good time to ask about Armed Ladies. I wanted to know if my son was going to be around someone who was carrying a gun. Though Hank was probably carrying a gun too. And then my thoughts traveled away from that—she was so petite, her thighs strong, long, slender, light-brown hair. I pressed my palm against her belly, also downy, and the faint smell of garlic, and after a while one of her hands began to massage my neck, and it was like she'd talked it over with Laurie somehow because during the early days and nights of our courtship her hand on my neck had bothered me. *Cut it out!* I'd whine, as we sat side-by-side at the movies, in the car, on a park bench. I'd lean away because it made me feel like a puppy or a kitten, and she was the mother, ready to lift me up by the scruff and carry me elsewhere. But I'd learned to love that sensation, and it was as if Diane knew just what I'd been missing, her fingers applying pressure right where I needed. Then she used both hands to guide me up onto the bed with her. "I'm ready," she said. "Are you ready?" She reached down to check. "You seem ready to me."

I peeled the Band-Aid off from between her breasts. "Let's see," I said.

∾

Afterward, I felt wide awake, thrilled, and relieved it had all gone well. Diane curled up close to me, warm, her head on my chest. I'd traveled past the point of exhaustion and now I was wired. I could have pulled an all-nighter, if necessary, but I knew I needed sleep. Ben would be bustling around in the morning, though, so if I wanted to ask some questions, now was the time. "You know," I said, "I googled you the other night."

She snuggled in a little closer. "Hmm," she said.

"And I've been meaning to ask you something."

I could feel her slowly drifting off. Her arm twitched ever so slightly. Still, I pressed on. "What's the deal with your Armed Lady group?"

She rubbed a palm into one of her eyes. "I'm all blissed out here and you want to talk about guns?"

"Just curious, I guess," I said. "And I like to know when my son is around guns."

"I used to work the night shift at the animal hospital," she said. "I felt safer once I was carrying. And it felt better to train with a group of women."

"Do you carry it everywhere?"

She repositioned her head and fiddled with my chest hair. "You are curious," she said. "You searched me already, though. Don't you remember?"

"Fair enough," I said.

"The truth is," she said, "I'm a good shot. You could come watch sometime. Maybe you'd like to try it. It's a great way to deal with frustration."

"I'll think about it," I said, "but I've got to take a piss. I'll be right back."

As I stepped over to the bathroom, she said, "I googled you too, by the way. I found some really nice photos of you in tennis shorts."

I yawned as I flushed the toilet and I walked back to the bed thinking I might manage to get a few hours of sleep after all. I'd wrap my arms around Diane and enjoy dreaming by her side.

I climbed in next to her and spooned myself around her. "I really like touching you," I whispered.

"I want you to like it," she said, pressing herself back against me.

"A sharp-shooting Armed Lady and a Transportation Security Officer," I said. "This bed is probably one of the safest places in the entire Capital Region."

"Yeah, right," she said.

I waited for her to say more. I stared up toward the plaster ceiling, barely visible, just flat darkness. I shut my eyes and focused on my breathing, on hers, and I listened for Ben's.

~

The next time I awoke skyscrapers of sunlight brightened the ceiling. I rolled over to find Diane and my arm brushed against the racket bag. I thought I'd taken it off the bed. She must have put it back on the bed when she'd left. It was a little after seven. I wasn't completely surprised she'd left, but why hadn't she said goodbye?

When I stood up and moved toward the bathroom, I smelled coffee brewing. And then Ben barreled into the bedroom. "Diane came over for breakfast!" he said. "She wants to know how you'd like your eggs this morning."

23

FROM THERE ON OUT, THE DAY passes like a dream, but more than that, like a dream I've dreamed of daring to dream someday. It unfurls before my eyes, the three of us around the kitchen table, feasting on scrambled eggs, hash browns, and toast. Before long I'm sipping my hot coffee and doing the dishes while I listen to Ben and Diane gabfesting once again, bustling around the apartment, gearing up for tennis. Ben's treating Diane as if she's his guest, as if she came over for him—a playdate. I fill three water bottles, pour the rest of the coffee into a thermos to pack along in honor of my father. I'd throw in clementines too, if I had any. And then it's time to put on my own musty tennis clothes. The shorts are a little looser around my waist—it's been a thinning year. I tuck in my T-shirt and lug the full racket bag to the front door, waiting for Ben and Diane, waiting, also, for the guilt to crush me, because it's one thing to sleep with another woman, that's simple animal behavior, hard-wired from the get-go, and no one, not even Laurie, would really hold that against me, though she—and Shannon—might have chosen differently. Still, it's another thing altogether to admire that other woman the morning after when she comes to the door in her compression shorts and skirt and tight top and bright sneakers. It's yet another thing to take her to the courts at Haven College, in the shadow of the hill on which Laurie died, the gravel road I carried her down in plain sight the whole time, Mary with her raised broadsword up there looking down. And higher up, way above the courts, a half-dozen vultures circle, riding the thermals, as they are wont to do. Maybe they are the guilt committee, summoned here to swoop down and tear at my flesh if I proceed any farther along this path, but the living dream continues and the vultures seem to soar off even higher, and the weather couldn't be better, crisp and clear, a perfect midspring late morning. It's not surprising that Paul and Vanessa don't arrive on time, and the privileged students must be sleeping in too, so for a while Ben, Diane, and I have the place all to ourselves. We do our jumping jacks and arm circles and we run in place and stretch and laugh and I'm the coach again, standing next to a hopper full of balls by the net, feeding the two of them on the other side, curious to discover what they can and cannot do. There's no use denying it, it feels close to blissful to be back on a court, at least as blissful as the fucking last night. My sneakers grip the grainy green asphalt and my hand grips the racket and there's the weight of the ball just so against the strings again and again—the *thwok thwok thwok* of it—our laughter traveling out to the woods and echoing back to us as Ben and Diane swing and miss or swing and make off-kilter contact. They have my focused attention and it's easy to see that I can help them the old Gallwey way, guide them forward, encourage them—show interest in the ball and be aware of your racket and find your quiet mind and have fun and let it happen—and that's what I'm doing when Paul and Vanessa show up, and the dream day gets even better. The happy couple says hello and smiles, but we keep the talk to a minimum because there is tennis to play, though it's not about a match, no push for games and points; instead we keep it light and spread out onto two courts and I find myself hitting with Paul, like I have so many times over the years, just trying to groove some ground strokes, crosscourt forehands, crosscourt backhands, get them landing deep, then smack it down the line, up on your toes, move your feet, stay loose, and breathe, breathe, breathe. I sink down into it or, better, elevate up into it, so thoroughly absorbed by the task at hand that I don't immediately notice when Diane, Vanessa, and Ben stop hitting just so they can watch, but then when I loop a forehand too deep and Paul lets it go by, they clap, and that startles me and I turn to see them kind of beaming at me, and Ben says "Wow," and Vanessa says, "Don't stop," and Diane says, "You look great," and I don't even hesitate before saying, "No, *you* look great," and then Paul says, "Let's all get back to it now." I'm happy to oblige, and I do so with full knowledge that this is what tennis can do for me, what it always has done for me, bring out the best I've got, whatever that might be, make it visible for others to glimpse, and even before I pummel the next forehand, I sense the day will continue to go well, that Diane will appreciate me even more, that I might even appreciate myself more, and it feels right and good and no longer completely unexpected when Diane spends the rest of the morning, and the afternoon, and the evening by my side, though it does catch me off-guard when she wakes up even earlier than I do and starts the coffee while I shower, don my uniform, and prepare to head back to work.

24

MONDAY MORNING, THE START of a new week, and there were three people in the apartment again, everything running on a familiar schedule, and we all hustled out the door together. Diane helped buckle Ben into his booster seat, and then she walked me to the driver's side. Back in uniform, in the light of day, the strangeness of it all threatened to paralyze me. Diane checked her phone, put her hands on my shoulders, atop the boards on the epaulets, and reached up to kiss my cheek. "You guys have a great day," she said.

"Already am," I said.

"Looks like I might have a trip coming up," she said. "We can talk about it over dinner tonight, but I might need some help."

"Whatever you want," I said. "Whenever you want."

"That's the way I like it," she said.

"Come on, Dad," Ben said. "It's time."

It was clearly going to be a busy day, right from the start. After work, Hank would drive by for a redo with the bike, and a little later Shannon was going to come over to look after Ben while Diane and I stepped out. The lack of sleep would eventually catch up to me, but I felt ready for almost anything. If I had to rush around all day, so be it. I started the engine and we both waved to Diane. "Here we go," I said.

~

I stopped by Neffer's as soon as I clocked in, but the office was empty and there was no sign of him around the break room. So I headed up to the checkpoint. Carelli was supervising and there were a bunch of shiny new blue shirts around, no boards on their epaulets and no badges on their chests. Another way the week was bound to be a doozy: a new cohort of TSOs, moving up on the floor for on-the-job training after two weeks in the classroom. The blueberries, as they were called, had to shadow TSOs at every station, their extra bodies making it more difficult to move around.

I was counting the blueberries—seven—when Carelli said, "Waldman, would you kindly introduce young Brian here to divestiture, lane two?"

Young kid, lanky, with bowl-cut brown hair, big-eyed, eager, a warm smile, and a pointy nose. The uniform was baggy on him. Maybe a basketball player. Early twenties, I guessed, just out of college, if he'd gone to college. A SUNY grad, maybe.

I told Brian to grab extra gloves before I led him over to the position. On the way, I reminded him to enunciate and project. Create calm. Command presence. Then I hung back and watched, like a coach scouting a possible recruit.

The kid had good posture as he moved up and down the line, talking to everyone, making eye contact, bringing the script to life. It didn't sound new—who could make it sound new anymore?—but it didn't sound old either. He spoke the words as if they mattered, as if he genuinely cared about the PAX and their travel experience.

Because he was managing all right, I could surveil the checkpoint a bit more, watch how the other blueberries were faring. First, though, I looked up at the observation deck to see who was studying me. Usually the instructors would be there, close to the glass, gazing down to see how their trainees were performing. All clear at the moment. Over on bag check, lane one, Sanchez was riding an older female blueberry pretty hard, asking her if she was sure she'd picked up the correct bag and was that the best way to carry it and how was she going to see anything in there without really moving the belongings around. "This is your house," Sanchez said, "and this bag is in your house. That makes it your bag. Treat it like you own it. Or maybe run while you can, before the Three Stooges from that cell show up." Sanchez wasn't the only one who took pleasure in convincing new hires to quit, but this older woman looked tough enough to take the heat. She had a blocky body and white hair that reminded me of the biker guy in my long-ago class, the guy who'd covered up his neck tattoo before every shift and then walked when the uniform gave him a rash.

I let the chatter wash over me, enjoying the sound of the accumulated wisdom of cowboys and grinders passing from one generation of Albany TSOs to the next. Then Brian hit a rough patch, flustered by the near simultaneous arrival of an old woman in a wheelchair, a young couple with a cat, and a flight crew. I stepped in to help. I radioed for a wheelchair assist. Kim's blueberry, a quick study, apparently, rushed over to claim the person-with-disability screening, because PWD screening practice was the hardest to get. I told O'Hearn at the mag about the cat couple. Then I showed Brian how to set a few bowls upside down on the belt so Kevin, on X-ray, would know which bags belonged to the crew. Brian absorbed the instruction and I sensed I wouldn't have to repeat myself.

That rhythm continued through one rotation and then another. I was riding my wave of Diane-tennis-postbirthday success, so my attention wasn't fully focused. Plus I expected there'd be a briefing and a Three Stooges update soon. But I embraced my TSA coaching role, close to content. Though I was on the floor, not up in the observation deck, I still felt above it all, blessed by a lingering elevation, and I noticed, not for the first time, that when the seas were calm the worlds of Homeland Security and my mother's hero, Werner Erhard, could overlap. Another way of understanding "multilayered security." It was the power of now, just a different sense of what the now held: threat, threat, threat or enlightenment, enlightenment, enlightenment.

Brian was working hard to follow SOP minute after minute, to say what he was supposed to say, all while also trying to earn respect. To move up. To win the job. To identify the terrorists. But could he feel the grace around him? Was it something I could share? Not just the recognition of it, but the way, when it appeared, you could lean back against it, let it hold you up, make you stronger. It might be easier to explain out on a tennis court. You didn't do anything but show up day after day and, suddenly, you're striking the ball right in the sweet spot again and again. Your miss-hits find their way in, painting the lines. The reflex volleys veer off at perfect angles. When you're serving, every toss rises to the ideal height and you can pound an ace out wide or down the middle at will. If, in between sets, you walk up to the vending machine to buy an energy bar, you reach into your pocket, pull out a handful of coins and it's exact change.

But Brian was sweating. Most likely he hadn't had a new lover spend the night. I walked over to help him through again. I'd share as much of my current good fortune as I could. I was well aware it wouldn't last forever.

"Listen, newbie," I said, "security done right is basically a state of grace."

Then, after our second full rotation, Carelli sent us off to break. Brian talked brightly about himself as we sipped our Starbucks. He was a teacher but he'd been unable to get full-time work, and even the part-time work was sporadic and miserable. An elementary school principal brought him in to help fourth-grade kids with test prep and he couldn't handle the pressure of getting twenty-eight nine-year-olds to perform. For the first time in his life, he suffered from panic attacks. News of the cell near the Canadian border didn't disrupt his sleep like that. Now he was hoping to go to law school, but he needed to bank some money first. He wanted to know how long it would take to become full-time and how often did people transfer and where was I hoping to go? I referred the first two questions to HR, ducked the third question, and asked what kind of law he wanted to practice. Brian said he was undecided.

On the way to the break room, I paused to bang a few knockers on "Clobber."

"Is that SOP?" Brian asked.

"My own private ritual," I said. "Another part of the day."

As Brian stepped up to the statue, two of his fellow blueberries, also heading to the break room, called to him. He left the statue alone and walked toward them. "Thanks for the help," he said. "See you later."

I didn't take his departure personally. It was good to see camaraderie on the job. I banged a few more knockers, hoping my sweet grace ride would continue through the rest of my shift and onward from there.

∾

Ben talked about the bike all the way home from school and he dashed out of the car when he saw Hank waiting for us on the stoop. Hank seemed lighthearted, following along, chatting as Ben wheeled the bike toward the park. I listened as Hank told the story of how Laurie had picked out the bike. She'd been tempted by a hot-pink bike, but Hank had told her that green would be a better color because it meant go go go. I tried to remember my own first bike without training wheels. A red Schwinn with a loud silver bell. I fell off in front of the driveway and scraped up my face. No one wore helmets back then.

And then wire-thin stepfather Morris drifted by, how he sold my father's Saab as quickly as he could, even though I thought it would be mine someday. He laughed when I told him he shouldn't have done that. I wound up trying to fight back tears. "What a Saab story," Morris said, laughing more. "You're not really going to cry about it, are you?"

Of course Ben should have his mother's bike. What had I been thinking?

We stopped at a grassy field by the playground. Ben didn't hesitate. Hank held the handlebars and I held the back of the banana seat. He pushed off and we were running alongside him, then chasing after him. My legs were fried from the return to tennis. Still, I kept up, and when Ben wobbled after a slight bump, I sprinted closer, but he held his balance and accelerated away. "I love it!" he shouted.

Talk about a grace ride.

I stopped next to Hank and we watched Ben circle the playground. "Thanks for giving me another chance with the bike," I said.

"Water under the bridge," he said.

"I looked for Neffer at work today, but he wasn't around."

"Neffer's a busy man," he said, giving nothing away, as usual.

"I heard about Rodgers's false sighting. Must have been a zoo for a little bit."

"She erred on the side we want her to err on," he said. "Extra attention is better than not enough attention."

Ben buzzed by us and sped away. We clapped and waved. "This bike is awesome!" he shouted.

I gave his happiness my full attention.

"You're still enjoying your time with Ms. Strand?" Hank asked.

"I am," I said. "We're going out for dinner later on."

"Must be nice to be around so much money."

"It's not about that," I said. I didn't need to confess that I couldn't stop myself from wondering if Alex would really come through with a substantial reward. A little added financial security wouldn't hurt, that was for sure.

"Right," Hank said, as if he could sense my inner confession. "Well, I'm going to head out after Ben comes back around, but I wanted to let you know I heard Elizabeth reached out to you. Tell her I miss her if she calls in again. Tell her I'm a work-in-progress, but I'm getting there. Can you do that?"

"Of course," I said.

Ben came speeding back toward us. "You're doing great," Hank shouted. "Keep it going! See you soon."

Ben zipped away again and Hank walked back toward his car. Whenever I imagined him doing his FBI work, I pictured terrible deeds. The way he talked about his past encouraged such thinking, but wasn't it at least equally possible that Hank also saved lives? Why hadn't I ever pictured him moving silently through darkness, risking his life to bring food to the starving, water to the thirsty? I watched him take a few more steps, and then he started to jog. Fine form, up on the balls of his feet, arms close to his chest. From the back, he looked like an overdressed boxer deep in training for his next bout.

~

By the time we were back on our block, Ben was a ball of sweat. Still, he couldn't wait to show off for Shannon and Diane. Shannon would get the first demonstration, because she was waiting on the stoop. Ben biked toward her along the sidewalk and she stood up and applauded. He went right by her, heading toward the next corner. I walked up and stood beside her. She looked like she'd just been working out, her skin glistening, her face radiant. She'd been playing less tennis the last few years, training for triathlons instead. I caught a whiff of chlorine.

Ben turned around at the corner and started racing back. I tried to look Shannon in the eye, but she continued to gaze at Ben. That's where her true affection was directed. She'd just been confused. She'd allowed her emotions for the son to envelop the father. "It's good to see you," I said.

"There's something I want to tell you," she said, and she seemed about to say more, but just then the Strands' Lexus pulled up and Diane stepped out, rushing toward me almost as quickly as Ben had rushed to Shannon. Diane wrapped her arms around me and started talking: "Alex was running errands, so I gave him a hand, and we were passing right by, and he said he wanted to talk to you before his trip."

I kissed her cheek and held her close for a moment. "You remember Shannon, don't you?"

"Of course I do," she said, turning to Shannon. "I was hoping to talk more with you at the cemetery—"

Before I could figure out what I should do next, Diane patted my shoulder and nudged me forward. "Go on," she said. "Alex gets cranky if you keep him waiting—"

I started walking away, listening as I went. I heard Ben laughing, shouting, "Watch this! Watch this!" I turned back. The two women were still there and they weren't attacking each other. They were smiling, besotted with Ben and his biking.

Meanwhile, Alex was out of the car, leaning against the front passenger door. No tie today, just a black mock turtleneck, a tweed sport coat, with buttons and a zipper, jeans, and shiny wingtips. "Good to see you out and about," I said, as we shook hands.

"I've been eager to get some time with you," Alex said. "It's been a bit chaotic around the house, though, and now I have to go through with my trip to Japan—"

I pictured him meeting up with Diane's mother in a golden temple. They'd wear long robes, sandals, sip tea as they gazed out over a garden of carefully raked rocks. "I've always wanted to see Kyoto," I said. "My mother dreamed of going. She—"

Alex didn't seem to be listening. He leaned his head back against the car and looked up into the clear sky. "I have so much to get done before I go," he said. "And I need to preserve my strength. My lawyers tell me this trip is unnecessary. They say they can take care of all the paperwork and I could have whatever conversations I want to have on the phone or the computer. But certain things ought to be done in person, even if they're difficult. Especially if they're difficult. Don't you think?"

I flashed to the airport bathroom and the robot-voiced AED, monotoning its instructions before Alex rose back up from the almost dead. That was done in person. What exactly was I being asked?

Don't you think?

Well, I think all the time. I think I think too much.

I leaned my head back too and gazed into the sky with Alex. A few wispy contrails slowly dispersed. "If there's anything I can do to help," I said, "just let me know."

"I suppose I'm getting to that," he said, then his phone chimed. "Time for more medicine." He took a plastic-wrapped capsule out of his sport coat pocket and washed it down with some orange soda he grabbed from the car. I glanced toward the stoop and saw Diane and Shannon walking away, following Ben. The two women waved and Diane called, "We're going around the block. Be right back."

Alex took another sip of the soda and then put the can back in the car. "I'm doing all the talking again," he said. "Not my best habit."

How could I tell him I truly didn't mind? I'd always been more than happy to listen to the father figures that entered my life. I tapped my fingers against the Lexus and remembered Lloyd and the Saab. I remembered plenty of conversations after tennis at Haven, standing by the dean's gold BMW, hoping to hear news of a promotion, a tenure-line opening. And, more recently, there was Neffer and his jerky by the Jeep. "How soon do you leave?" I asked.

"I'm leaving tomorrow," he said. "My doctor told me there were no restrictions, though he warned me to stay away from blowfish. I won't be gone long. But here's part of what I want to tell you: My debt to you hasn't changed. If anything, it's grown more significant. I've learned quite a bit from the way my wife responded to my near-death experience. I've had my suspicions for a while. Still, I'd never have known all I know now if you hadn't helped bring me back to life."

"I was just doing my—"

"You've told me. But let me go on, please."

"I'm listening," I said.

"It's been a pleasure to see this intense connection developing between you and Diane. There's a new light in her eyes. I wanted to believe it came from her relief about me, but I realize it's actually much more about you."

"I don't know."

"That's fine," Alex said. "But I *do* know. What I don't know, however, is if she's talked about her career plans with you since she quit her job."

Now that Alex was waiting for me to speak, I wasn't sure what to say. Whenever Diane talked about not missing her job, I could almost see myself walking into the HR office, saying farewell to the TSA. I hadn't pressed Diane about her plans and all she'd mentioned so far was the desire to travel, to find a house of her own, to explore animal hospital ownership. "Nothing particular," I said. "I know she's looking forward to doing some traveling."

"I'm not surprised," Alex said, rubbing his forehead with his thumb and fingertips. "I hope you'll get to meet her mother someday. It may be illuminating. We were going to meet her in San Francisco on the day you saved my life. When she heard what happened, she canceled her trip and refuses to reschedule. But enough about that. Weren't you about to tell me something about your mother?"

"My mother liked yoga and meditation," I said. "She talked about studying Zen in Japan someday. She settled for a lot of time with EST folks around Big Sur."

"EST," Alex said, smiling. "Who doesn't want to do some self-re-invention on occasion?"

"Did you always know what job you wanted?" I asked. "You were a lawyer and then you became a consultant, right? How did you know it was time to switch?"

Alex laughed. "There were other jobs, too, and not all of them were that admirable. There were defeats as well. Enemies made. I dusted myself off and looked squarely in the opposite direction. Then I got back to work."

I could hear Ben's voice, though I couldn't see him yet. "Hurry up!" he shouted.

Alex stood up straight and rolled his shoulders. "Maybe you're asking about more than jobs, though? I know how difficult it can be to find a new partner. I looked for Faye for a long time and it went very well for a while."

Ben came into view and then the women turned the corner. Shannon began sprinting after Ben. "I'm accelerating!" she shouted.

Ben cackled, rising up from his seat to pedal faster. He zoomed toward the stoop, shouting, "I'm going to win!" Shannon was right behind him, slowing down so he could have his victory. Meanwhile, Diane was walking quickly toward the Lexus. "You both look so serious," she said. "What were you talking about?"

Alex stepped back around the car and opened the driver's door. "Gary was just promising to help ease me on my journey tomorrow," he said. "I told him it would be a pleasure to see him at work without any of the emergency procedures."

"It'll go fine," she said, leaning against me.

"I hope all of you have a nice night," Alex called out, looking over toward the stoop at Shannon and Ben. Then he climbed back into the car, honked, waved, and sped off.

Soon after that, Diane and I called out some farewells of our own, shouting to Ben and Shannon, who were jogging and biking off for another lap around the block. Once they were out of sight, Diane took my hand and said, "Sushi!"

~

As we walked over to the Japanese place on Madison Avenue, I noticed it was becoming easier to be with Diane in public without getting lost in the swirl of my thoughts. It helped to have something like an agenda. We'd eat dinner and discuss whatever was about to happen in Kyoto when Alex arrived.

But Diane was excited about other things. We sat at the sushi bar, our stools close together, ordered our drinks and food, and then she pulled out her phone to show me vacation rental listings. I'd told her some of the places I'd hoped to travel with Laurie and she'd been researching possibilities. "We'll leave Japan off the list for now," she said. "Take a look at this villa outside of Montepulciano. A friend gave me the names of a few amazing restaurants. We can rent bikes. Ben will love it."

I listened to her and leaned close to marvel at the tiny images of vast vineyards and ancient wine cellars. It wasn't an outlandish possibility. I was due a few weeks of vacation and if I could finesse the cost somehow it would be nice to give Ben an international adventure. The kid deserved at least that much.

"After Italy," she said, "we can go up into the Alps or across to Greece. What do you think? Do you think Ben's babysitter would want to come along?"

"You mean Shannon?"

"She's a sweetheart," Diane said. "We had a good walk. I can tell she thought the world of Laurie."

I was nowhere near ready to talk about Shannon with her. I drained my sake cup and the waitress appeared right away, asking if we wanted another bottle. Couldn't hurt to split one more. While we waited for it, I said, "I love the whole vision. Don't get me wrong. But you know the TSA salary range, don't you?"

"You're with me now," she said. "I'm giving you everything. Remember?"

The waitress filled our cups and set the bottle down. "*Kanpei!*" Diane said, and we clinked cups.

I glanced over at the sushi chef, slicing away. "I'm getting hungry," I said.

"We've probably got a few more minutes," Diane said, standing up and offering her hand. "I know something we can do while we wait."

Eventually, I'd have to push her about her career plans. There were other questions, too. But her hand was there, reaching for me. I stood up and took it—it was warm, her grip still strong—and I let her lead me to the women's room. I sensed what she wanted, but pretended not to know. "I'll wait for you," I said.

"Come on," she said. "No one's watching."

Maybe I'd hit the sculpture just right, or maybe the stars had aligned, or maybe the karmic wheel had spun my way once again. Such temporary happiness wasn't without precedent. I had tennis memories of elevating into the zone. There were those long-ago afternoons on the court with my father. A handful of effortless matches, hitting winners at will. There was the magical courtship with Laurie. How stupefied and enthralled I'd been when she handed over those lilies.

I stepped into the bathroom and she locked the door behind us. The women's room wasn't much different from the men's room. The same glass-bowl sink. The same piped-in music. The same dried flowers in a tall orange-brown clay vase. The word *ikebana* came back to me as she flicked off the light.

The switch itself gave off a dim red glow. Diane rested her purse on the toilet tank, leaned against the wall, and opened her arms. I moved toward her. She reached for my belt. "I'll have to stay at home tonight," she said, "so this is our chance."

I hesitated for a moment. *I can be spontaneous, I just like to know when.* This was when. I pulled her dress up. She had her hands on me and she was humming "Edelweiss" again. "Time to bloom and grow," she said.

I knew better than to voice my doubts, but I couldn't resist. "How long before this ends?" I asked.

"Why do you think it has to end?"

"It's what experience has taught me, I guess."

"Fuck experience," she said.

"I'd rather fuck you."

"That's just what you're going to do, darling."

Still, I had another question. "Don't you worry it's too good to be true?"

"It feels too good," she said. "That's true."

I laughed.

"I'm so wet," she said. "Can you feel that?"

"I can."

"Tell me," she said. "Say it."

"You're so wet."

"That's it," she said, easing me in. "All we have to do is let it happen. Isn't that what you were saying out on the courts? Let's practice what you preach. Let's keep blooming and growing forever. We're capable of anything. We can do whatever we want."

It was dark and she was humming in my ear. I flashed to those stories of TSOs using their break time to fuck in airport bathrooms. Plenty of people had lost their jobs that way in terminals across the country. But I didn't think there were any cameras here.

I adjusted my stance and lifted her a little higher. Innovation. Integrity. Team spirit. Quiet might also be a good attribute, given our current location. I wanted to cover her mouth, but I didn't have a free hand.

"It feels incredible when you do that," she said. She wrapped her legs around me and held me even tighter.

I laughed again. "Whoa," I said.

"Do you feel anything ending?"

"Well, I'm getting close here."

"Me too," she said, "but I'm not talking about that. It all feels like a beginning to me."

I couldn't really speak anymore. I chased another flash of Nora Flint, hoping she might once again cast her deflating spell. The sink full of dirty dishes. Another breath. But it was no use. I tried to pull out.

Diane didn't release me. "I want to give you everything," she said.

"I'm going to—"

"It okay," she said.

I held myself as still as I could.

"Stay with me," she whispered. "You saved Alex's life. Why shouldn't I save yours?"

She raked her fingernails down my back and, somewhere deep inside, she squeezed me tighter. I couldn't wait any longer.

"I'm right with you," she said.

I let it all go.

~

After dinner I thought we'd walk back to the apartment together and I'd give her a ride home, but she called an Uber while I took care of the bill. "Shannon told me she didn't want to stay out too late," she said. "But tomorrow's not too long to wait, is it?"

"It'll feel like a long time," I said.

"That was so nice in there," she said, as we left the restaurant. "I agree," I said.

Outside, buzzed, puzzled, full and tired, I walked her to the car. We kissed good night and I strolled back home alone. I took my time walking, trying to make sense of Diane and whatever was happening between us. And then, suddenly, I sensed Laurie nearby. Had I offended her spirit? I turned and glimpsed her, right by my side. There was something different about her and I got it almost immediately. She was pregnant. *Way* pregnant. Deep in the third trimester. The sight of her belly out to there, almost bumping into me, nearly made me laugh. Or cry. Was that Ben again, or some future never-to-be baby, the one we'd been talking about trying to have after her birthday? She hadn't carried so low before, if I could trust my memory, but it was all a blur. So much was a blur.

And now, here she is, and I can see her mouth moving, but I can't hear a thing. I slow down, let her set the pace, and I do my best to read her beautiful pale-red bee-stung lips. Those lips, her voice—I miss her so hard I might fall over. I move closer to listen. She's not talking about the baby. She's talking about my new job and I remember the conversation she is for some reason reenacting. Didn't it take place in our kitchen? But here is where she is and she's saying she likes the idea of steady work and she's sure I'll be good at it if I put my mind to it. She pauses to lean against a streetlight, as if to catch whatever remains of her breath. *It's like I told my brother*, she says. *He wanted to enlist and I thought he should finish college but he said he wanted to protect people.* She rests her crossed arms on the shelf of her outrageous belly. I want to rest a hand there too. I'd love to plant a kiss right above her belly button and talk about something different. So many questions. Why this visit? Had I gone too far too fast? And, most important, I want to beg forgiveness, about Diane, about everything else. When I reach out to touch her, she fades away a little. Then she starts waddling forward again and continues the old conversation. *I told him he didn't need to protect me,* she says. *They always told him that was his job. I worried he'd miss—*

I miss you, I'm about to say. *You.* But right in front of me some partying college kids bustled out of a car, dressed to the nines, ready to hit the Lark Street bars. I gave them space and walked on, trying to block out their raucous noise, hoping Laurie would reappear.

She's sitting on the stoop, waiting for me, so I sit beside her. I place an open hand on her belly and this time she doesn't fade away. She glances down, smiles, and then it's back to the old conversation. *I'm sure the TSA will be fine,* she says. *At least for a while. Then we can see. You won't follow in his footsteps—*

What about now? I ask. *What should I do now?*

Shh, she says, and I can almost feel her hand on the back of my neck, guiding my head down ever so slightly.

I bend and press my ear against her belly and I hear the pulsing, feel the fluttering, and there, right there, a kick comes at me, a little bang. I sit back up to peer into my dead wife's face. She's disappearing. *Whatever you want, baby,* she says. *Whatever you want.*

Her lips are still visible, her eyes slowly closing, and I want to believe she's smiling as she vanishes, but it might have been a grimace. I can't deny the possibility. *Honey,* I say, *I'm so sorry. I'm lost without you. Don't go.*

Then she's gone again and I hear the door to the building open and shut behind me.

~

When I turned around, I saw Shannon walking down the steps. She sat next to me, unaware of how shocked I was to suddenly see someone alive and breathing. A change in the air. An electric spark, and yet I longed to shut my eyes tight and bring Laurie back.

"The boy's sound asleep," Shannon said. "I saw you out here."

"Diane told me you wanted to head home early," I said. "I didn't mean to hold you up."

"So glad you and Diane are thinking about what I want," she said.

It took real effort to look over at her. I made eye contact for a moment and then looked up into the sky where a half-moon was slowly rising higher, a hazy ring around it. "Shannon, I don't know what—"

"It's okay, Coach," she said. "It's late. We don't need to get into anything tonight. You've got more than enough going on. Were you on the phone?"

I kept gazing into the dark sky, watching the stars appear as my eyes adjusted. "Do you ever see Laurie now?"

She slid closer. "I'm aware of her, but I've never seen her. You mean like a ghost or something?"

I nodded. "I just walked home with her, I think."

"Have you seen her before?"

"Not like this. She was so pregnant."

"What was she saying?"

"I was asking her what I should do. I was asking her not to go."

"Did you ask her about Diane?"

A fair question, and I heard surprisingly little judgment in it. Still, maybe I'd talked too much. I slapped my thigh, ready to stand and end the conversation.

"Sorry," Shannon said. "That wasn't super-nice."

I stayed where I was. "I'm guessing she knows all about it," I said, "if that doesn't sound too kooky."

"No kookier than anything else these days. You could ask me about Diane if you wanted. I wouldn't mind. I'd give you one woman's sense of another woman."

"Tempting," I said, "but I'd rather ask you about you. What has this year been like for you?"

She glanced back up at the apartment window. "I don't know what to say about the year. Too much for a late-night chat, probably. But I can tell you that being with Ben is the best part of my life right now. And I can see it's the same for you. I see how you are around him. You stand up straighter."

"Do you ever want kids of your own?"

"What do you think, Sherlock?"

I wasn't feeling like a very talented detective at all. Why had Laurie come to me so pregnant? I focused back on Shannon. "I think you'd be a great mom," I said.

"You're still not asking me about Diane, are you?"

"Is there something you want to tell me about her?"

"You're going to have to ask. For now, I'll just say what I wanted to say earlier, before everyone else arrived."

"Go ahead."

"You might deserve it, you might not, but I've decided to wait and see what happens. There's Ben, and I've chosen him. It's more than that, though."

"Do you know something about her?"

"You're going to have to really ask me if you want to ask me, Coach. I don't want to be that woman who offers unsolicited advice, especially in a situation like this."

Maybe it was enough to know I could ask whenever I wanted. Maybe I was deciding to wait and see as well. "I'll keep that in mind," I said.

"Okay," she said.

"I like the woman you are," I said. "For the record."

"Yeah, yeah," she said. "Go in and get some rest. I'm betting you need it."

She pecked my cheek, stood up, and walked to her car. She waved before climbing in. I watched her drive away and then, before climbing the stairs, I glanced up once more at the half-moon. The other half was there too, in darkness. I couldn't remember if it was something I could really see or if my brain just filled out the circle. I opened my eyes wider. As I stared, the hazy ring around the moon seemed to rotate.

25

THE NEXT MORNING I WAS BACK to solo-parenting, getting breakfast ready, packing the lunch, when the phone buzzed on the table. Ben, sitting right there, answered it and handed it over. "She says her name's Elizabeth," he said. "She wants to talk to you."

I took the phone. "Good morning," I said.

"Have you heard from him?" she asked.

Maybe she'd learned her abruptness from Hank. She sounded upset, though, so I kept it simple. "We've been texting a little," I said.

"How did he seem?"

"Hard to tell," I said. "But, listen, I've got to rush out the door. I don't mean to be rude. If there's something I can—"

"He used to do this thing before he headed off on his missions," she said. "He'd call me and say a lot of sentences beginning with *Just in case* and *I want to make sure you know*. Well, he left me one of those messages this morning and I thought he might still be with you."

"I'm hoping to see him later."

"Tell him I'm thinking of him. Tell him we can talk, okay?"

"Funny," I said. "He wanted me to tell you the same things. Have you tried calling him?"

"When he doesn't want to be reached, no one can reach him. You know that much, don't you?"

If she was still on the West Coast, then it was the middle of the night for her. I imagined her sitting on a hotel bed, talking in the dark, worried. "There's a lot I don't know," I said. "I don't even know where you're calling from."

"I haven't gone far," she said. "San Francisco. You can tell him if he asks."

"He says he misses you."

"He's a good, honorable man," she said. "I know he misses me, but I need him to miss me more."

"Can I ask you something?"

"You're the one who said you had to rush."

I stepped out of the kitchen, so Ben couldn't hear my next question. "Do you think he'll ever forgive me for what happened to his sister?"

She went silent and I could hear the quiet of whatever room she was in. "He'd have to learn how to forgive himself first."

"But it wasn't his fault."

"Depends how you look at it, I guess."

Wasn't that what Laurie had been trying to tell me? She worried about Hank's lifelong need to protect her.

"Also," Elizabeth said, "he might be seeking forgiveness for a few other things, too."

Ben stepped out of the kitchen to find me. He had his schoolbag over his shoulder. "Come on, Dad," he said.

"That must be your son," Elizabeth said. "Sometimes it feels like Hank talks about him all the time. I don't think he's ever sent a postcard to anyone else his whole life."

"Dad!"

"Go ahead," Elizabeth said. "I'll call again if I hear anything. If you do see him, tell him I miss him too."

~

In the car, Ben had his own questions. "Can we call Diane?"

"She's running around this morning. We can call her after school, though. Did you miss seeing her for breakfast?"

"I wanted to ask her more about my book show-and-tell," he said. "It might happen today."

"What did you want to ask her?"

"She was telling me what to do if I felt shy."

"What was her advice?"

"She told me to imagine that everyone in the room was tiny. Like little ants. She also said that I'd get used to it the more I did it."

"That makes sense."

"Do you ever feel shy?"

"Of course."

"What do you do?"

Sometimes my nose would bleed before matches. Sometimes I couldn't sleep at all the night before. "I guess I practice," I said. "You did great in front of the audience at Mom's ceremony. Do you want to try the report out on me? Pretend I'm your class?"

Ben pulled a book from his bag as we took our place in the car line. "You have to promise not to interrupt," he said. "You have to stay quiet. And you have to pay attention."

"Is that what your teacher says?"

"Those are the rules."

"I'm pretty good at following rules."

Ben held the familiar book up so I could see it in the rearview mirror and then he began. "*If I Built a House* is about a boy named Jack. He has a big face and a tiny body. He tells his mom and dad all about the house he wants to build someday. He draws the plans himself. It will be a big house with things like an aquarium and an art room and a giant slide."

How many times had I read that book out loud? I waited a moment to make sure the show-and-tell was over. I didn't want to interrupt. I rolled closer to the front of the line. "I'm sorry we don't have a house like that," I said.

"It's okay. Diane does."

Before I could begin to reckon with that, Irene opened the door. "I just practiced my show-and-tell," Ben said.

"Can't wait to hear it," she said.

I watched him go, wondering how far ahead he was already thinking. He was a few steps beyond me and I thought I was the one moving quickly. Then the phone buzzed again. The caller ID read Command Center. It was a number we'd all been told to store in our phones the first day of training. We were supposed to call in when we were running late, for any reason whatsoever. I'd had to use it a few times over the years, but this was the first time a call had come my way.

"Waldman, Neffer here. You still have your son with you?"

"I'm just dropping him off."

"We'd like you to bring him in today for a bit of the morning. I'm aware it's short notice, but as you probably know Alex Strand is flying again today and it seems someone has arranged a little media circus for you after all. There's a desire to broadcast some good news."

"What do you mean?"

"The folks upstairs believe your son would increase your heroic aura and make better PR. I told them it was a lot to ask. It's completely up to you."

Ben was almost at the school's front door.

"What do you think?"

I'd worked hard to arrange a life so that Ben's schooling was almost never disrupted. I didn't like the idea of messing with the book report schedule. But I didn't want to disappoint Neffer or Strand or Diane. And I liked the idea of maybe impressing my son. "I'll need to hustle to get him."

"Go on, then. Clock in and bring him right up to the checkpoint. I'll explain more later."

∽

It wasn't until I was driving Ben away from the school, following my usual route to work, that the scope of what I was doing began to hit me. I hadn't flown anywhere since at least a year before Ben was born. All these days at the airport, but I'd never walked my son into the terminal.

I tried to revel in Ben's excited questions. "Can I wear a uniform?" and "Will they search me?" and "Can I stay the whole day?" and "Will Diane be there?" I shared the little I knew and said we were lucky to have a chance like this. "You have to stay with me and listen carefully, okay?"

"I promise," Ben said.

I led him from the employee lot to baggage claim and then through a door next to the men's room that opened into a narrow hallway. Ben, full of energy, almost bounced forward with each step, oblivious to the cameras watching us. The first time I'd walked through this corridor by myself I'd been so nervous I'd almost forgotten how to enter my code in the security door. I was going to get fired on day-one of on-the-job training. Fortunately, I'd been joined in the corridor by one of the old-timers, a tall, ex-window salesman named Bill, who'd reminded me how to use my card and code. "Swipe, enter your last four, wait for the green," Bill had said. "And then don't forget to close the thing in my face."

Whoever was watching the cameras this morning must have been briefed by Neffer and the suits. I unlocked the door and held it open for Ben and no alarms went off. Together we cut across a piece of the tarmac near the Southwest gates. Ben slowed down to look out toward the runways. It would be a blast to walk him out to an airplane, greet some other airport workers, but that would be big trouble. Besides, Ben wasn't asking for that. He was just gazing out toward the vast expanse of asphalt-covered marshland. I put a hand on his shoulder and pointed to the yellow line on the tarmac that led from one door to another. "We have to stay on this line," I said.

"Okay," Ben said, leaning in closer. "Did you ever bring Mom out here?"

"I never did."

"Why not?"

"Well, today they asked me to bring you in. They never asked me to bring her, so it would have been against the rules."

"I don't think she would have liked the smell anyhow."

I laughed. "You're probably right," I said. Then I pointed to two great blue herons lifting off out of the cattails beyond the runways.

"Mom would have liked that," he said.

The birds appeared ungainly at first, their legs and wings folded in ways that seemed to work against each other, making flight improbable. Then their bodies straightened, parallel with the ground, and they were suddenly elegant and immense, gaining altitude. We stood together and watched them swoop off toward the larger marsh out beyond the long-term parking lot.

"Closest thing we get to pterodactyls, right?" I said.

"I think that's pelicans, Dad."

"Come on, Dino-man," I said, smiling, and we followed the yellow line to the security door that opened into the terminal right by the break room. It would be nice to bump into Bill again, but he'd retired a few years back. I hoped we wouldn't run into August or Sanchez first. Fortunately, Kevin was at his locker. "Whoa," he said. "If I'd known it was bring-your-kids-to-work day I would've brought my own."

"Neffer's orders," I said. "Some kind of media thing."

Kevin reached down to muss Ben's hair. "What's up, little man?"

Ben smiled and chatted with Kevin while I wondered what it would have been like to bring Laurie through. She'd never asked. I'd never offered. A few more coworkers stopped by and said good morning to Ben. The kid looked proud, wide-eyed and standing tall. All I had to do was keep it that way. When Sanchez and August walked in, they kept their distance, glowering. They were studying the photos of the Stooges on the bulletin board again. "Make sure your kid knows about these photos," Sanchez said. "They always say kids don't miss a trick."

"Which photos, Dad?" Ben asked.

"I'll show you another time," I said, determined to keep my distance. "Right now it's time to clock in. And there's something I want to show you upstairs."

Kevin lingered with Sanchez, August, and a few others. As I led Ben past the small crowd, I heard Kevin say, "I take it as motivation, man. If I save some lives, then I can bring my kids in."

"What do you want to show me?" Ben asked.

"We're almost there," I said, and then I led him to the main concourse, right up to "Clobber." "Here's what I do whenever I walk by this sculpture," I said. I reached up, grabbed one of the larger knockers, and slammed it against the wood.

Ben laughed. "We're allowed to do that?"

"That's what it's here for."

Ben reached over, raised a knocker up, and let it drop.

"You can do it louder than that if you want," I said.

Ben slammed a few more, as did I. We were making a serious racket. Passengers glanced over, but they didn't break stride, lost in their own travels. I could feel the metallic clanging in my teeth. That didn't stop me from banging more. Then I saw Neffer walking our way from the checkpoint. I felt glad to see him. He approached Ben first. "Good morning," he said, kneeling down. "Remember that Band-Aid you gave me?"

Ben nodded.

"Well, I've been meaning to give you something back," Neffer said. He reached into his sport coat's inside pocket and pulled out a TSA Junior Officer sticker. "Mind if I put this on your shirt? It will help you at the checkpoint."

Ben smiled, even though I'd already brought home dozens of the stickers. Sometimes Ben gave them away himself to kids in the neighborhood.

Neffer pressed the sticker onto Ben's chest and stood up, stepping my way. "Now, about this sculpture," he said. "I've seen you knocking here before, Officer." He reached over and banged one of the largest knockers. "It's not on the placard or anything, but I've heard the artist was inspired by a D. H. Lawrence poem. I only remember the last few lines. Care to hear them?"

"Seriously?" I said.

"Don't look so surprised," Neffer said. "Your brother-in-law isn't the only one who reads poetry." He kept his hand on the knocker he'd banged as he recited the lines.

> What is the knocking at the door in the night?
> It is somebody wants to do us harm.
>
> No, no, it is the three strange angels.
> Admit them, admit them.

"I'm impressed," I said.

"I'm glad," Neffer said, "but now we have a media circus to attend. Let's clobber this thing once more with feeling before we go."

I drifted toward Laurie, wherever whatever remained of her might be. Strange angel, spirit, dust. I knocked again because I wanted to thank her for last night's visit. And I wanted her to see me alive, enjoying my time with Ben, the two of us moving on as best we could. Then I knocked one last time to tell her I'd still be cautious. And more spontaneous. And I'd never forget her, no matter where we lived, or with whom. I wanted her to rest in peace. Maybe it was as simple as that.

Then why was I making so much damn noise?

Ben stayed close as we walked up to the checkpoint. "I like it here," he said.

I rested a hand on his shoulder again. "What do you like about it?"

"It's fun," he said.

Neffer laughed. "We should get you to say that when the cameras are rolling."

Diane texted in just before the shift started. *Could b even wilder tonight. See u soon.* At the checkpoint, the chaos of the newbies was lessening a bit as they settled into day two. Brian was shadowing Singh over at the document checking station and he seemed to be doing fine.

Ben started in with another flurry of questions—"What is that woman doing?" and "How does that machine work?" and "Why do they have to hold their arms up like that?" I wanted to explain it all as best I could, but the man in charge of the whole place, the airport's Federal Site Director, Arnold Bentley, was walking my way. Carelli stepped over and asked if he could show Ben the supervisor's podium. "Please?" Ben said, and I let him go.

I'd never spoken to Bentley one-on-one. My main memory of the guy was from a few years back, soon after he'd arrived on-site, when he came to introduce himself during a briefing. He hadn't come across as much of a leader. He'd slouched into a chair and complained about a head cold. "I have just one more point," he said three times, for three different points. Then he'd mumbled a final conclusion about the Global War on Terror and the destructive, borderline traitorous work of so many journalists.

The guy still seemed to be suffering from a head cold. He was making an effort at least, offering his hand. But the handshake was limp, the hand skeletal, the thank you almost inaudible. Then he mumbled more about clearing his desk and off he went.

Neffer shook his head as he watched Bentley shuffle away. "I'm glad that happened before the newspaper folks arrived," he said. "The less time he gets in front of TV crews, the better off we'll be."

"You're expecting TV crews?"

"Your lady gave you zero warning? Must have been too busy giving you other things."

I still didn't mind being ribbed by him. I shook my head and let it go.

Neffer leaned against the closed door of the small room we used when PAX requested private screenings. "Well, here's what I couldn't get to on the phone," he said. "TSA HQ is embracing the rare shot at good publicity. There's basically nothing I like about it. Maybe it's another way of testing me, but no one will say that. In any case, they're letting the media cover the reunion between the hero, the hero's son, and the back-from-the-dead man. They want to capture it as-it-happens. A joyous checkpoint moment."

"Okay."

"You let them get the handshake. A hug or two. Tell them you didn't have a choice—"

"I was doing what anyone would do."

"There you go. You could say you were just being a decent human being. You could say you're a part of a team and this was a team win. This is simply the way the TSA does business, day in, day out."

"I get the message."

"I need you to deliver the message. And I need to trust that you won't be distracted by that beguiling thinny-thin-thin woman."

"I'll do my—"

"I know about your best," Neffer said. "And I believe in it. What I can't believe is that I'm almost out of here and your brother-in-law is floating around somewhere behind the scenes, supervigilant about a high-level threat. He won't tell me any more than he's already told me."

"It's his job."

"I know that," Neffer said. "And I'm counting on you to do your job. Chloe is counting on you too."

Over at the podium, Ben was standing next to Carelli, staring at a computer screen, a walkie-talkie in his hand.

"We'll have you on bag check, lane three," Neffer said. "Your hard-working newbie Brian will be shadowing at X-ray, so it's a chance to inspire the new guy, too. Carelli will bring Ben over for a few shots. You tell them you can't leave your post and that helps keep the whole spectacle short. You say, *I need to get back to work.* Then we let them go their merry way, and once they're gone you can head off to drop Ben back at school, okay?"

"Understood," I said.

"Have I mentioned I don't like anything about this?"

"You have."

"We're here to do our job and this is not our job," Neffer said. Then he shook his head, stood up straighter, and checked his watch. It was the gold antique today. "You don't have any food on you, by any chance?"

"I've got some lunch in my locker."

"After all I've shared with you," he said, smiling. "Man, I'm hungry." He clapped his hands. "They'll be here any minute. Get to your post."

I stepped to lane three and before I could even get my gloves on, Brian waved me over, pointed to the image on the screen, and said, "Could be a knife."

The only way to get good at X-ray was to put in the time. You paid attention and built your image repertoire, and after hours and hours of practice you could recognize objects almost immediately. "Toy car," I said, and I quickly scanned the PAX line, looking for Diane and Alex. No sign of them yet. No cameras either. Then I checked to see who was waiting for a carry-on. "Bag goes with that guy over there?"

Brian nodded.

"Probably a gift for his kid or something like that. You want me to take a look?"

"I guess not."

"You're one hundred percent sure?"

"No."

"I'm on bag check and you're on X-ray, right?"

"Right."

I finished pulling on my gloves and gave them a little snap. "Then tell me to search the bag."

That's where I was, doing my job, pawing through another dad's belongings, when Diane, Alex, three reporters, and a bunch of camera-carrying men and women began to make their way through the checkpoint. They weren't going all the way through, so they didn't pass through the scanners. They all gathered by the X-ray station. Neffer was moving from line to line, reminding everyone to maintain focused attention.

Alex was leaning heavily on Diane. He looked like he'd gotten worse overnight. Maybe he was trying to justify the gate pass for Diane. But he seemed paler. How much did he dread this trip? The spectacle of it couldn't please him either.

I finished up with the search—it turned out to be a black Hot Wheels Corvette Stingray. I ran the bag back through again with the car in a separate bowl. Then I returned the bag to the waiting father and tried to steady myself for whatever was to come.

Brian was distracted by all the hoopla, so I made a point of looking over the screen. Neither Diane nor Alex was carrying much. One man-purse and one medium-sized woman's purse. Alex must have checked at least one suitcase. I wanted a chance to wish Alex an easy trip and I would have liked a chance to do much more with Diane. Brian started to ask me a question, but then the first reporter was right there and some flashes popped. Diane hugged me. "This is the man who saved my stepfather's life," she said.

More flashes popped and my vision blurred. It felt like they were shoving cameras and phones right into my face. Diane was gone again. I heard voices: "Let's get a handshake" and "Hold it" and "Smile" and "One more." My heart raced as I did my best to cycle through my lines. I glimpsed someone standing beside a cameraman, holding a mic connected to a long pole, staring very intently at Diane. At first I thought it looked a little like Thomas, but the beard was all wrong. Still, the guy seemed familiar. Or maybe it was just good old Smallbany.

Then Carelli was leading Ben over and more bright lights flashed. I focused my attention on my son's face. He didn't look scared. As far as I could tell, he remained thrilled. "Wow, Dad," he said. "Thanks again for bringing me here. This is great!"

I leaned down and spoke into his ear. "Glad you're having fun. We'll head back to school in a few minutes." Then I stood up straight and spoke my lines as clearly as I could: "I need to return to work now."

I expected the words to function like a cue. Time to clear out the checkpoint so we could all get back to our jobs. "I need to return to work now," I repeated, but the words had no effect. Neffer was nowhere in sight. Some PAX in lane two were trading snide comments about how desperate the TSA was for good publicity. "Doesn't matter if they slow the whole place down," said one guy. "The news won't show how this line isn't moving at all," said another.

Carelli began urging the reporters and cameramen to leave. "Time's up," he was saying. "Thank you for coming by. Please step back to the front of the checkpoint. Director Bentley will be making a brief statement down by baggage claim in just a few minutes."

Diane was grabbing her purse off the belt. Alex was stepping toward her, but first he stopped next to me and said, "Take good care of her."

"I'll do my best," I said.

"And watch out for her too," he added.

"Of course I will," I said. "Have a safe trip."

Despite Carelli's efforts, a few reporters pushed forward, shouting more questions as the cameras kept pressing in: "How did it feel?" and "Do you think the TSA gets a bad rap?" and "Do you like your job?"

"We're a team," I said, trying to stay on-message. "I need to get back to work with my team."

Diane rushed over into the crowd and gave me another hug. More lights flashed. "My hero," she said. She kissed my cheek and moved her lips to my ear. "I'll come find you on my way back," she whispered. "I might need some help."

"I'll be right here," I said, and then she was gone, hustling to get her arm around Alex.

There was applause and a few more flashes before Carelli finally cleared out the cameras and the reporters. Diane and Alex walked away from the checkpoint. I rested an open hand on top of Ben's head and, for a moment, I felt truly proud. Together we watched Diane glance back toward us. The look on her face gave me a chill. Why? I couldn't put my finger on it. She waved and blew a kiss. Ben waved back.

I kept watching. Something about them held my attention. Did I expect them to stop and bang "Clobber"? That wasn't it. The feeling was very different from the joy I'd felt standing by the sculpture with Neffer and Ben and the spirit of Laurie.

"Showtime's over, everybody," Carelli called out. "Back to work, please."

When I looked down the concourse again, they were turning toward Alex's gate. Neffer walked over. "We'll give the media folks a chance to vamoose. Then you get this boy back to school."

"Can't I stay for the whole day?" Ben asked.

"I wish," I said. "That would make the job even more fun."

"You both did great," Neffer said. "I believe it actually might not have been terrible, but we won't know for sure until we see the coverage. And we'll see how Director Bentley does downstairs. I'll come back to escort you guys to your car in a few minutes."

While I waited, whatever was nagging at me drew me toward tennis and led me back to an afternoon during my early years on UAlbany's tennis team, when I still believed I was getting better, rising up toward a shot at playing number-one singles, with the chance to make some noise in the NCAAs, at least regionally, and no one could ever say for sure, of course, but a pro career of some sort wasn't yet completely off the table. Melissa, my girlfriend back then, would come to most of the home matches, sit up front in the bleachers and cheer me on. She saw me win and she saw me lose. I was a work-in-progress. Who wasn't? She had faith in me. Then, one day, I walked out on the court to play against a sophomore from Stony Brook. The kid didn't look old enough to be in college. He barely looked old enough for high school. He was a baby-faced string bean and he didn't break a sweat as he blew me off the court. After losing the first set at love, I was determined to take a game, build on that, wear the kid down, grind it out. I'd clawed my way back into matches many times before. The kid must have sensed my willingness to run harder. No problem. He led me from side to side, up and back, like a puppet on a string, and then, at will, he'd crush a winner. I couldn't tell whether it was out of boredom or kindness that the kid eventually switched back to his first-set tactics, finishing off points as quickly as he could. I never got a game. Never even managed a break point. When it was time to meet the kid at the net and shake hands, I struggled to walk. I couldn't remember ever feeling so dismantled, but I tried to stand up straight, hold my head high. Someday maybe I'd be able to say that I'd been absolutely thrashed by the latest incarnation of Agassi or Sampras or McEnroe. I could live with that. I'd be in good company. I shook the kid's hand and wished him luck. Then I turned to Melissa, sitting shoulders hunched on the bleachers, and I saw on her face the look that resembled whatever Diane had just shared with me.

I didn't find out right away, but that had been a farewell glance. Later, I'd learned Melissa had once dated the guy who'd shellacked me. Turned out she'd been trying to lure that baby-faced string bean back for a while. She waited until she'd traveled back and forth to Stony Brook a few times after that match before officially ending it with me.

"Some people," Paul had said, "need to step from one boat directly into another."

She claimed it hadn't been planned at all. She said it had nothing to do with how brutally I'd been defeated. It was complicated, she insisted. But I knew I'd been betrayed. Used. It had all been there in her face when I hobbled up to the net. She showed me that face once more, just before she walked away for good, two heavy bags slung over her tiny shoulders.

Then it hit me. I jogged over to Brian. "They were each carrying one bag, weren't they?"

Brian was devoting all his attention to the bags coming through. "Who?" he asked.

I walked back to Ben, replaying the scene in my mind. As they walked down the concourse, it looked like Alex had his own bag and Diane somehow had her purse and another bag. Was that really what I'd seen? Was I really going to let it bother me? Maybe I'd check when she came back through.

But it *did* bother me. And who was that guy with the mic who wasn't Thomas? Seemed to have a lot of extra bags looped over his shoulders.

Neffer was back, talking to me, saying it was almost time to go.

What would she put in a bag that she didn't want X-rayed? I'd missed something. A gun? Armed Lady. But maybe the purse had just been bouncing on her shoulder. I turned to Neffer. "Did you notice how many bags the Strands had with them?"

Neffer stared at me. "What do you mean?"

"I'm not sure, but I think they might have showed up with two and walked away with three."

Ben spoke up. "Diane had two bags with her. Alex had one small one."

I knelt down to look him in the eyes. "You're sure?"

Ben nodded.

Time to run after Diane and find out what was going on. *We're capable of anything,* she'd said. *We can do whatever we want.* I couldn't make it all fit, but, suddenly, her words terrified me.

Carelli came over and before he could speak, I nudged Ben toward him. "Stay here," I said. "I'll be right back."

"Wait a second," Neffer said. "Talk to me. It's another drill, isn't it? They're testing me, right?"

But I couldn't wait. What was I going to say? *It was the look on her face.* That wouldn't help. The best I could offer would be: *It was too good to be true.*

And that guy with the beard! He had those blue eyes that had been driving Sanchez wild!

"Call my brother-in-law," I said. "Tell him one of those guys from the photos was a bearded cameraman and just passed an uncleared bag to Diane. I'm hoping he already knows somehow." And then I was off, running down the concourse.

26

As I ran past "Clobber," I had no idea what to do. I was a TSO. I should wait for Hank and the LEOs. But there was no time to wait now.

I slowed before reaching the gate. Preboarding was complete. Alex was gone and a line of passengers was filing peacefully onto the plane. Diane was standing by the window, not far from the door to the jetway. She looked furious. She had one bag in her hand and a purse slung over her shoulder. The bag was black, with plenty of Velcro and zippers—something that might once have been used to lug cameras around.

That was the uncleared bag she'd been handed.

I couldn't be the only layer of security at this point, could I? The people shuffling forward in line didn't seem to sense any danger. The gate agent was oblivious, scanning one boarding pass after another. Diane gazed out at the plane, still unaware of me.

I switched off my radio so she wouldn't hear any chatter and walked up beside her. "Hi," I said, trying to create calm, for her and myself.

She startled, gripping the bag tighter. Leakage. "It's you," she said. "I thought you were working. Are you on break?"

I still couldn't put it all together, but this woman wasn't who I'd thought she was. Could it be that maybe, just maybe, she was being forced to do whatever she was doing? I wished I could believe it. But I sensed the truth was simpler and more familiar: She'd been toying with me. "Are you all right?" I asked.

"I just need some time," she said. "Let me wait here by myself for a while. I'll catch up to you on my way out."

I stared at her and I could almost see her standing in my kitchen, resting a hand on my shoulder as she poured my coffee, then sitting down beside me, pulling her chair close. With a little more effort, I could see her out on the tennis court, so comfortable with Paul and Vanessa and Ben, watching me with such clear admiration. And there we were, on my bed, and she was holding me with all her might.

It had been too easy. I knew it had been too easy. When had she worked out what she was going to do? Whatever this was, it could have been unfolding from the moment she appeared at the checkpoint in her yoga tights. She'd rushed into the bathroom with Alex's phone and who knows who she'd been talking to. The pat down in the clothes closet and everything else—just part of a plan. She'd studied the checkpoint, she'd learned I was vulnerable, she'd waited for an opportunity, and she'd reeled me in. But why? To do what exactly? To be a part of a jihadist's plot? To blow up Alex's plane?

"Are you waiting to watch the take-off?" I asked.

"Sweetheart," she said, and I could hear the strain behind the word. It had never been real. It certainly wasn't real now.

"What is it?"

"I'll come find you when I'm done."

"Done with what?"

She sighed. Her hand still held the bag tightly. Was there a timer? What did Sanchez's blue-eyed Curly still have with him?

"Alex was worried about this trip," I said.

"He's going to divorce my mother," she said.

"I'm sorry." I risked putting a hand on her shoulder. "How about we sit down?"

She stepped away from me. "You don't understand."

Help must be coming. I just had to stall her long enough, keep her talking. Up and down the concourse, the cameras were rolling. Someone could see what was happening, even if the PAX and personnel around me remained oblivious. The line inched forward, the PAX boarding like lemmings.

I needed to stay calm. All that old talk about disguise and deception with my tennis players. Disguise the serve. Disguise the spin. Pay attention because your opponent will be trying equally hard to deceive you. I'd repeated those truths every season even though deception had never been my strength as a player. On the court and off, I was a grinder. What you saw was what you got, despite the fact that life kept trying to teach me the opposite.

I could learn, couldn't I? Make some new rules. Try following them?

Maybe my message had been unclear. Maybe Hank and the LEOs were rushing to protect Director Bentley down by baggage claim.

"You look thirsty," I said. "I'm going to get a drink of water. It'll give you a little time alone. Can I bring you anything?"

"I'm fine," she said.

"I'll be right back," I said. I walked to the water fountain on the other side of the concourse. As I leaned down for a drink, I switched on my radio and told the dispatcher to send LEOs right away. Then I switched the radio back off.

Diane had turned her face to the window again, staring out at the plane. Was she hoping to catch sight of Alex, peering back at her? Boarding was almost complete. She had some sort of timer in the bag and a bomb somewhere on the plane—that was my best guess, as insane as it seemed. She must have a gun, too. She was waiting for the plane to get up in the air. Would she push the button herself? She'd told Ben to think of other people as tiny ants.

I could hear my mother talking about acceptance. *This is the way it worked out. You don't like it? Too bad.* Twists of fate. The turning of the karmic wheel. These ideas invented by humans to explain terrible accidents. But they could also explain how we can take each other for awful rides. Lift each other up one day, destroy each other the day after.

By the time I was standing next to her again, I couldn't believe how scared I was. She had the bag slung over her left shoulder now. "Have you talked with your mother?" I asked.

"He's going over there to tell her in person. The whole reason she went there was to stop him from telling her."

I tried to keep my voice steady. She wasn't moving farther away, but she wouldn't look at me either. "Maybe they can work it out," I said. "Maybe that's why he's making the trip. It might wind up being a good thing."

"I can't let it happen," she said. "He'll change his will. I'll lose everything. I need to look out for myself. And my mother."

My hands were shaking. I shoved them into my pockets. How much time did I have? If I was right about the bomb, how high did the plane need to be for it to work? "I hated my stepfather too," I said, "but—"

"I love Alex," she said. "You idiot. I love him like a father."

"I'm sorry, I didn't mean—"

"It's okay," she said, and I thought she was about to cry. "Or it's not okay," she went on. "I know. Or I don't know—"

"Can I say something strange?"

"Go ahead."

"I get the feeling you're about to do something terrible. And if you love him, it's even more terrible."

She still wouldn't look at me. She moved the bag from one shoulder to the other. "You can walk away from me right now," she said. "That's what I'd recommend. There will be some chaos. We can still leave together. None of this will come back to me."

"Can you tell me what you think is going to happen?"

She tilted her head from side to side. She used her free hand to rub and then scratch at the base of her neck. Her skin there looked red. Her fingers seemed twitchy. "Well, we were off to a nice start," she said, "weren't we?"

"That's how it felt," I said. I expected to hear people running our way, but I didn't want her to see that in my face, if she ever turned from the window to look me full in the face.

"Well, Alex taught me about opportunities," she said. "This is the one I saw. It's the one that crossed my path. It gives me a way to hold on to what I want."

"I don't believe you're thinking about killing a bunch of innocent—"

"I'm not the first or last."

I stared at her and shook my head. What could I say? Now wasn't the time to tell her how wrong she was. Keep her talking. Make sure she doesn't look back toward the checkpoint. The LEOs would be arriving any second. "You think you can blow up a plane—"

"We could have an extraordinary life together for a while," she said. "You might enjoy it."

"I'm just an ordinary guy," I said. "I thought you knew that. I thought you liked that."

"I've decided what I want," she said. "You should do the same."

"You think you can blow it up, kill all those people, and then go on with your life?"

She shrugged. The bag shifted on her shoulder. A few more passengers were waiting to board, but the line had stopped moving. She stepped closer to the window. "What's taking them so long?"

How many terrorists, at the end of the day, were just acting out family dramas? It had to be far more complicated than that, of course. Despite the job and all the briefings, what did I really know about it? And yet, how many terrorists craved more love and attention? How many longed to hold onto whatever was being taken away from them? How many yearned for the possessions of others? I thought I understood the search for surrogate parents, father figures, substitute mothers. I knew it was easy to get lost, to act self-destructively. But I never imagined it could go this far wrong.

"What's in the bag?" I asked. "Tell me the plan here."

"I thought you had it all figured out."

"I'm trying."

"You don't have much time. Think about what you want. Think hard."

I took my hands out of my pockets. My palms were damp. "I don't think you really want to do whatever you're about to do," I said. "I'd like you to give me the bag." I reached out and she jumped back.

"Don't try to touch me again," she said. Her eyes remained open and bright. No affection for me at all. Just cold calculation. She glanced back up the concourse, toward the checkpoint. "Shit," she said. Then two flights attendants from the plane started leading the PAX back out through the jetway.

27

I FLINCHED WHEN THE AIRPORT warning system kicked in. Diane stood still, observing. Lights flashed all through the terminal and a high-pitched alarm pulsed on and on. The PA system started repeating the evacuation message: "There has been a report of an emergency. Proceed calmly and leave the building immediately."

The passengers and airport workers were remarkably calm as they walked toward the checkpoint. I'd watched some of the shaky videos online after the Los Angeles International shooting, people running as fast as they could while LEOs with guns drawn screamed for everyone to get down. All it would take was one gunshot, one loud explosion to change this whole scene. But, so far, this Albany crowd was treating the announced emergency as an inconvenient fire drill. A few people had their phones out, filming for YouTube and occasionally offering wry commentary.

"Equipment malfunction," a short, old woman was saying, her long silver hair swaying back and forth as she talked. "That's my bet."

"False alarm," said the older man next to her. "We'll probably be stuck here for hours."

I stayed close to Diane. She seemed focused on the PAX exiting the jetway. One of the flight attendants remained by the door, repeating instructions. "Please proceed directly to the checkpoint and exit the terminal," he said. "Please stay calm."

I figured they were bringing the PAX back through the airport because they knew about a bomb on the plane. Diane took a few steps in the attendant's direction, staying near the window. If she reached into the bag, I'd tackle her immediately. Then, at last, I saw the LEOs racing our way.

During the past six-plus years of TSA time, I'd watched LEOs at work almost every day. I'd seen them respond to tests. I'd seen them perform their drills—with dogs and without. I'd seen them routinely issue citations to the PAX who were foolish enough to stash firearms in their carry-ons. I'd seen them handle with surprising decency the protesters who occasionally wanted to leaflet the airport and film pat downs. I'd also seen LEOs in line at Starbucks. I often strolled by them on my way back and forth to the employees' lot. I didn't know their names and they didn't know mine, but I'd give whoever was on duty a wave and a hello and I'd usually get the same in return. I'd come to believe the LEOs I shared the airport with weren't all that different from my fellow TSOs. They looked like action comic characters with their guns, Tasers, batons, and bulletproof vests; but at the end of the day, they were neither heroes nor villains by definition, just men and women, cowboys and grinders, doing their jobs, trying to make ends meet.

I tried to hold onto that idea of solidarity as the LEOs closed the distance. Then I lost track of that thought because I saw a man in a familiar blue suit sprinting ahead of the LEOs.

I was glad to see Hank. Then I was pissed off. The whole visit had nothing at all to do with the birthday. I'd been used again. Or was I being saved? How much had Hank kept from me? I was still sorting it out when I saw Diane move her arm and open her bag. I lunged over to tackle her, but she was quick and she dodged me. She stepped closer to the window and now she had the gun out of her bag. She pointed it at me and positioned herself behind me.

Hank and the LEOs had their guns drawn too. "Good morning, Diane," Hank said. "You need to put down your gun right away."

I couldn't see her face anymore. She must have been afraid. At least as afraid as I was. I could feel the gun against my back. She seemed to be holding it steady. "Diane," I said.

The LEOs were clearing the space. Hank walked closer. "Put down your weapon," he said. "Then tell us what you want. No one needs to get hurt here. We already have your friend, as you can see. We wanted to make sure we got him first."

Another three LEOs were approaching and they were dragging the bearded "cameraman" along with them. "Ricardo," Diane said, shaking her head and staring at the guy we'd been calling Curly. "Shit."

The LEOs stopped behind Hank and stood their prisoner up. "This was all my idea," Ricardo said. "It's not her fault."

"Shut up, you idiot," Diane said. "You don't have to protect me."

"People always have to be reminded they need protection," Hank said. "At least that's what I've observed over and over again. Anyhow, we've been tracking good old Ricardo for quite a while. It was a pleasure to finally scoop him up."

I stared at Ricardo. Maybe he'd found Diane and put her to use. Maybe she was the "opportunity" that crossed his path. Maybe they were both using each other. The guy was wriggling his arms behind his back, as if trying to free himself from the handcuffs. One of the LEOs turned him around and started shoving him back toward the checkpoint.

"Your bomb never even made it onto the plane," Hank said. "Turn around and look out the window. You can see the bomb guys gearing up to take care of it."

I turned for a moment to face her. She wasn't going to look behind her. She was staring straight ahead. "Come on, Diane," I said.

"Shut up," she said, jabbing me in the back.

"Nothing irrevocable has happened yet," Hank was saying. "I actually believe Ricardo will get most of the blame. He groomed you for this. He preyed on you. He and his pals have preyed on others before you. We know this. Your life can keep going forward if we all walk out of here right now."

I wanted to help. I needed to clear my mind. Focus. Could I somehow spin around and grab the gun out of her hand? That would be harder than tackling her and I'd failed to tackle her. I glanced at Hank for guidance.

Then Alex emerged from the jetway and saw Diane. He must have seen the gun too, but he stepped out of the line. The flight attendant at the gate called out to him. "Sir! Please proceed to the checkpoint and exit the airport!"

Alex didn't listen. He walked right up to Diane. "What are you doing?" he asked.

"Waiting for you," she said.

"I don't understand," Alex said.

"So nice of you to stroll over," Diane said. "I'm sure Gary won't mind if you take his place." She grabbed Alex by the arm and yanked him closer to her. Then she started pushing Alex forward, leaving me alone. "Let us walk out of here," she said to Hank, "or I'll shoot him."

"Would you please explain what's going on?" Alex asked.

"You're doing what I tell you," Diane said. "That's what's going on."

Hank held his ground. A few PAX dropped down and hid behind chairs. Others began running back to the checkpoint. I started to move toward Hank, but maybe I could somehow get behind Diane.

"Out of our way," she said to Hank.

"I need to stay right here," Hank said. "I just want to talk."

"Sure you do," she said.

I couldn't imagine that Diane would really shoot anyone. But I didn't know her. I needed to stop her. Alex was shuffling forward, still talking. "You and your mother will be more than fine," he was saying. "I thought I made that clear. Why would you act like this?"

"Shut up," she said, pushing him to take another step.

People will use loss to justify anything. That's what my father had told me. What was Diane losing? A father figure she claimed to love. The wealth of the Strands. The mansion she lived in. An inheritance she thought would be hers.

Somehow she'd joined up with Ricardo and together they'd made this plan that satisfied both of their desires: bring down a plane and kill Alex at the same time.

I thought of Diane's mother, Faye, over in Japan, arranging flowers and visiting temples. She probably wouldn't be coming back anytime soon. Maybe the healthiest thing Diane could have done was chase after her. Instead of trying to kill Alex, she should have taken his place on the plane.

But I didn't know her. Why was that so difficult to accept? I couldn't save her and I didn't understand her. She'd betrayed me.

"Diane," Alex said. "Don't do this."

Ricardo wasn't cooperating with the two LEOs who were trying to push and pull him in the direction of the checkpoint.

Then I saw Carelli and Neffer rushing down the concourse to help. I was glad to see them, but I wondered who was watching Ben. I didn't want him anywhere near whatever was about to happen. Why had I brought him to this place? I was failing again. At the same time, I had an idea. "Diane," I said. "Ben's here with me."

"Ben?" she said. "Where?"

"He's still at the checkpoint," I said. "Remember?"

Diane's face softened for a moment and she glanced toward the checkpoint. Here was something she hadn't fully considered. Maybe she wanted a chance to explain. I couldn't dwell on that. She lowered her gun ever so slightly, distracted. I didn't think about it. *Let it happen!* I ran right at her, ready to tackle her to the floor this time. But then she turned and I rammed into Alex instead.

The two of us fell to the carpet. I heard the first shot. Alex's whole body jerked and blood started covering his leg. Someone needed to stop the bleeding. Apply pressure. I moved closer. Alex was staring in the direction of Hank, the LEOs, and their guns. "No!" he shouted. "Don't shoot her!"

"You want them to shoot me," she said. "Trust me."

"Diane," I said, "don't—"

I got one last look into her emerald-green eyes, unblinking. I thought I could see her finger, about to pull the trigger. Then the LEOs started shooting. It was so loud. I couldn't count the shots. I couldn't turn away. Her right shoulder blew back. She glanced over at it. She looked inconvenienced, about to complain. Her right leg buckled beneath her. She stayed on her feet, the gun lower, but still gripped tight in her blood-spattered hands. She fired a shot into the carpet. Then a bullet slammed into her chest and she tilted backward.

I wanted to get back to Ben, keep him away. He didn't need to see any of this. I had to stop that from happening. But how could I? I was crawling on the dull-brown carpet. I was staying low, trying to move toward my son.

But there was real chaos now. I heard others screaming and shouting. Beyond the wall of LEOs, plenty of people were still dashing up the concourse, back toward the checkpoint and the exit. No one was chatting or filming anymore. They were flat-out running. I saw a father and mother pulling their two daughters along. "Just drop the bags!" the father shouted. "We don't need them. Come on. Come on!"

I stood up, hoping to break out into the open and run with the crowd. I heard more shots. Alex screamed "No!" EMTs hustled forward. I looked up the concourse for Ben, but I couldn't see him anywhere.

"Stay down, Gary!" Hank shouted.

I crouched back down. Somehow, Ricardo was free, racing toward Diane, his hands cuffed but in front of his body again. There was more shooting. Ricardo was reaching for the gun that Diane had dropped. Hank aimed at Ricardo, fired one shot, and Ricardo crumbled.

It suddenly grew much quieter, though the echoes of the shots still rang in my ears. And then there was Hank, standing right in front of me, leaning down, offering a hand. "You're okay," he said.

I looked around at the aftermath. The mullet EMT and his partner, as twitchy as before, were tending to Alex's left leg. "You're a lucky man," Nonmullet was saying.

"Again," Mullet said, getting a stretcher ready.

Then I saw Ricardo, sprawled-out lifeless beside Diane. The LEOs were covering his whole body with a blanket and getting ready to cover Diane. There was blood all over her face, her neck at an impossible angle.

How could I have been so wrong, so blind? I'd been falling for her and she'd been using me the whole time. *What you don't see . . .* I had to learn to see better. I promised myself that, somehow, I would learn to see better.

Hank was still waiting. I reached up and took the offered hand. I felt myself pulled back onto my feet.

"I'm grateful," I said. "I'm so glad you showed up."

Hank clapped me on the back. "Just looking out for your son," he said. "He needs his father to stay around."

The reporters and cameramen apparently hadn't traveled far. They were rushing up the concourse to get the story as the bodies of Diane and Ricardo were wheeled away.

I moved closer to Hank and put a hand on his shoulder. "Well," I said, "it's nice for him to have an uncle around too."

Hank smiled. A rare sight that made his face look much more like his sister's. "You know," he said, "I'm sorry I had to keep you in the dark about so much. We needed to flush Ricardo out of hiding. You were awfully brave today. You might even be better at this kind of work than I thought. Maybe you've got a future in it after all."

I shook my head. I'd been so suspicious of my brother-in-law, so trusting of Diane. I'd had it all backward.

Neffer came over to stand beside us and he spoke directly to Hank. "Damn straight he's got a future in it," he said. "If that's what he wants."

I was nowhere near ready to discuss my future, but I felt certain my TSA career was over. It was time for a different job, and I hoped Hank and I could someday trade stories about our decisions to switch careers. Everything had changed again and would no doubt keep changing. There was so much beyond my control—maybe that was the exception, the one thing that would *not* change. The sooner I accepted my lack of control, the better off I'd be.

Then the camera lights were flashing again and the reporters' questions were coming at me. Hank was there to help with the details. I tried to focus, but I couldn't get the image of Diane out of my mind. That gun. The blood. The unblinking eyes. I glanced back toward where her blanket-covered body had been, but it was gone. I'd begun to imagine everything with her, but I hadn't imagined this.

And I wasn't the only one who'd been imagining a Diane-filled future. I looked around for Ben. He was running up the concourse, Kevin lumbering along behind him. "Dad!" he called. "Dad!"

I knelt down and watched him speed my way. He seemed so tall! When had that happened? How had those gangly legs become even longer? He was growing, changing, right before my eyes. I was exhausted, probably deep in shock, but I realized Ben didn't need me to stay the same. I'd used my loss to justify hiding out, hunkering down. That wasn't what Ben needed. He needed his father to grow and change with him. I yearned to become the father he needed and, in that way, I might just manage to become the father I longed to be.

And then he was in my arms, so warm, soaked in sweat, breathing fast. I closed my eyes and held him tight. "We're all right," I said. "I love you so."

"What happened?" he asked.

"I'll tell you all about it later," I said, standing up, holding him close.

I tried to keep him from studying the scene too much. He didn't need to see all the blood and chaos. "We'll get through this," I said, though I wasn't sure how we'd do that. It was another line borrowed from the therapist. All those months ago he'd reassured me that Ben was young and resilient. "Time will help us," he'd said. "You'll both keep talking."

I vowed to do it. I would keep talking. I would tell him everything. I wouldn't distort the truth at all. I'd learned that much. But it could wait. For now, I was hoping my son could be more resilient than I'd been. And wiser. And a better judge of character. And more self-confident. I wanted to be able to help him. And help myself. I squeezed his hand, more determined than ever to become the father it seemed I'd been seeking forever. No one else could do that for me. No one else could do that for him. No surrogates. No substitutes. It was far and away my most important job.

Ben twisted his hand a little. "Not so tight," he said.

So I loosened my grip.

Then I brought his hand to my lips and kissed it, just below the knuckles. Laurie's pointy knuckles.

Meanwhile, the reporters were becoming impatient, firing more and more questions at me. I didn't know when or how or if I'd be able to answer them all, but standing tall between my son and my brother-in-law, I did my best to start. I'd try to get one thing right and move on from there.

Epilogue

ONE YEAR LATER, WHEN IT'S time to mark Laurie's birthday again, our lives look very different.

I've left the TSA behind and I'm coaching tennis again. On this particular Saturday afternoon, I'm finishing up a set of doubles with the men's 4.0 group at Albany Tennis Club; I stepped in because they needed a fourth when one of the regulars twisted an ankle and drove home to ice it. The average age of the remaining three guys is in the midsixties. I keep the ball in play, trying to give each of them a chance to look good. I applaud their shots and urge them to recover some of their youthfulness. I quote Gallwey quoting Suzuki: "Childlikeness has to be restored with long years of training in self-forgetfulness."

I'm talking to myself at least as much as I'm talking to them. A lot has changed during the year, but I still have a tough time figuring out what to remember and what to forget. I want to accept that I'll never know Diane's whole story and that I'm not somehow to blame for her violent death. Hank told me as much as he could about how Ricardo had met Diane at the shooting range in Troy where the Armed Ladies practiced. Ricardo courted her, as he'd been trained to do. He groomed her and slowly edged toward asking her to help him get a bomb on a plane. Then, when he learned of her concerns about Alex, the divorce, and the will, everything accelerated

The other two guys in that cell—Moe and Larry—had been apprehended as well. Apparently, they'd been racing to see who could bring down a plane first. "Getting them behind bars was a nice way to end my FBI career," Hank said. It remains difficult to stop myself from wondering how I was so blind. It's foolish to think I could have saved Diane, but why didn't I figure it all out sooner?

Hank tells me not to be so hard on myself. He says he barely figured it out in time. He's been helpful in other ways, too. He's the one who put me in touch with the people at the Albany Tennis Club, where they have eight beautiful red-clay courts. It's part-time work, but I enjoy it, and I also found assistant coaching work at Emma Willard, a top-notch private school across the river. In addition to the coaching, I'm working toward an MA in education at UAlbany. Money's tight, but a substantial reward from Alex Strand has been making it all possible, and once I get the MA, more jobs should open up.

Right now, I check my watch. I'm scheduled to go off-duty at five—just a few minutes away—and then I'm supposed to meet up with Ben, Shannon, Neffer, Hank, and Elizabeth for a picnic dinner next to the courts. My partner and I need to break serve here to take the set. I'll turn it up a notch to finish on time. We're already ahead love-fifteen. I bounce on my toes and wait for the slow lefty serve to come my way.

I look down at my feet for a moment and see a reminder of my Albany International days. When I left, Neffer gave me a pair of Nike tennis shoes, an outrageous shade of blue, lighter and brighter than the titanium blue of my TSA uniform. Neffer has moved on as well, promoted to Federal Site Director at Stewart International Airport, just sixty miles north of New York City, right outside of Newburgh. Kevin's a supervisor there now and they've both tried to lure me back. "I need all the grinders I can get at my new airport," Neffer says. But he also says, "I'm happy you're back out on the courts."

The serve spins in, slicing away from my backhand. I take a quick step and then let myself slide toward it—one of the luxuries of clay, so much easier on my knees than the hard asphalt at Haven. I slice it back crosscourt, keeping it low, near the center line so the lefty has to take it on his backhand side. Anticipating a bit of a floater, I close on the net and put myself in perfect position for my next shot. The ball is shoulder height when it reaches me. Just punch the volley down the line or sharply crosscourt and the point will be over.

That's what I'm thinking when I see Neffer approaching the gate to the courts.

"Officer Waldman," he shouts. He's walking hand-in-hand with Chloe and he's carrying two six-packs of beer. "Focus, please! Pay no attention to the cold beverages I've brought for the occasion."

I feather a drop-volley crosscourt, where even the thirty-year-old version of the lefty couldn't have reached it. "I'll be right with you," I say.

"We'll see about that," the lefty says, getting ready to serve again.

I want to keep my head in the game, but then Shannon's car pulls into the lot and Ben's out of the backseat almost before the car stops moving.

Shannon had waited, just as she'd said she would. She'd done more than wait. She's been staying over almost every night, talking and talking with me and Ben as we all keep struggling to make sense of our lives. The old list still runs through my mind—ex-player, babysitter, friend—and I'm well aware that's far more than I deserve. With each passing week, though, it's increasingly obvious that the old list is incomplete. I'm hesitant, frightened of making another terrible mistake, but Shannon is my lover, Ben's mother-figure, and the list will most likely keep growing.

My partner seems eager to get off the court too. He pounces on the next serve, ripping a forehand up the alley for a clean winner.

The lefty is not about to give up. "Come on," he says. "We got this. One point at a time."

I wave to Shannon and Ben and watch them hug Neffer and Chloe. Then I prepare for another slow lefty-serve. I want everyone to see me play the point, but I also want to set it up so my partner gets a shot at the game-winner. I'll be the old human backboard. Just hit another safe crosscourt return and see what happens next.

But as the lefty is in the middle of hitting his first serve, Hank's Charger speeds into the lot, horn honking. The serve goes right into the net.

"Sorry about that," I say. "That's my brother-in-law. Take another first serve."

Hank and Elizabeth walk up hand-in-hand to join the crowd. Hank, wearing blue jeans and an orange San Francisco Giants sweatshirt, looks like a younger, more relaxed version of himself. He and Elizabeth have been spending a lot of time in Albany together. It's been nice to have them around, for many reasons. Paul and Vanessa moved away to Philadelphia, but Hank has stepped in as my running partner and more. Elizabeth, it turns out, is a doctor with a specialty in orthopedics. She's finalizing arrangements to join a practice associated with Albany Med, and the two of them have begun looking at houses a few miles outside of downtown Albany. "We want to get some land," Hank says. "Space for a big dog. Might even see if we can handle chickens. And wouldn't it be nice if Ben had a cousin or two?"

Right now, he shouts out, "What's the score here?"

"Love-forty," I say. "Set point."

"Close it out," Hank says. "Pizza's in the car getting cold."

"You should all get comfortable," the lefty says.

Hank laughs. "Come on, brother," he says. "You know what to do here. You want to keep playing a game or you want to picnic with us?"

I'd happily keep playing. But if I have to choose, the choice is clear.

"Hey Coach," Shannon shouts. "Don't forget to have fun out there!"

My old words, circling back. I grin and look over at my people, these people I love and, for a moment, I think again of how close I came to losing them forever.

Think about what you want, Diane had said in the airport. *Think hard.*

Well, I still want to wash those final bloody images of her out of my mind.

I want to have done a better job, with everything. I want to do a better job with everything in the future.

And then there are the familiar impossibilities, the yearning for what I have already lost forever: My mother, my father, my wife. I can't stop missing Laurie. I wish Ben could have grown up alongside her.

The serve spins toward my backhand again. I slice it crosscourt, a little more bite on this one, and I charge the net. The lefty bends down to get the return and tries to poke a lob over our heads.

The ball rises up.

The late-April sun slips lower in the sky, sparkling a bit on the red clay and deepening the green of the baseball field beyond the fence. Maybe, on a day like this, all my wants don't have to be impossible. Maybe it's almost reasonable to hope that with assistance from Shannon, Hank, Neffer, and others, I can coach Ben toward a full life, a life that will include love and joy as well as loss and grief and hurt. We won't be able to control it all, no matter how hard we try. That will have to be okay. More than okay. Maybe that's something we can keep learning together, father and son, in the years to come.

My partner backpedals into no-man's land. He reaches up for the ball and overheads a rocket right down the middle. The ball bounces up high and flies, untouched, over the fence.

I'm already at the net. I wait there for the other guys and then we shake hands while the small crowd applauds. I turn to them. "Give me a few more minutes," I say. I need to help sweep the courts for the next group. I grab one broom and my partner grabs another.

"Wait," Ben shouts. "I want to hit some!"

It's only then that I notice my son has brought a racket. Not a new one. An old classic. I've seen it before. Ben lifts it above his head and holds it aloft, like a torch or a sword. It's Laurie's old racket—I see that now. It must be the latest gift from Hank. It's too big for the kid. Too heavy. He'll barely be able to wrap his hand around the grip.

"Can I, Dad?" he asks. "Please?"

I smile, set the broom down, and tell my partner to do likewise. I'm not about to miss this chance. I'll let it happen. I wave my son onto the court. Tennis can't solve everything. I know that much. But it can occasionally offer comfort. "Come on," I say. "I was hoping you'd want to play."

Acknowledgments

WITH THANKS TO THOSE WHO read and/or talked about these pages repeatedly and managed to give insightful, indispensable advice every single time: Rob Arnold, David Blake, Carrie Brown, Jessica Cherry, Doug Dorst, Ellen Ferguson, Danny Goodwin, Ike Herschkopf, Adam Johnson, Eric Korsh, Julie Orringer, Todd James Pierce, Angela Pneuman, Harry Schwirck, and James Steiner.

With gratitude to all those at my day job at the University at Albany, SUNY, especially my colleagues in the English Department and the New York State Writers Institute.

And much gratitude as well to all those at Albany International Airport, workers and travelers alike, for tolerating my rather inept presence when I worked for a while as a Transportation Security Officer-in-Training. A special shout-out to the Elite Eight—you know who you are.

For the gift of time, space, and invaluable, generous support, I am seriously indebted to The Netherlands Institute for Advanced Study, the New York Foundation for the Arts, the Virginia Center for the Creative Arts, and the Hanse-Wissenschaftskolleg (HWK) Institute for Advanced Study.

I am also grateful to everyone at SUNY Press, especially James Peltz, for believing in this book and making it much better. The imperfections that remain are all my own doing.

Even more gratitude to William and Carol Schwarzschild, Jeffrey Schwarzschild, Daniela Stoutenburg, Arthur Schwarzschild (we miss you like crazy, Arthur!), Mark Merin, Cathleen Williams, Carl Albert, Susan Schaefer Albert, Bill Schaefer, and Elaine Albert.

And, finally, infinite forever gratitude to my love, Elisa, and our love, Miller David.

About the Author

Edward Schwarzschild is the author of the novel *Responsible Men* and the story collection *The Family Diamond*. While writing *In Security*, he worked for several months as a Transportation Security Officer-in-training at Albany International Airport. He wrote a long essay about that experience that first appeared at *Hazlitt.net* and then was reposted widely before being published in *The Guardian*. Other essays and stories have appeared in such places as *Tin House*, *Virginia Quarterly Review*, *The Believer*, and *The Yale Journal of Criticism*. He's been a New York Foundation for the Arts Fellow in Fiction, a Fulbright Scholar at the University of Zaragoza in Spain, and a *Fiction Meets Science* Writer-in-Residence at the Hanse-Wissenschaftskolleg (Institute for Advanced Study) in Delmenhorst, Germany. Since 2001, he has taught in the English department at the University at Albany, SUNY, where he is Director of Creative Writing and a Fellow of the New York State Writers Institute. Further information about Edward Schwarzschild is available at his website at www.edwardschwarzschild.com.